Secrets of the U'tanse

Henry Melton

Secrets of the U'tanse

Henry Melton

Wire Rim Books
Hutto, Texas

WRB

Printing History
First Edition: December 2016
ISBN 978-1-935236-66-5

ePub ISBN 978-1-935236-67-2
Kindle ISBN 978-1-935236-68-9

Website of Henry Melton
www.HenryMelton.com

Character images © 2016 by Djamila Knopf
http://shilesque.deviantart.com/

Printed in the United States of America

Wire Rim Books
www.wirerimbooks.com

Acknowledgements

Proceeding from the idea to a finished novel has many steps, and in my case, many people who have contributed. I can't draw, so you'll find the cover artist **Djamila Knopf,** who has helped me keep a distinctive style for this series, on the facing copyright page.

I have several other helpers that have pointed out plot flaws, misnamed characters, grammar mistakes, and many typos. At each stage in the process, once I finish my first draft, a little voice in my head says, "It's done now." Then, each marked-up copy arrives from my helpers and knocks that idea aside.

There's something I've noticed working on all these books, each helper—whether they call themselves an editor, a beta-reader, or a proofreader—each one finds errors that none of the others found. Every one of them has saved me from embarrassing flaws. So, thank you, all of you.

This book was marked up by: **Jonathan Andrews, Jim Dunn, Linda Elliott, Mike Lynch,** and **Tom Stock.**

Contents

We Are Aliens   1

Boat Cave   3

Long Swim   11

Factory   17

Monitor Elehadi   23

Brainstorming   29

Supply Run   37

New Home   43

Meeting Holana   51

Semaphore Practice   57

Secrets   65

Dinner   71

Impossible   77

Charging New Home   83

Taking of the Survivors   89

Betty's Pump   95

Looking Homeward   101

Underfoot   107

Gifts   113

Mechanics   121

Clearing the Rock Pile   127

Wrapping Up   133

Back to Work   139

Ba   145

U'tanse-That-Swims   151

In the Garden   157

Reassignments   163

Cyclops Updates   169

Weeding   175

Blackout   179

Damage Report   185

Status Meeting   191

Out of Power   197

Test Run   203

Visiting Home   209

Sally's Run   215

Aarison's Speech   221

Upstream   229

Up the Mountain   235

Sally's Choice   243

Encounter   249

Sally's Escape   255

To the Sea   261

Open Mouth   267

Back to Base   271

Fire in his Eyes   277

Index: Cerik Terms   281

Index: U'tanse Terms   289

Index: Slave Races   291

Index: The Ko Calendar   293

Southwest Lands of Ko

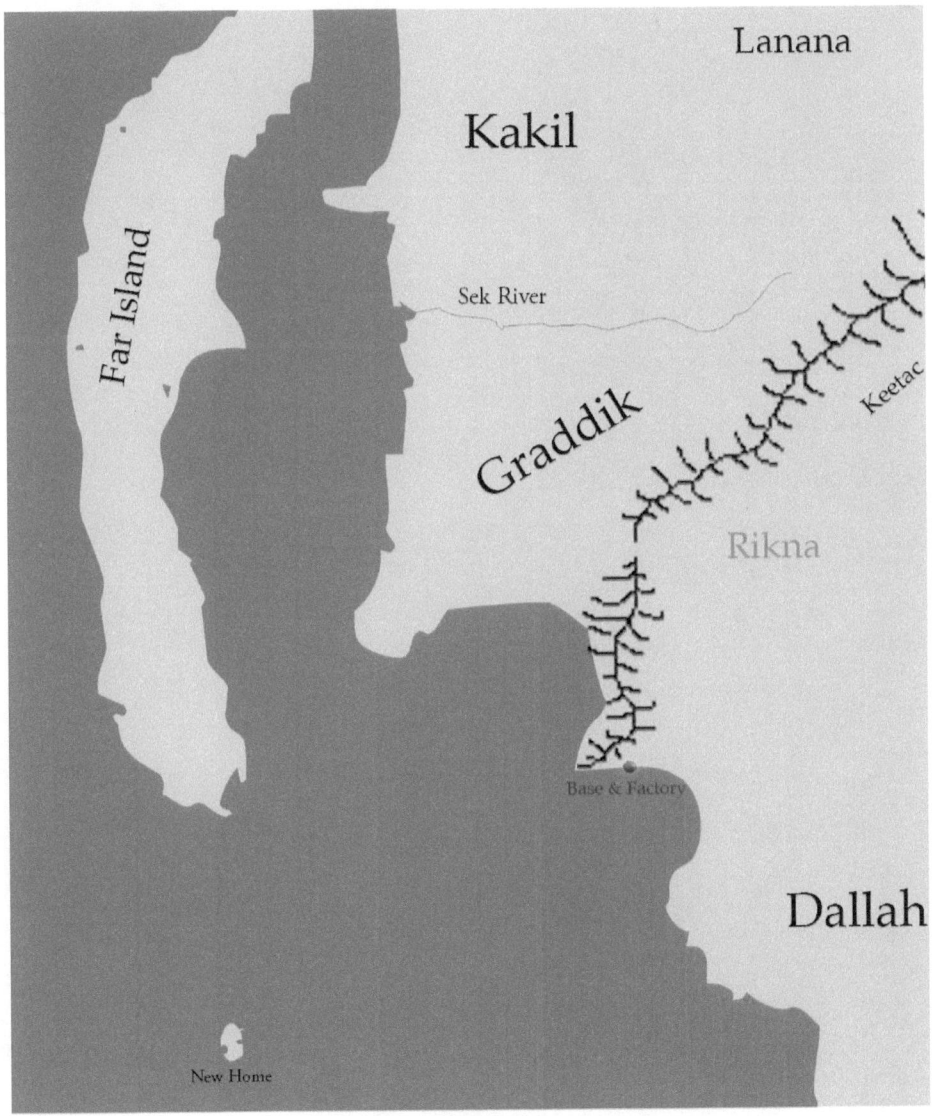

Lanana

Kakil

Far Island

Sek River

Graddik

Keetac

Rikna

Base & Factory

Dallah

New Home

We Are Aliens

Everything we know about ourselves comes from the Book, the memories of Father Abe, the only man who remembered Old Earth. The story feels like mythology, with our home planet being scorched by the glare of Betelgeuse, an old star that exploded. Human technology collapsed and the Cerik were there waiting to move in to claim lands and prey.

Abe and Sharon, Father and Mother to us all, fought the Cerik for all of humankind, and they won, at the cost of their own freedom.

Every cutie from the nursery doubts the tales, at first. Then, when they grow up and get a taste of the raw, unfiltered air outside our burrows, they know the truth first hand. We, the U'tanse of Ko, are not natives to this world.

Unlike every other animal on the planet, our lungs burn and our skin forms ulcers from the simple exposure to the air. It is a rare plant or animal that we can eat without being poisoned. Without the filters we could not exist here.

For generations, we U'tanse have been slaves under the claws of the Cerik, dependent on technology we alone can supply. That is, until the Free U'tanse, a collection of castoffs, came together and formed their own family. Their very existence, hiding in the rocks, depended on keeping themselves hidden from the Cerik—a difficult task on a world populated with telepaths and seers.

Boat Cave

Joshua saw a flicker in the skies, just above the shoreline. He paused in his swim. Most of the time movement up above was a *ska*, or a flock of them. But this time the red glint of sunlight reflecting off metal clearly showed it was a flier.

None of the Free U'tanse fliers were due to be in the sky right now. It had to be Cerik. If they saw him, they'd kill him on sight—worse, they'd send hordes of warriors to search the area. Maybe Base would remain hidden, but Factory was too exposed, with nothing hiding it from sight but a painted drapery concealing the cliff-side dock. Hunters on the ground would certainly find it during a determined search.

He reached for the tube on the side of his breather and rotated the connector, switching to the longer hose. It was harder to pull air through it, but he let the float ride on the surface while he sculled with his hands until his whole body was a couple of feet below the waves.

There were no betraying thoughts leaking from Base or Factory—everyone was too well trained. The Cerik pilot flying in his boat above, however, was churning with frustration. His thoughts weren't on his job at all. Instead of searching the landscape for signs of escaped U'tanse, the claws of his right hand were slicing the air. In his imagination, he was ripping the eyes from his superior, who had called him a *dakka*-hunter.

Joshua had seen such revenge fights before, when he had been telepathically monitoring the race of predators who ruled the planet. Blazingly fast, they moved in for the kill, attacking the weakest part of those armored bodies, the ocular ridge on their head. Then they roared their victory as they ate the eyes of their enemy, dead on the ground.

Joshua hid deep in the water and let the predator fly on by, heading down the coast. In spite of the danger, he felt a guilty relief at the chance to rest. Taking on the job as Cyclops's assistant, it seemed his chores had become endless. He was sure he could take a break, but every time he rested, he imagined the blindfolded face of his father looking at him.

Through the glass goggles, he saw the nearby fish dart away. To them he was likely a dangerous hunter himself. Luckily, he was the big fish and they were all small. He'd seen larger ones through the submarine's windows, but they were rare this close to Base and Factory.

Within a couple of minutes, the Cerik boat moved down the coast, lost in the haze. The pilot had noticed nothing more than some egg-shaped rocks near the shore.

Joshua frowned as he surfaced and took the time to retract the air hose onto its spool. The process was hardly smooth. His underwater breather mask was still a new invention, and while he was overjoyed at the ability to have filtered air to breathe while swimming—it greatly increased the range he could travel—the tubes that allowed him to breathe deeper underwater were difficult to deal with. There had to be a better way to handle the process.

As he stowed the hose, he reached out with his *sight*, looking for the egg-shaped rock that had attracted the attention of the Cerik. He checked his tow bag and stroked the water with his arms, getting back into the rhythm. It wasn't every day that he swam the three miles over to the hidden cave, but he'd done it enough times that the cave appeared right when he expected it.

When he *saw* the "rock" he winced, and swam faster.

The dark opening in the pale, wave-splashed rocks was right at the water line, and he could see it flicker into view between the waves. It was totally invisible from any higher angle. No flier could see it, luckily. Not twenty yards away, an egg-shaped metal tank was wedged in the rocks.

His heart pounded. If the Cerik had circled back to check .... He didn't want to think about it.

During the chaos of Kakil clan's invasion of Rikna, when the Free U'tanse suddenly came into possession of two more boats, the flying shuttles that tied the continent together, it brought their little fleet to three. But they needed places to hide them and clairvoyant scouts had found this cave. Joshua had been with the crew that removed its seaweed and rubble. Cleaned out, there was room to hide the smallest of the boats, even when the lone moon was at its closest approach, a Large Moon high tide. After another twenty minutes or so of slow, even strokes, he entered the shadowy entrance. The opening in the stone was barely tall enough to let the flier itself in. The boat had to be landed in the surf and floated sideways through the opening by hand.

Joshua checked on Den, the pilot's, location with his *sight* before he approached, just to be sure the hideout hadn't been compromised. Den was sleeping in the boat, and all was safe. Still, as he pulled himself and his gear out of the water up onto the rocky ledge, the hatch opened, illuminating the dark interior. Several more egg-shaped metal tanks were clustered around the boat, kept from rolling in the highest surf with stones propped into place.

Den looked at the large tow bag Joshua pulled out of the water and asked, "My supplies? I guess I lost track of the day."

"Yes. Just give me a minute to catch my breath."

Den moved closer and helped him with his breather. "I can't understand a thing you're saying with that contraption over your head. Come on inside where the air is filtered."

Joshua shook his head. "Not yet. One of your tanks is visible outside."

Den's bearded face dropped. "No! Not again!"

Together they waded out into the surf. Den didn't even wait to get a breather. They snagged the four-foot-long egg and together carried it back. Den scanned the skies the whole time, stumbling on the wet rocks.

They moved inside the boat and Joshua took advantage of a towel and a spare tunic. Although the pilot was ten years older than he was, Den was about his size and the clothes fit.

"I'm sorry about that. It must have gotten loose at the last high tide. It's pretty cramped in here."

Joshua didn't dwell on the lapse. They both knew what was at stake if they were discovered.

Den had started unpacking the supplies from the tow bag.

He opened the seal on a small tub and stuffed one of the small dried *jenna* into his mouth and crunched it between his teeth.

"Ahh! I fish for these myself, but with the no smoke rule that I have to cook everything over a hot plate, mine just can't compare to the home grilled and seasoned versions you bring me."

Joshua shrugged. "You should thank Ciara. She made all your food. She insisted on taking over that task. She was a cook back at Rikna, specializing in carry-off meals for workers at remote jobs."

Den stroked his beard and frowned. "Base or Factory?"

"She started at Base, but just moved over to Factory."

He sighed. "Just my luck. A new girl and here I'm stuck babysitting the boat for the next month. There'll be a dozen guys making their move on her before I get back."

Joshua shook his head. "She isn't the only New Home girl who moved. I hear the idea of coming to Base and Factory is quite popular among the Rikna survivors. Too many women there, and too many guys here. It's inevitable. Most of the girls start out coming to Base, just to get them used to the idea of living under the rock, but most of the guys work at Factory."

Den took another bite of the fish and grinned. "Then why did your Sally go back to New Home?"

Joshua frowned, a familiar tight knot in his chest. Almost automatically he stretched his *sight* off to the west, far across the ocean waves and zeroed in on the island where the Rikna survivors were making their New Home. Sally was knee deep in the shallows of the bay, raking up sea weed and collecting it in tubs. He saw her pinch the protein-rich *dakka* slugs off the leaves and drop them into a separate pot.

He dismissed the vision and answered Den's question. "Oh, she wasn't mine... not officially. And she didn't go back permanently. They needed her to help with the youngsters—*ineda* training, mostly. Most of the people at New Home don't know how to properly block their thoughts."

Den dug into his supplies, fishing out the orders from his boss. Keeping his eyes on the paper, he said, "Rumors mentioned a big fight between you two."

Joshua closed his eyes and leaned back with his hands behind his head. "I'm going to take a little nap. I've got to get back to Factory before dark."

Den grunted and let him be.

Eyes closed and letting his breathing settle into a peaceful rhythm, Joshua could almost pretend he was dozing. But he had new habits now, and getting some actual sleep was not on his list.

His *sight* was nowhere as powerful as that of Cyclops, his father, but from what people told him, it was respectable.

First, he viewed the signal flag under the stone mountain that hid Base, the center of operations for the Free U'tanse. They had a new set of flags now, once they discovered that some of the clairvoyants had trouble making out color shades. The one draped over the railing near his father's office inside Base was green with a large black circle, the sign that all was well.

There was a matching green flag in the dining area at Factory. It was draped poorly, as if someone had just tossed it over the railing. He supposed someone had changed it to the white flag with a red X when the Cerik boat had passed over, and then put the green one back later.

Joshua hadn't bothered to look for it when he'd been swimming, since he'd seen the flier directly. *I wonder if I'd have gotten any advanced warning if I'd looked?*

That was the problem with the signal flags. People with *sight* had to check on them regularly. It was better than nothing, but so many people, especially the new refugees, had been used to a constant flood of other people's thoughts. Alerts had been instant and only the *tenners*, the small number of men who were non-telepathic, went ignorant of important events.

Most new refugees understood, intellectually, the importance of hiding their thoughts under *ineda* so that the Cerik telepaths wouldn't be able to find them. However, endlessly blocking their thoughts didn't come naturally. Nearly everyone was born telepathic, and habits of a lifetime didn't change easily.

Once again, he turned his attention to New Home, only this time as a focus for his telepathy. He shook his head disapprovingly as a flood of thoughts poured through. It was mostly harmless stuff—the thoughts of people living their lives in an underground burrow near the seashore. The same thoughts could be found from many of the Cerik-controlled Homes across the globe.

New Home was different, hurriedly populated with the refugees of the destroyed Rikna Home, every one of them supposedly killed in the *flick* blast that turned their old burrow into a molten crater. It was important to keep their existence a secret from the rest of the telepaths on the planet, both U'tanse and Cerik. Free U'tanse, rogue U'tanse, weren't supposed to exist. Any that escaped their Cerik master were always hunted down and killed.

But the refugees had been careless. Someone had let slip thoughts of their old Home. A telepath on the mainland noticed this survivor, walking free on the shoreline, and the word spread.

Throughout the many Homes on the planet, certain people started thinking about the idea of U'tanse living free of their Cerik masters. And whether the Cerik originally discovered thoughts from New Home or just overheard a slip from their own slaves, the word was out, and it had come to the attention of the Names.

And then the overflights began, as these clan leaders began hunting for the rogue colony. To their minds, the rogues were to be eradicated as soon as possible.

Thank God the Cerik telepaths are so rare. He sighed. They hadn't discovered the critical piece of the puzzle, that the rogues were not on the one massive continent of Ko. New Home was off on a lonely island in the sea—a place no Cerik wanted to be.

"I didn't think you were really asleep," said Den when he heard the sigh.

Joshua opened his eyes and looked over at the grinning face. He sat up. "I guess it's a lost cause. Sleep'll come when I'm exhausted."

"Then talk to me for a bit. I'm so lonely here, I'm listening for idle thoughts half-way around the world just to keep from going crazy."

Joshua stretched and leaned up against the wall. "You said you'd be here for another month?"

"Possibly. It all depends on the Cerik. I have to be ready to spring into action and get the boat to safety if there's any chance the Cerik locate this cave. It's all part of my job, I guess. I didn't know I'd be signing up for this when I volunteered to take the boat-piloting training."

"Tough break, then. I won't even ask what your plans are if you have to run for it. I was told to keep my eyes off your orders, just in case I was captured."

Den nodded. "I have trouble thinking like that—plans and backup plans. I just wanted to fly."

Joshua looked over at the piloting position where a human chair was bolted into place instead of the original gripping bar a Cerik pilot would clutch with his rear talons.

"I guess flying is something I'd like to learn how to do, someday. Lots of commands to learn, I guess."

Den smiled, "Yeah. I've got to play with it a little—although some systems are strictly off limits."

"Like what?"

Den shrugged. "Like the shouter, for one. It's quiet here, with nothing to listen to except the surf. I'd love to be able to use the shouter to talk to the other pilots. But when I asked about it, Patrick's face went white. It seems there's a side-effect of the shouter. When you listen in to any other signal, it adds that boat to your navigation map display."

Joshua frowned, nodding, "So … if you were using a shouter and were overheard by some Cerik pilot, he'd instantly have a location fix on your boat?"

Den nodded. "Yeah. It makes sense for a bunch of pilots working together. It's deadly for someone who wants to keep his boat hidden from all the others."

"That's bad luck for us. I hadn't thought about the shouters before. It would have been a great way for *ineda*-blocked telepaths to keep in communication with each other. Maybe we should find a way to change that feature."

Den looked skeptical. "Do you know anyone who can decode and modify Delense machine instructions? I don't."

Joshua considered it. "We've got some pretty talented people at Factory. I'll ask around." He smiled. "That's how I got my underwater breather."

Den looked over at the still-damp harness. "I wish I had one of those. Just getting out of the cave for a few minutes would be great."

Joshua grinned at him. "We'd need an official reason, though. Something more serious than going out to see the fish."

Den's face wrinkled in hard thought. Then he said, "The cave is cramped for space, with all the storage tanks. I don't have room for them all above the high tide level. That's where I store all my gear, and they get in the way. I might even have to dump them into the water to get the boat out in an emergency. Not a good idea to have them floating around in the water so close to Factory. If I could store them outside, underwater, then this place would be less cramped."

Joshua nodded, "You'd need a net to keep them secure. And an underwater breather to let you work there un-observed."

They grinned at each other as they considered how to phrase the request. Joshua nodded. "I'll see what can be done."

Long Swim

A fresh-caught rock creeper—very easy to catch when he could keep his eyes wide open underwater—made a tasty meal between them, even just filleted and seared on the hot plate. Joshua made a final check for the warning flags draped inside Base and Factory and then slipped back into the water.

The swim was much easier without a tow bag. It was tempting to reach the closest shore past the fallen stone pillars and just walk the rest of the way. The hidden cave was near the tip of a finger of land broken in pieces by volcanic eruptions. At the highest of the tides, Den's refuge was an island, but at other times a man or Cerik could jump from boulder to boulder, from slab to slab, and make it all the way between the cave and the mainland. It would be hazardous and very visible. The swim along the coast was safer and easier.

Although, with the possibility of a Cerik flier overhead at any time, even swimming along the surface made him feel exposed.

If those idiots at New Home hadn't leaked their thoughts, I wouldn't have to worry about this.

Frustrated, he spooled out an arm's length of breathing tube and began swimming under the surface.

Water had been a refuge from the Cerik since the beginning of time. The Delense, another native species of the planet Ko, had lived in the swamps and rivers, relying on their cleverness and the water to keep from being eaten by the fast and powerful Cerik.

The Cerik hated the water. Joshua had known that before, but once he started reading the Tales of the Cerik being compiled by George the *tenner* at Kakil, he realized just how much the powerful, leaping predators really *hated* the water. Over and over again, these legends—the only history the Cerik had—told of mighty hunters being frustrated by the sucking mud under their feet or by clever, amphibious Delense eluding them by slipping into the water, where the hunters could not follow.

The underwater breather, with its goggles, gave Joshua a better view of the undersea world than he was used to. Everything was clearer, and since he didn't have to turn his head every breath, he could do more looking. He swam at a slower pace than before, his eyes taking in the varied wildlife all around him. In spite of all the hours he'd spent swimming in the sea, goggles under the surface turned the place into a whole new world.

There were many more kinds of fish than he could keep track of. He'd seen some, on the few trips he'd taken in the submarine, but nothing like the variety he was seeing now. There was a puff, a disturbance in the mud, and then it settled. Some critter had seen him and vanished before he could spot it.

Maybe the submarine makes too much noise and scares these little ones away. I wish Sally could see this.

He'd never been among the crew who caught the bushels of *jenna* that made up a substantial portion of the colony's diet. Surely they would have seen more of these fish, but Joshua didn't know of more than a half-dozen varieties that made their way onto the dinner plates. Maybe the *jenna* were just too stupid to avoid the regular fishing areas—or were the majority of the fish poisonous to U'tanse? They were aliens who had come from another world called Earth, after all. They were lucky they could eat anything native to Ko.

Maybe, if he had the time, he'd ask around.

A little later, among the rocks and the crawlers, he saw something different. He kicked a little harder and swerved to get a closer look. Something straight as a ruler stretched about thirty feet across the rubble, ending in a wide circular patch. He slowed to a stop above it. Covered in mud, it was the same color as the stones, overgrown by the same underwater plants, but it had to be some kind of manufactured item.

He unspooled more breathing hose and swam down to it. He could feel the pressure as the mask clamped hard on his face and breathing became impossible, but he got close enough to brush some mud free of the surface. It was a pipe, about a foot in diameter.

His lungs labored. He had to get back up. He couldn't pull a breath through the full length of the hose. He kicked his way back to the surface and pulled off his breather, gulping in unfiltered air.

He put his breather back on and blew the tube clear. He had to take another look. He breathed deeply three times and then swam down. Halfway down, he noticed that the hose had collapsed flat. No air was coming through that.

But he pushed lower. He put his hand on the surface of the circular patch, realizing it was just a crust. It collapsed into fragments under his touch. In the dim light, the void below was covered in mud. Some creature stirred and Joshua backed away, swimming back to the surface.

Metal… mostly corroded away. Something the Delense left, then, but now the den of something I don't want to disturb.

The hose was normal at the surface. He reeled it back in, and then tested it again. Everything worked fine within a couple of feet of the surface, but more than five feet or so deep, his lungs couldn't pull in enough air.

I felt pressure when I was deep. Is that it?

He'd need to talk to Ace. The *tenner* knew all the science of it.

But as he looked around, he had a different problem. Swimming underwater with his attention focused on the fish and the bottom life, he'd drifted off course. The shoreline was so far off that he couldn't see any details through the haze.

It wasn't serious, since he could *see* his way home, but it would take longer than he'd planned. He stowed the long breathing tube and started concentrating on more powerful strokes. Twice he saw something long, with segmented body scales swimming below. It just might consider him a meal. He shifted course to get to shallower waters.

…

High clouds reflecting the ruddy light of the fading sun stayed with him right until he approached Factory's hidden entrance. He ducked under the surface to clear the drapery—a huge shield woven of *shash* and then stained to match the rock layers around it.

Floating at the dock inside, the submarine was still shiny from its most recent paint job. Workmen were cleaning up. Artificial light was too risky for work after sunset.

"Hey," called one of them. "The kid's back. Tell Patrick."

There were hands down on the floating platform helping Joshua out of the water. He felt limp as a wet rag after the longer-than-normal swim. At the top of the ladder, he saw the clothing bin—a strong reminder of the influx of women who had migrated from New Home. At first, Factory was a male-only facility, and some of the dock workers and swimmers like him would be walking around on the dock naked from time to time. It was a hot, sweaty environment, and an occasional dunk in the water was refreshing.

But then, a few women arrived, and suddenly there was a need for a clothing locker. Long-abandoned corners were swept and Ace came up with a set of lettering guides that made the labels on the doors and corridors look trim and tidy—not the scratched hand-lettering that had been the rule before.

But the biggest change was the men themselves. Beards were trimmed. Hair was combed. Clothes were washed much more frequently. It was still five or six men for every woman, but the place was a little more civilized than the all-male environment it had been.

Patrick himself walked up just as Joshua finished dressing. The senior boat pilot put his hand on his shoulder. "I was worried about you. We were making plans to fly out over the water once it got dark. Even with the *sight*, I'd lost track of where you'd gone. It's a big ocean out there."

Joshua frowned. "Sorry. I swam more underwater with the new breather, and it was so distracting—all the fish and clutter on the seabed. I got off course. Took me longer."

Patrick nodded. "So the breather worked okay? No lung damage?"

"It worked great. This wasn't my first swim with it, but it was the first time I had the longer breathing tube. It was like being in a submarine, seeing all the fish."

The man nodded. "I can remember being blown away, the first time I flew in a boat—seeing the world outside from high above. I can understand it being distracting, but be careful! I never want to have to report to Cyclops that I've lost his son."

Joshua took the rebuke. "It was my fault—all of it. I'll definitely keep my *sight* on my destination from now on. But it's great being able to make a swim, even when the Cerik are overhead."

The pilot nodded. He was grounded—all the pilots were—except for emergencies. Cerik in the sky meant he couldn't be.

Joshua asked, "How is the paint job coming?"

It had been Patrick's suggestion to camouflage the submarine, since he could see it so clearly from the air.

He sighed, "The first try hid it better than nothing, but we guessed wrong on the color. I could still see the outline—like some big sea monster. We're changing the paint. I guess it's just a matter of trial and error."

Joshua nodded. "Things change color under the water. And it's not just one change either. When I went deeper to look at an old Delense pipe on the bottom, I noticed that everything changed color a little—more washed out and bluer."

"What did you find?"

"Nothing. Just old, corroded metal. Nothing new."

Patrick looked off toward the bay, obscured by the drapery, but not to his *sight*. "I've seen things too, down on the bottom. The Delense never really cleaned up this place as well as they could have."

Joshua asked, "Maybe it was good enough to conceal their clutter from the Cerik. Has anyone ever examined how well our predator friends can see, compared to humans?"

Patrick shook his head. "I don't know. They can see better in the dark, everyone knows that, but colors and stuff like that—you'd better ask your father. He'd know if anyone ever tested them."

Joshua sighed. "One more thing to ask him, if I ever get back to Base."

Factory

Factory almost felt like home to Joshua. Both it and Base had been carved out of a massive basalt layer with tunneling machines that used rotating tongues to etch away the rock. People had speculated that Base was built at a later time than Factory, but no one knew for sure. The Delense were long gone and no one had decoded any kind of history from the writings they'd left behind. The semi-aquatic slave species had apparently created literacy for the sole purpose of writing technical manuals.

Base, where he'd been born and raised, was a little more refined in its architecture, with nicer features like the bathing pools on every level. Factory was strictly utilitarian.

Base could only be entered from an underwater opening, but air and fresh water flowed easily through pools in its chambers. Everything was built perfectly for the burrowing quadrupeds who had created the technology of the planet.

Factory was designed to get the power from the hydroelectric plant on the mountain above to the various workshops in its interior. There was only one freshwater bath, and it doubled as a heat exchanger, positioned near the metal furnaces.

Once he passed through the airlock doors that separated the dock from the interior, Joshua could feel the muggy air coming from the bath. His skin was drying, and he tried to scratch between his shoulder blades. He yearned for a nice, long soak. The new breather kept the corrosive components of the air out of his lungs, but there was nothing he could do to protect his skin. Leathers and swimming just didn't mix. He would need time to heal, and until he could take the time to do it right, he'd have to suffer the itch from his little skin lesions.

"Hey, Ford! What's up?" he yelled across the work floor. Stamping machines forming shapes in metal and punching holes in the fixtures made raising his voice necessary.

The gray-haired man at the control panel waved at him with his right hand, the one missing the two little fingers. He tapped the screen with the other and the pounding slowed to a crawl.

Joshua said, "Don't stop on my account."

Ford shrugged. "It's just a small lot—replacement parts. What's up? Want me to make something for you?"

"Um, no, not just yet. The new breathing mask works great."

"No leaks?"

"No. I just got back from from a three-mile swim, both ways. I got a mouthful of water a couple of times, but the blow-valve worked just like you said it would."

They talked about the problem with the hose in deep water, but Ford just shrugged. "Too much pressure for sure, but I don't know how to solve that one. Maybe you should ask Ace."

"I will. But for shallow water, I have no complaints about the breather. Den wants one, too."

Ford nodded. "I don't guess you measured his head? The seal has to fit the shape of your face. It's not flexible like the leather breathers."

"No. I forgot about that. I'll probably swim out there again before too long."

"Well, let me know when you'll need it. It'll take me a couple of days and I'll have to make arrangements to get the right leather for the seals and the valve." He shrugged. "This is mostly a metal-and-glass operation here."

"Great," Joshua said, "but I won't know how soon I can get you the measurements. It's not the highest priority right now. I've got more tasks on my plate than I can keep track of."

Ford chuckled. "Don't we all? My rule of thumb is to prioritize by who's asking and how loud they're yelling."

. . .

Joshua thought about Ford's advice when he stopped by the kitchen and wheedled Ciara into fixing him something to eat.

"Den was most appreciative of your dried *jenna*. It was the first thing he dug into from the supplies I brought and he raved about how good they were."

She shook her head, not looking his way, hunched over a cooking pot stirring. Ciara was a little plumper than Sally, or Joshua's mother. She tasted the dish she was preparing. "Poor man. Those weren't anything special. He must be on bag rations, stuck out there."

She fixed Joshua rice with toasted creepers, claiming he'd need the protein when she saw the skin damage he'd need to heal.

"I can send Anra around to help," she offered.

He shook his head. "No, I'm trying to improve my own healing abilities. I'm not in a hurry, so now's a good time to practice."

Ciara shrugged and let him eat in peace.

Healing himself was a personal goal, but part of his motive was an uneasiness around Anra. Her healing skills were excellent, but the girl seemed too happy to put her hands on him. Bernard noticed it and made a couple of comments, once he began spending most of his time at Factory. It started about the time Sally left to go back to New Home, and Joshua was in no mood to complicate things.

Bernard had said, "Don't be so surprised. Cyclops runs everything, and now you're moving into position as his Second. Every unattached female in the place is going to take a closer look at you."

Joshua didn't like his analysis, but perhaps Bernard was right. He was older, and had more experience.

All the more reason to steer clear of any those smiling faces.

He ate every scrap, down to the last grain of rice and the last crunchy bit.

Walking toward the bath, he did a sweep, checking all the alert flags, and then checking the bath itself.

Hurried footsteps came up behind him.

Joshua turned. "Hey, Bernard. I was just thinking about you."

The man nodded, panting. "I was on semaphore duty. Still am. But there was a private message for you from Cyclops. Short one. 'B-N'. Do you know what that means?"

Joshua frowned. "Yeah. I guess we'll have to talk later then. I've got a job to do."

Bernard nodded. "And I'm still on duty. Gotta go."

Joshua hurried toward the bath, but his *sight* was over at Base, locating his father. The man was still talking to others in the map room. Now was not the time to signal him.

He shifted his attention, locating Kakil, the Cerik clan off to the north. Elehadi, the Name of Kakil, was probably the most hated Cerik among the surviving refugees of New Home. He was not on his High Perch, where he spent most of his time. Joshua had to locate him. That was the meaning of the BN shortcut code—monitor Elehadi.

It was full dark with the moon in its more distant position. A crescent Small Moon gave little light, but there was still plenty of activity. Torches burned, each illuminating a circle of huts where warriors rested. One Cerik looked much like all the rest, even through *sight*. But a few were distinctive. Elehadi had his habits. Joshua had to locate him quickly.

As Joshua reached the bath he had to concentrate on his own footsteps. There were four others mostly clustered around the wallow near the steam vents. Metal-shop guys were talking with one of the forge operators about a new batch of metal stock. Joshua would have loved to settle in near there and chat, but not while he was on a job. He found another place where he could rest on his belly, mostly submerged in the warm water, just far enough from the others so that he could ignore their words.

He closed his eyes and let himself get comfortable with the warm water and ignore the faint chemical tang in the air. He concentrated first on adjusting his body chemistry. The long open-air swim had left numerous places, particularly on his back, where his skin cells were damaged. Ulcers were starting to form, and he needed to make sure his cellular defenses were hard at work. Once kickstarted by his focus on the damage, his body knew what to do.

With his more conscious mind, he turned his *sight* back north to Kakil, hunting for Elehadi.

Joshua searched a path he knew the Name followed regularly. There was a private hunting meadow that was off-limits to anyone other than Elehadi and his telepath, Stakka. The two Cerik had strong *ineda* to keep other telepaths from monitoring their thoughts, but to confer privately they needed to make sure no one with more readable minds were within listening distance.

His focus flickered to that meadow, but Elehadi wasn't there, nor were the wide ring of warriors who normally maintained that privacy when he was present. Joshua's memory flickered back to the days when Samson, one of the rare U'tanse warriors in service to the Name, had been part of that guard. It had been Joshua's duty to listen into Samson's thoughts and report what he discovered.

It had been an easier time then, reading a human's thoughts. After Samson's death, he'd had to interpret Cerik minds and because of that had become much more fluent in the Cerik language. Both species had much in common. They had two eyes, two arms, two hands, two legs, and used spoken language. But there was so much that was different between them. Those hands on a Cerik were articulated claws. They saw others only as prey. Written text was beyond them, and they certainly had no history other than verbal tales.

Reading the minds of other species was inherently hard without training. Joshua remembered the day he tried to find a lost *chitchit*, and although he'd made contact with the little animal's mind, he couldn't even interpret what it was seeing through its eyes—their minds were so different.

Was searching at night throwing him off? If he were using his eyes, he'd be at a big disadvantage against a Cerik. They were predators, with senses to match.

But he did have one other option. His ally, the Ba.

Hidden beneath Elehadi's private meadow, a Ba rested just under the surface. It was a secret known only to Cyclops and himself. A Ba was hardly anything like a human. They were circular and flat, able to dig through layers of the soil without being seen. And they had learned the Cerik language. Captive slaves like the U'tanse, several of the Ba had escaped to freedom—at least the freedom to wander on this planet. They, too, yearned for their home far away across space. They spoke of that place where there were Ba on Ba on Ba.

A treaty had been struck in secret, and a living mind was listening directly under Elehadi's secret refuge.

Joshua reached for that mind, resting, almost hibernating, and doing nothing more than listening.

The mind, still like a pond of water, fed him a strange sound. It was ripples, like sound, only lower. Ba could hear it, but this wasn't sound like anything a human could hear.

Then it shifted, rising in pitch.

Joshua took in a breath. He recognized it—a boat coming in for a landing right on top of the Ba!

Monitor Elehadi

Ace had explained it to him once.

"Josh, it's a matter of distance. When the boat is high in the sky, it can pull air for a longer time before the beams reach the ground. When closer, they have to cycle much faster to keep from losing too much power. So the higher the pitch, the closer a boat is to the ground."

Joshua never quite understood the science of it, but the rule of thumb worked. Some boat was coming down, and Ba could feel its force.

Not on top of him!

But through the Ba's mind, it felt like a compression as the boat landed.

But there were still thoughts, vague and indistinct, coming from the Ba. There was pride. There was a feeling of being supported by the whole planet. Ba could hold the weight, no matter what.

Joshua focused his *sight*, now that he had an exact location. Two Cerik exited the boat, and stood aside as the boat lifted away in a wash of blown dust. Both had their thoughts locked down tight, but the larger one was Elehadi. The other was large and powerful, too, the Name of some other clan, probably. But which clan?

Joshua tried to put aside his worries for his pancake-flat alien ally and concentrated on the sounds the Ba could hear.

<Now we're here. If this is a trap, you won't survive it.>

Elehadi shifted his weight backwards, making it more difficult to leap—a sign that he wasn't about to attack. <There are easier ways to take a Name. I brought you here because this is the only place where we can talk. It's just

23

you and me. No pilots, no guards, no one who can hear us. No one whose weak minds could be read.>

The other Cerik inhaled the night air, sniffing for anyone hidden in the dark. He exhaled. <You're right. Other than that *hatsen* upwind.>

Elehadi never let his eyes off the other. All Names were deadly enemies, no matter what the circumstances. Inviting another into his territory was unusual, to say the least.

<We need to discuss the U'tanse.>

The other shifted his weight. <You caused this problem. You're like a *sendt* up against a rock wall.>

Elehadi hissed, then said, <The U'tanse problem started when Tenthonad brought them here in the first place. We've got a swarm of... *helpers* who can turn into a poisonous Ferreer hive without warning.>

<You did that, forcing them into a corner. They had to change or die.>

Elehadi waved his claws. <So now we have to creep like a *lulur* around our own slaves in fear that they will turn into a mind-eating telepathic hive? Better to kill them now, quickly, before they can take that power.>

The other Name rattled his hind talons on the pebbles. Then he said, <We can't. The instant we move, the other U'tanse will find out and their fear will convert them into Ferreer. There's no way we can kill them quickly enough.>

Joshua, took in a deep breath. *The other is seriously considering Elehadi's plan. He's thought about it before. How many other Names want to kill us all off?* He refocused his *sight* on the dark meadow to the north and listened even more carefully through Ba's mind.

Elehadi said, <We can't wait too long, either. You've heard the stories. Even treating the U'tanse like favored pets hasn't stopped the occasional outbreak. Everyone tainted by the Ferreer has been killed off so far, but we've been lucky.>

The other grumbled, <You speak the truth. Even the Sanassan's U'tanse aren't immune. When I was Second, I had to burn a valley to take out a lumbering crew that had turned. My Name at the time tried to keep the news from our other U'tanse, but I suspect that some of them knew. We all pretended it was lava eruption. I fear the day when it will happen again. I have kept a spare power cell in our stores, just in case.>

Joshua made a firm mental note. *Their Name has a power cell all prepped and ready to* flick *Sanassan Home.*

Elehadi's chest rumbled in satisfaction. <We all have to be prepared. I need more power cells. Every Name has to be ready to *flick* their U'tanse at the same moment, all across Ko.>

<If the U'tanse find out—>

<We are Cerik. There are no better hunters. We will circle our enemies in the silence and the dark. That's why we're here, under our *ineda*, with no ears listening in. It will take time to get the word spread.>

<This should really be decided at the Face, not in secret between Names.>

Elehadi paced back and forth, careful not to advance on the other.

<It will never happen! Our slaves listen in to everything that happens at the Face. It doesn't matter that we forbid them to be present. It doesn't matter that every Name *should* have been *ineda* trained. We have weak-minded Names, and not every Name has reliable *rettiks* to attend them. Telepaths know every word that is spoken, all over Ko. Our slaves may pretend ignorance, but there are many secrets behind those down-turned eyes.>

Sanassan's Name grumbled, <Like the ones who have escaped their burrow.>

Elehadi hissed. He shifted his stance. <We hide our claws. In their burrow, our slaves pretend they don't know. Their names refuse to talk about it among themselves. No one wants slaves smelling the tempting breeze. They know we can't ignore U'tanse that run for the hills. Every day I send out fliers, hunting for them. Soon we'll find a trace, and we'll kill all of them. Even the U'tanse know *that* is coming. >

"Joshua." There was a touch on his arm.

He jerked, startled. Anra, Factory's leading healer had swum over to where he was resting.

"Sorry," she said. "I heard that you might need some help with your skin damage."

It took him a moment to shift gears from the intense monitoring of the Cerik Names in the dark meadow, to seeing an albino-white-haired woman in the water next to him. He'd heard that she tended to wear a light gown in the bath, just to avoid the sexual overtures sure to come her way in the male-dominated facility, but seeing the way the wet fabric clung to her skin made him think it was a lost cause.

He shook his head. "Can't. Not now. I'm on monitoring duty, and I need to get back to it." He deliberately closed his eyes and tried to refocus on the meadow.

She quietly moved away, and only when the water quit swirling and he knew she was gone was he successful in reconnecting.

Sanassan was talking. <When my telepath told me of the U'tanse walking in the sea, I sent my own boats to search my shoreline, but it was a waste. The rogue slaves were probably from Rikna anyway. I'm surprised you haven't found them yet. Maybe you should put those excess warriors of yours to use. Search for them the old way—following the game trails.>

<What I do with my own clan is my business. If they're on my lands, I'll find them.>

Joshua listened for another half hour before Elehadi opened his mind just enough to call Stakka, his telepath. Shortly, Sanassan's boat arrived and with a few parting insults, the visiting Name left. Elehadi rested in *dan* for a few minutes, until Stakka arrived.

<For your Name!>

Elehadi came back alert. <Was there any trouble with Sanassan's boat?>

<No, the pilot and his two *rettik* stayed on board until I gave the word to go pick him up.>

Elehadi paced around the meadow. Stakka followed, behind and to the right.

<Sanassan will be ready when the day comes. I could wish all the Names would be as wise.>

Stakka asked, <Will you call all the Names here, one at a time?>

<If I must. This matter has to be kept quiet. I know of no other way.>

<It will not be ready by the Face.>

Elehadi hissed. <I won't forgive what was said before! I need something to make them revere my Name by that time.>

Stakka was silent. Elehadi turned to him. Even in the dim light of a faint moon, they stared at each other.

<Telepath, speak! I won't mistake your words for theirs.>

Stakka couched lower. <For your Name. The last Face was too soon after the burning of the Rikna burrow. The fear of U'tanse-Ferreer was still on them all. And . . . the Names too near you were all in fear of what happened to the Name of Rikna. Everyone knows of your greatness, and your

desire for their lands. Now there is this rumble over the escapes. If you could display the heads of the rogue U'tanse at the next Face, it would do much to still those words.>

Elehadi was quiet. Then he asked, <Why have we not found them yet?>

<Pilots have given up sniffing a dry trail. I have checked their thoughts. Some would fly in *dan*, if they could.>

Elehadi hissed. <I will stir their blood!>

Stakka lowered his head. <A fearful hunter is not a hunter, he is prey.>

Joshua, listening carefully, recognized the line from one of the Tales. It hadn't been three months before that he'd read a translation made by George of Kakil that his father had copied. That particular line came from a story of another Name, long ago, who tried to instill fear into his hunters, and lost half of them to the bogs.

Elehadi must have remembered it, too. He said, in a calmer voice, <We have used too many power cells in the search, keeping the boats in the air. I needed those to move my warriors! With the restrictions from the last Face, it will take too long to get more cells from Tenthonad. They are trying to keep me on the ground!>

He thought for a moment, then said, <Pass the word. Cancel the regular boat searches for the U'tanse. Instead, breeding pit duty for the warrior who brings me a U'tanse head from the coast. If a pilot wishes to participate in the search, then he must beg the favor, and put restrictions on those. The pilot has to be eager to find them.>

Stakka asked, <You are seeking overland searches?>

<Why not? Too many of my warriors rest and await the herders to push a runner their way. Let them wander the hills and find their own meat.>

Joshua memorized the details. Stakka would be appointing one of the Rear Talon *tetca* to schedule the boats. A change to predictable flights was just what Cyclops had been looking for. If they could monitor when Cerik boats were due, the Free U'tanse could time the submarine and their own boats to avoid those periods.

Stakka hurried off. Elehadi started to leave, and then paused. He sniffed the air, and then headed on back to his perch.

On a hunch, Joshua waited a moment, trying to listen even closer through the Ba's mind.

He jerked, splashing a little in the water when he sensed the Ba shifting its position, many feet vibrating and shoving. Like a knife moving sideways through the soil, the Ba moved off, parallel to the line of hills behind the meadow.

Joshua checked again on Elehadi, now moving at a comfortable pace away from the meadow.

When his eyes came open, Joshua looked around. There were only a couple of other people in the bath. He shifted to a shallower ledge and faced Base. In his mind, he could see his father standing at his desk.

Joshua moved his arms, sending a message in code; *monitor complete, high confidence message was understood, I have questions.*

His father, across the bay and under the massive rock dome that shielded Base from discovery, sent back his reply; *high confidence message was understood, I have questions, stay at your current location, expect a message via courier.*

Joshua settled back down in the water, relieved that his father had been able to monitor the exchange as well. But there were so many things he really wanted to discuss with his father. Had the Ba left its post? Why?

Brainstorming

Joshua concentrated on healing his skin. He was a little relieved that Anra had left. Yes, he was trying to improve his self-healing skills, but he was also uncomfortable around healers lately.

They were all women. It was only logical, since generations of U'tanse had consistently conserved the skill of Mother, the first female U'tanse, to carefully monitor and repair the cells of her own body. It was necessary to allow every mother to choose which of the father's sperm would most faithfully preserve their survival skills while eliminating the deadly genes exposed by inbreeding.

Anra's white hair had come from Mother, and it only showed up in a couple of percent of the women. Joshua doubted that there was any link between the hair color and her healing skills, but it was easy to think that. Mother had a fearsome reputation, both among her descendants and among their owners. It wasn't in the official Tales that George had translated, but there was a whispered story among the Cerik that told of her raising Father from the dead and taking over the body of Tenthonad's telepath, just as the Ferreer were reported to do.

Yes, Anra could probably heal him faster than he could manage on his own, but since Sally left, he didn't like being that close to the other women. It was irrational on his part, but healing was often a hands-on experience, and he didn't need the distraction.

He dismissed the irrelevant thoughts and cleared his mind.

Stay where I am? That was his order. There were plenty of things he could do while stranded at Factory, but he had things to check at Base as well.

He moved his focus there. His father was resting on the bed near his desk. Joshua suspected he was running tired, as well.

His mother, Debbie, was down in the gardens, alone for a change, tending her crops. She had helpers, but whenever she wanted to be by herself, she'd go weed her test beds.

He shifted over to the nursery. It seemed like ages had passed since his whole world had been bound by the walls of those few rooms. Until children could reliably protect their thoughts from the Cerik, that's where they had to live. His sister Veronica still lived there, although she had the skills to leave. She just wasn't ready to live under *ineda* all the time. The surface thoughts of someone living in an enclosed nursery was no danger. No Cerik could locate them from that. There would be no hint that this nursery was any different from all the Homes in all the clan lands across the planet. The U'tanse skills of *sight* and telepathy together gave them a great advantage over the predators.

He lightly touched Very's thoughts and smiled. She was playing games with the cuties, and in a way her thoughts were like theirs. Not all the time, though. Little Timothy was taking cautious steps, trying to get from the crib to a springy-toy just out of his reach. Very watched, resisting the urge to go help him. She picked up her drawing book and moved to a chair to be closer, just in case the little boy fell and cried.

Is she carrying that thing around again?

The drawings were worrisome. Ash, Veronica's best friend, was the real artist of the group, but when Veronica started having her bad dreams, he'd had the idea of getting her to draw her disturbing visions as a way to keep from worrying about them.

Perhaps it was a good idea. Joshua wasn't sure, himself. But one thing had become clear. His little sister was having dreams about things far beyond the range of the nursery—bad things that hadn't happened yet.

I wish I could sneak a peek at what she's drawn recently. That was what Sylvia did, when she got a chance between changing the diapers of the little ones, including her own little Timothy, and managing the squabbles among the older ones.

Joshua was really jealous of his father's *sight*. Cyclops no longer had eyes—he'd lost them in a fire when he was young—but his clairvoyance was so finely tuned that he could read text from books far across the world.

That was so rare a skill that no one thought it possible. The Free U'tanse didn't want anyone to realize it, not even other U'tanse.

But as much as her dream journal might give them hints about upcoming dangers, the nightmares were dangerous to Veronica. She appeared to have no control over them, and they scared her. If she knew—really knew—that they were prophetic visions, the little girl might be traumatized even more. Thus far, even when her earlier visions proved predictive of the breakout of attachment in the dying Rikna Home and of his burns in the explosion, Joshua and his parents had decided to keep that information from his sister.

I just wish they would stop. I don't want Very suffering from scary monsters in her dreams, and I sure don't want her to feel trapped by horrible visions of a future that she can't change.

But if there were predictions in that drawing book, then Sylvia had to sneak a look and pass the information on to Cyclops.

I fear the day when Sylvia can't make sense of the drawings. I don't want to be the person who has to ask Very what she saw in her dreams.

He sighed and checked the healing process. It was good enough. Infections had been staved off and new skin tissue was growing into place. It was time to dry off.

. . .

"You should have asked me first," Ace said the next day. "But there are ways around it. It's obvious you can't breathe through a siphon once you go too deep. Your lungs are supplying the power, like a vacuum pump. The problem is that there's no way you can pull that much vacuum, just with muscle power. Animals were never designed for that."

The engineer, only a couple of years older than Joshua, tapped the diagram he drew of the underwater breather. "You need a compression pump, up here on the float. In theory, a mechanical pump there could compress all the air you need to match the pressure against your chest put there by the weight of the water above you." He waved his hand. "Unfortunately, the deeper you get, the bigger the pump." He shrugged. "If the idea is to hide from the boats flying overhead, then it's a lost cause."

Joshua sighed, "I've been having an idea lately. But I'm getting nowhere." He had hoped that a good brainstorming session with Ace would clear his head. He'd slept uneasily after that last monitoring session watching Elehadi.

There were too many changes happening too fast, and with no easy communication with his father, he felt trapped. Cyclops was in charge, not him. It was his job to wait for new orders.

"The breather works," pointed out Ace.

"Yeah. But I want to do more. With the Names aware of us now, I don't feel like Base and Factory are as safe as they used to be. The only place I really feel safe is underwater." Joshua grinned. "I realize that's just me, but the Delense felt the same way, back before they gave in and became slaves to the Cerik. Even the submarine was originally their craft."

Ace nodded. "But it's ours now. We've rebuilt it. Half the works are now U'tanse design."

Joshua said, "Only... there's just one of them. Can we build more? A whole fleet of them?"

Ace let out a sigh and shook his head. "Pieces, maybe. I've been all through the Factory, and if the hull was fabricated here, the machines have been replaced with other things."

Joshua scratched the back of his neck. It itched there, and maybe he'd need to check the skin when he had time. "We've been making eggs. I was surprised at the ones we used during the Rikna evacuation—the man-sized ones with built-in air filters. You've made some as storage containers, too—different-sized ones."

Ace smiled. "Yeah, we've got the fabricator working great. We can make elongated metal egg shapes, complete with the protective surface, in a wide variety of sizes. After that, it's just a matter of cutting openings in them."

"How big? What's the maximum size?"

Ace looked at the ceiling thoughtfully. "To make a submarine hull out of it?"

"Yes. How big?"

Ace shook his head. "The diameter of the fabricator is the limit. I could make one a hundred feet long, but at best, only five feet wide. Not that we'd be able to move a hull that size out of the fabrication bay. Certainly we can't duplicate something the size of the submarine. Even if I could, the eggs aren't as thick and as sturdy as the submarine hull—they'd have to be braced internally to prevent them from collapsing if they got too deep under the surface."

He turned to a display panel and his fingers started dancing over the circular control pads, much faster than Joshua could follow. Shortly, some diagrams started to appear, annotated with squiggly figures. Joshua could tell it was Delense script, but that was never something he'd studied.

"Is that...?"

Ace nodded, "Yes. It's the original diagrams for the submarine. Or, *a* submarine. It doesn't quite match the one we have today. But I ran across this diagram a few months ago and filed a shortcut to it. I've never really studied it in detail."

"Can you read Delense?"

Ace chuckled. "I can translate it with the index. It takes a while. Someday I'd like to be able read it cold, but I can't yet." He waved at a dense set of text. "The interesting part here is a list of design constraints. The size of the hull limits the size of the engine, which requires chemical batteries of a certain size and weight—"

"Chemical batteries?"

"Yeah. The sub was invented before the Delense had power cell technology. That's one of the things we changed with our sub. There was nothing left of the batteries but a corroded mass of sludge when Aaron discovered it at the bottom of the bay. I hear there were only a handful of people here at that time. I'm surprised they were even able to get it up off the bottom, let alone get it to work again."

Joshua had heard stories of those days, before even his parents had joined the Free U'tanse. As much as he'd wrinkled his nose at the Cerik, who only had a verbal history, there was quite a bit of his own family's history that had never been written down. He added that to his mental checklist of things to be done.

"So," he asked Ace, "can you take the size of the egg hull you can make, and apply those design limits to it? Can you make us a little sub? Even a one-man sub that could make a regular run between Base and Factory without the Cerik boats being able to see it would be valuable. One that could go all the way to New Home would change everything for us."

Ace frowned at the text and pulled out a scroll of metal with the translation index on it. "It will take a while." He fussed with the scroll. "I need to get this all on paper. It's a pain to deal with."

...

Blaaa! Blaaa! Blaaa! The alert blast echoed down the hallway shortly after Ace and Joshua had finished their mid-day meal. Fainter echoes, returning from farther passages, followed.

Joshua automatically looked to where the semaphore station would be, even though it was through hundreds of feet of rock and machinery. His *sight* showed Bernard intently copying a message, one letter at a time.

He then focused on Base. His father was standing tall, holding his arms wide, right arm up at the quarter position, left arm straight.

No, let Bernard do his job. No need to interpret the codes myself.

Checking Kakil, Joshua saw more activity than there had been since Rikna's invasion. Elehadi's plan seemed to be spreading rapidly through his clan. *The idea that an ordinary warrior could get a chance at the breeding pits has fired their imaginations.* Joshua was dismayed at how quickly things had changed.

The Sanassan's Name had made a comment about there being too many Kakil warriors. He probably wasn't joking. Elehadi's aggressive "annexation" of neighboring clans had acquired their warriors and the best herders. He had more warriors than he needed, especially now that the other clans had restricted his ability to move his warriors around by boat. Too many hungry, idle Cerik meant lots of fights and too few runners to keep them fed.

It was just hours after the announcement, but it looked like a dozen or more hunting parties were headed toward the shoreline. None appeared heading in their direction, so it wasn't like they'd been found. It was just that the search had expanded.

Joshua checked the Kakil landing field. Pilots were fighting each other for the privilege of taking out a boat to hunt for signs of rogue U'tanse. He recognized the signs of a *koodak* where contestants were bringing fresh-killed prey as gifts to the Rear Talon *la* to decide which pilot could get access to a boat first. At least he didn't see any boats in the air.

Joshua was just considering how much the contest might delay the searches when Ace asked, "What's going on?"

Joshua blinked. *Oh yeah, Ace's a* tenner. *All he knows is that the alert sounded.*

"Sorry. Kakil has gone into heavy search mode. Many new search parties. Base is sending new orders. I've got to run see what the semaphore said."

Ace nodded. "Go. There's nothing more you can do here. The numbers don't look good enough for a little sub anyway. Anything we could make would have limited range, and it'd be a death trap for the pilot if anything went wrong."

Joshua nodded. "Keep thinking about it. I've got to go." He ran.

Supply Run

Joshua had to dodge people as he made his way through Factory's corridors. The three blasts on the horn had sent people to pre-assigned positions. He had no permanent assignment at Factory so he wasn't in on those plans. It was just chaos to him.

Bernard waved a hand toward the papers as Joshua came in. Semaphore codes from Base had the flagger's attention, so he didn't have time to talk.

Joshua looked over the sheets laid out side by side, the ink still damp and shiny.

People monitoring Kakil had determined that the *koodak* ritual gave them a window of time to get a resupply mission off to New Home with little chance of being spotted if they moved fast. There was a list of manufactured items to be loaded into a boat. The submarine would pick up food supplies from Base and take them back to Factory. If the *koodak* was still undecided by the time they were all loaded, they'd fly the boat from Factory to New Home.

Joshua was assigned to go along to New Home, with new written instructions to arrive with the food supplies.

Patrick entered and began reading from the first sheet.

"Joshua, can you help with the loading?"

"Sure."

Patrick picked up a pen and began copying part of the list. "Then drop this off at stores, and tell Wender to put the cradle in the water. I'll be down there as quickly as I can."

Joshua took the paper and ran.

. . .

The cradle was a raft made of fat, thin-shelled pipes. It was light, but sturdy enough. It had wheels, and the crew just rolled the fifty-foot-long framework off the dock. Joshua swam in the water, helping push it past the concealment drapery, out a few dozen yards past any obstructions. There was a smaller loading cradle just like it for the other transport.

He felt the shaking in his body before he heard anything.

"It's coming," he yelled to the three other swimmers helping to maneuver the unpowered structure.

Everyone held on, careful to stay low in the water.

Boat B appeared like a *ska* overhead—at first just a dark patch in the sky. But then it lowered quickly, and the downdraft threw up sea spray everywhere. Joshua had his breather mask and goggles on, but it didn't help him see. The boat's shadow moved over and then the cradle sagged deeper as it took on the weight.

"Reel us in!" came a shout from one of the other swimmers.

The cable tightened and began pulling boat, cradle, and the swimmers back behind the drapery. A few minutes later, the cradle was lashed in place next to the dock and a plank was laid out to the opened hatchway. Joshua was barely out of the water before the supply pallets of sheetmetal, pipes, and other materials were being wheeled into the boat.

Two men were huddled in conversation. Joshua moved closer to hear.

Patrick asked, "Are you sure?"

Carson, Boat B's pilot, nodded. "It was faint, but I could see the shimmering trail in the water. It vanished where the inlet meets the bay. I guess that's when the submarine went to deeper water."

Patrick nodded. "The submarine left just minutes before you arrived. Paint residue, it has to be. Let's hope it dissipates quickly. I didn't see it after the first paint job."

Joshua tossed on a robe and joined the crew loading the supplies. His clairvoyant peek at Base a few minutes later showed that the submarine had entered through the underwater passageway and the loading was just starting. His mother was there on the docks, checking some paperwork that was being attached to the food crates. At the pace everyone was working, the submarine might be back within an hour or so. And then he'd be off to New Home. No telling how long it would be before he could return. It could be only a day. It might be months.

He shook off the idle thought that months there with Sally might be a perfect way to spend the time.

What did he need to take with him?

When the first stage of loading was done, he hurried back to change into better clothes and to bundle his underwater breather for easy carrying. He got a standard breather and leathers from stores for regular use. He was likely to be outdoors some.

He also caught a few moments with Ace.

The man shook his head. "It still doesn't look good. We could make a small sub powered by a chemical battery, but its limited range would make it nearly useless. I could do without tanks for breathing air and use a snorkel system, but that wouldn't get you deep enough to avoid detection from the air."

"It's a power problem? Can't you use a power cell? Those store lots more energy than chemical batteries."

Ace nodded. "Right, but that's push-pull energy. We need lots of electricity to run the motor on the sub to spin the propeller. Converting power from a cell to electricity, at least in those quantities, takes a module even bigger than the motor itself. The numbers just don't work out—not for a hull we can fabricate."

Joshua urged him to keep thinking about the problem. Looking over at the final supplies being loaded, Joshua had no more time to talk.

. . .

They were in the air, heading high and at a diagonal southwest, avoiding any hint at where they were really heading. Carson yelled at him, "Report that I can't see any sign of the submarine paint trail that I saw last time."

Joshua replied, "Got it."

He'd have to wait for the next scheduled semaphore session, when he was at a stable location, but it was good to know.

Carson was planning to weave an erratic course, and that would take longer than usual. It gave Joshua time to pull out his orders and reread them.

For Joshua from Cyclops:

It has been months since our regular flights to New Home stopped, so I'm charging you with the important task of mending relations between us and them. I'd advise you to spend much more time listening to their problems and concerns than trying to convince them that our policies emphasizing safety are correct. In many ways you are the perfect spokesman. You were right there during their rescue and were nearly killed for them. You don't want to mention that, but they will know it.

Specific tasks to accomplish:

Train someone with distant clairvoyant skills in the full semaphore alphabet. The warning flag system is too limited. Set up a regular schedule between New Home and our Base and Factory operators. If we don't talk regularly, we'll never be able to work together. I've included an illustrated chart to leave with them.

Now that you've spent time at Factory, and you've learned some of their capabilities and limitations, I want you to do the same thing at New Home. By now, they've had a chance to explore the Delense technology left at their island. Maybe they can do some things that Factory can't, and we already know Factory can make things they need. We need to set up a viable trading system, just like between Base and Factory, and like we do with the Festivals. Learn what resources they can provide and help them realize what they can do with them.

Talk with Sally and work out your disagreement. It's a miniature version of Base versus New Home. Solve your problem, and maybe we can solve the bigger one.

There was more, but the personal note sounded more like it was from his mother. He'd just have to see whether he and Sally could resolve their points of view. He could understand what she had said. The people of New Home were important to her and she thought Cyclops was too arbitrary in his decisions. He just couldn't agree that the newly freed U'tanse had enough sense of how to keep everything secret.

He folded the papers and stared out the viewport. Endless water passed below. Carson was still making random course changes, even though they were well out of sight of the land. Everyone was taking extra precautions. The stakes were too high not to.

A color change in the sea outside caught Joshua's eye. He leaned closer to the viewport. His *sight* added clarity. There was a wide mound just below the surface, like an island not yet born. He barely had time to notice the fish swirling over a hot spot, and then the boat moved on, leaving the sea mound behind.

Maybe it'll be an island someday. He remembered something Sally had said about New Home. The Delense had built a facility there, some time before their extermination. But the stream that had channeled through the burrows originally had gone dry. Supposedly, part of the hillside had shifted, tilting the ground. U'tanse survivors from Rikna had to build a dam above the living areas to re-direct the stream into the old dried channel. The island was still changing, growing larger over time.

It's like that Cerik tale about the Name who tried to colonize Far Island. The story had talked about an island that had appeared out of the sea. The tale had been a precautionary tale, with the Name finding only bare rock and eating his Delense to survive long enough to sail back to the mainland. That was the only mention of Cerik sailing on water boats. Had they ever gone back to Far Island, now that they had true flying boats?

Joshua was content that Cerik stayed on the mainland, never considering islands at all. All it would take would be someone like Elehadi to make the mental leap and New Home could be discovered.

It was bad enough that they could detect the thoughts of U'tanse there. If just one Cerik was able to locate them by their thoughts, it would be all over. Luckily, they didn't have that skill.

Joshua's deepest fear came from his days when he monitored Samson. That giant had deeply believed that what was best for the U'tanse was showing unswerving loyalty to his Name, Elehadi. Would Samson have betrayed his own people to his master? Possibly. He'd certainly destroyed the Rikna Home, and himself along with it, when it had been overcome by attachment.

How many other U'tanse feel more loyalty to their Cerik Names than to distant U'tanse who are less than strangers to them?

Joshua had been born free, with no Cerik master. Trying to understand Samson's loyalty as a slave had been the hardest part of his monitoring duty.

It was something he never fully understood. Samson had been fully aware of Elehadi's casual disregard for the U'tanse, yet his sense of duty had driven him to his final task.

Carson interrupted his thoughts. "We're approaching New Home. Sometimes the wind makes landings rough. Hang on."

Joshua could see the edges of the land out his viewport. Somewhere, Sally was on that island.

He gripped the bar attached to the hull and waited out the noise and shaking.

"We're down."

"Thanks, Carson. It was a smooth trip."

Just as he got to his feet, he sensed the unshielded thoughts of a number of people, excited that they'd arrived.

Joshua frowned. *They should stop! It isn't safe.*

The hatchway opened, and he stepped out on the island. People were coming from all directions.

New Home

It was unlike any place he'd ever been before. Even on his earlier visit to the island, the Rikna refugees had been fearful and nervous. He had checked up on Sally from time to time, but he'd never given the place a good look recently. It felt like everything had changed. The mood was more open and alive.

Everyone out in the open air wore breathers, of course, but only a couple of people were in leathers. He could see the airlock into the burrow—the U'tanse-designed hatchway built on top of the original opening. But that was hardly the most shocking to him.

Open fields, rows of crops, stretched across the land from the high-tide line up to the hills. A Cerik pilot could *not* miss it, not even the stupid ones.

New Home had no fear of being seen.

"Joshua!" A man came striding his way, his hand outstretched. "It's good to see you."

"Otto." He shook the elder's hand. "We've got some supplies for you. Carson has a list of everything."

"Wonderful. Wonderful. I'll get people to unload it." He waved a couple of men over and started the process.

Joshua looked from side to side, every step showing how developed the place had become. Nothing was hidden. Nobody had given a thought to security. His grip tightened around his bag, but he forced himself to relax the scowl that had formed. His father's advice echoed in his head. He had a role to play here, he couldn't sabotage it. *No yelling. Don't throw up any barriers between us.*

Otto smiled, "You're impressed by how much we've done since you were here last?" He looked fondly over the fields.

"Um. Yes."

Otto sighed, "It's really not as productive as we'd like. We can't eat most of what we grow. It's all native plants, out here in the open air."

Joshua remembered the last time he'd looked in on Sally. "Is it feed stock for creepers?"

The man nodded. "Some of that—we eat a lot of bug stew here—but a lot of it is for materials. We have our own *shash* fields—we almost wiped out the stocks that grew naturally along the stream. There's also a bush we can beat to extract usable fibers." He fingered his tunic. "It's rough, but it's all we've got."

Otto pointed off to the left as they approached the airlock. "Over there, we have our local variety of *kel* trees. A lot of them get cut early for small structural use, but I have hopes we'll get some mature ones for bigger timber. We didn't even start that stand. I don't know how they got here to the island, but it's all we have for building, other than just stacking stones."

They went inside and Joshua removed his breather. He was conscious that he was the only one in leathers, but he had only a single change of clothes.

He fingered the leather sleeve. "I take it there are no large animals on the island?"

One of Otto's assistants chuckled, "Well, nothing that we can use for leather. But there are some sea creatures we find on the rocks sometimes." He tugged his belt off and let Joshua feel it. The leather was like hundreds of fingernail-sized pebbles, all merged together into a flexible strip. "We call them nobblies. The meat is almost too tough to eat, but we can get maybe five or six strips like this off their hide."

Joshua smiled, "Full leathers might be a bit uncomfortable, then."

They laughed. The assistant shook his hand. "I'm Derry. Sally is a first cousin."

Joshua tried not to react. Most of Sally's relatives were at New Home. "Nice to meet you. If I get a chance, I'd like to see a nobbly. I don't recall anything like it."

"I'll keep an eye out. There's a better chance of seeing them at low tide, so it's a few days yet. How long are you going to be here?"

Joshua looked at Otto. "I don't know. We've really been hiding a lot the past few months. There've been boats flying along the coastline every day, and at irregular times. Our boats and the water craft are all hidden where none of their scouts can find them. That means we don't get to use them either."

He shrugged, then continued, "Just yesterday, Elehadi of Kakil changed up the way scouting missions were scheduled, and that gave us a brief opportunity to send you these supplies. Carson will take the boat back just as soon as a new gap in their hunt happens, but I'll be here long enough to train someone in the semaphore code so we can communicate more freely."

Just then, another assistant, Ruth, came in with questions about where to store the new supplies. Otto left to deal with it. Derry was given the task of finding places for Carson and Joshua to stay.

He said, "There are a number of rooms in the Delense burrow still vacant, although we'll have to get someone to clean them out. Unless, that is ..."

"Yes?"

"Um. Did you intend to stay with Sally?"

Joshua sighed. "Well, when she left we had some unresolved issues. I'd better not impose on her."

...

By sunset, the boat was unloaded and the corridors of New Home were busy with people, mostly women, either organizing the goods, or planning what to do with them. Joshua was swamped with the random thoughts. No one seemed to care about *ineda*. He wanted to warn them, but kept his thoughts to himself.

The agricultural supplies were the most welcomed. Debbie had included a variety of food stocks that New Home didn't have, as well as packets of seeds and cuttings that would enable their indoor gardens to grow more nutritious foods.

Ellen, the head gardener, sought him out with questions. She held up a screw-lid metal cylinder. "I don't understand this. What are 'potato creepers'?"

He took the can and unscrewed it. There were about a hundred of them, with their legs wrapped tightly up against their bodies.

"You know potatoes, right?"

Ellen nodded. "Oh, sure. We had them back at Rikna. I'm very grateful to see you brought us some. We'll get them cut and planted just as soon as we can."

Joshua smiled. She frowned at his expression. "What?"

He said, "You look and sound like a younger version of Elizabeth."

She smiled sadly. "She was my mom."

Joshua said, "She saved my life, during the explosion. I only knew her from a few minutes together, but she made an impression on me."

Every minute of that day was burned into his memories—the raid into the Rikna Home to rescue the people who hadn't had their wills absorbed into the hive mind. In fact, Ellen's thoughts—vivid memories of that hurried rush up the mountain trail to reach the shelter on the other side of the pass before the Home was obliterated by the flick of an overloaded power cell—were leaking from her.

She said, "I was in the party just ahead of you on the trail. I could hear how you kept urging her on. Thank you for that."

There was an old ache, the pain of her mother dying in the explosion, spreading her arms to shield Joshua and young Lucy from the flash.

Then Ellen straightened. "Now, back to the creepers?"

He replaced the lid. "They're dormant now. They'll stay that way until you let them out in damp soil. They're a native species, but they can live in filtered air and have a taste for the potato plant. They found their way into Base and infested our crops. At first, we just plucked them off and disposed of them as pests, but Debbie, my mother, was always experimenting. She let some of them grow larger and found that they were a good source of protein—more bug stew." He grinned.

She grimaced. "We have that already."

He handed her the can. "It's your choice. Keep them away from the potatoes and have a better crop, or allow some to chew on the leaves and have a protein supplement. They're fairly tasty. You might try a few and see what you think."

She shook her head. "We're starved for Earth-native crops. The potatoes, corn, and rice you brought are our highest priorities now. We had them all back at Rikna, but seeds were the last things on our minds in the escape."

Joshua helped her interpret the notes his mother had included with the shipment. He'd spent plenty of time helping her tend the garden growing up. There were basic food stocks, packets of seeds, and shoots of what Debbie had named "cotton," like the fabric mentioned in the Book.

New Home's internal gardens were wider than those at Base, but the roof was lower. He commented, "It's lucky you have power for your lights."

Ellen nodded. "That's new. We had to live by torchlight when we first arrived. It was only after they redirected the water that the electricity came back on line. Even now, we don't have any blue lights for Earth crops. I don't know how that will affect them."

He nodded; his mother had taught him all about how Earth plants always grew better under lights with a more blueish tint than the red light of Ko's sun.

"I'll be sure to pass that on. Factory can make lights with different colors. We can ship earth-lights the next chance we get." He sighed. "It's frustrating. We could have included those, if we'd just realized it. We've got to get better communications."

Ellen shook her head. "We're telepaths. I've never understood why you have to resort to flags and things."

Joshua didn't argue. She wasn't the person who needed convincing.

...

"Sally's going to be upset she wasn't here," Lonna said as the group gathered around a table. They were looking at a full bowl of something pungent. The smiling, motherly old woman reached for one of the wooden scoops and helped herself to a dab of the main dish.

Joshua tried it. "Chewy. Not bad." The seasoning offset the slight bitterness.

Lonna smiled, "Don't ask what kind of critter supplied those lumps. Just enjoy the result."

He nodded. "Someone told me Sally was on the other side of the island?"

"Right. A party headed out a couple of days ago. We've explored the coastline, but the interior still had a few places we've only *seen*. Sally and her girls discovered a second burrow last month, and they're anxious to see what other things the Delense left for us."

Sally and her girls? Joshua remembered seeing Sally with a group of five slightly younger girls one of the times he'd peeked over at the island to see how she was doing. He hadn't thought anything about it at the time. Or rather, he'd been glad she wasn't spending a lot of time with one of the few men of New Home.

Before Rikna Home's destruction, most of the male workers had been sold off to other clans. The remaining population was heavily female although there were children and some of the elderly who hadn't been considered workers. During the window of time between the founding of New Home and the start of the overflights, there had been a few exchanges. Women came to live at Factory and Base, and some of the men there went to become part of New Home. But all that halted suddenly when the highest priority became hiding out from the searchers.

Joshua said, "I'd love to know what you find. We're happy to send you supplies—it's our duty since we brought you here—but you're going to need more things than what Base and Factory can supply. The All-Ko Festival is coming up in a few months, and if we could find something to trade with the other Homes, New Home could become much more independent."

Otto asked, "I've been wondering about that. I had hoped to talk to Cyclops about Festival. Base has been trading with the other Homes for some time now, right?"

Joshua quickly surveyed the others at the table. Everyone in this little group had a tight *ineda*. He'd just have to trust that critical information would stay secret.

"Certainly not by that name, and we've never revealed that our 'Secret Home' was anything more than just a hidden group owned by a Name who wanted his ownership of U'tanse to stay secret."

Some of the clans had long-standing resistance to the U'tanse, but even they appreciated the manufactured goods that could only be had through those off-world hands. Sometimes a Name would swallow his pride and purchase the traditional twenty-seven U'tanse from another clan to start his own Home. But it wouldn't seem unusual if a resistant clan tried to skirt the rules and created a hidden Home.

Otto frowned. "I remember a woman at the last Western Festival I attended. She was interested in trading her spice plants for leather pelts, but she never revealed which Home she was from."

Joshua nodded. "My mother. She's been our primary contact to the Festivals. We try to stay out of sight."

"So, you think New Home should try to attend Festival?"

"You should certainly make the effort to have something to trade. Either work though us or develop your own story—one that won't raise any questions. Certainly you could never go personally. You're too well known and you supposedly died at Rikna."

Otto said, "We don't have any transportation off the island."

Joshua tapped the table. "And that's why I need to train someone in semaphore. There's a lot to be discussed. Lots of plans to make. Don't try to convince me; I'm just a messenger."

Otto thought a moment. "Semaphore requires good clairvoyance."

Joshua had been through the training process and had seen how it was done. He'd made a list. "And a good memory, and the ability to write down the codes rapidly. There's also a lot of idle time between messages, so they'd need patience. It's important to have someone who can keep secrets. Do you have anyone in mind with all those skills?"

Meeting Holana

Cyclops was still at his desk when Joshua retired to the room they'd set up for him. Joshua faced the wall in the direction of Base and rested both hands on top of his head. His father must have been waiting for him, because he started waving his arms.

According to the Book written by the ancestor of all the U'tanse, semaphore was the name of a way of signaling with flags back on Earth. Unfortunately, Father didn't explain how it was done or what different signs were used. Cyclops and Patrick had started using codes they'd made up to communicate between Base and Factory before Joshua was even out of the nursery. Over time, they'd enhanced the codes, including common phrases as well as the full alphabet. It was almost like talking, after having used it regularly over the past year.

Cyclops sent, *"Any problems?"*

Joshua moved his arms, *"Calm here. New information. Gardening needs blue lights. New Delense burrow discovered. Candidate chosen for semaphore training."*

Cyclops replied, *"Noted. Private code follows: Ba remaining in meadow but in a new position. Overflights resumed. Can predict schedule, but not course of boat. Tell Carson to remain until we have safe time. Will notify. Arms tired."*

Joshua closed with, *"Arms tired."*

It was more like his brain was tired. He'd had to be more social than he was used to. Everyone seemed to be watching him and listening to every word he said. A couple of times he'd had to back up and rephrase what he'd said when it was clear the New Home people were reading more into his words than he'd intended.

Carson kept quiet during the meal, but privately, he'd mentioned that several people had asked if they were going to keep the boat here at New Home. He just shrugged and said that he was just the pilot, he didn't make the decisions.

Joshua knew the answer. For quite a few reasons, the boat would be based back at Factory, no matter what the New Home people wanted.

Soon enough, Otto would make a formal request. He just hoped he'd know how to answer diplomatically when the time came.

...

They found an isolated chamber far enough from the main passageways where the semaphore trainee could work with no distractions. Joshua made sure there was a table where messages could be written and displayed, and he discovered just how poor New Home's supply of paper was. They made do with beaten *shash*, and had no regular production set up. He made another note on his list of supplies that New Home needed.

Lonna arrived with a short girl in tow. She looked about his age, but she wore a tunic that draped down low. She wore her hair, a slightly darker brown than most, down nearly to her waist.

"This is Holana."

"Hello, I'm Joshua," he said. "You're here for training?"

She smiled. "I guess. That's what they tell me." She looked around the room. "You'll have to explain it all."

He nodded, then pulled out his papers. Lonna smiled encouragingly at Holana and then left.

"Have a seat, Holana."

She looked at the chair and the bench. "Which one?"

He shrugged. "If this works out for you, you'll be spending a lot of time in this room. You might as well get comfortable."

She looked at the chair before she chose the bench.

Joshua started off easy. "You're from Rikna. What did you do there?"

She smiled. "I was still looking at a lot of things. My mother wanted me to help with the weaving, but I was easily distractible and got into trouble."

"Distractible?"

She shrugged. "Oh, you know, I was weaving a pattern into the fabric and there'd be ... things happening outside."

Joshua thought back to his own days in the nursery, when his clairvoyance was developing. "Outside the room, or ... what?"

She waved her hand to the air. "Oh, everywhere. My *sight* had kicked in, and I was interested in everything."

He nodded. "That's one thing we need to test. Are you ready?"

She looked worried. "Um ... now?"

"Yes."

She took a breath. "Okay."

He considered what to test her with.

"Can you *see* where Rikna Home was?"

She frowned. "Yes. I've looked. It's just a big hole in the ground now."

"Let's go there, now." He remembered the same exercise his father had used with him, testing his *sight*.

Her eyes drifted away from his face, not focused. "Oh, it's filled with water."

His *sight* zeroed in on the location of her former home, too. There was rubble, forming a rough crater, left by the explosion. But the river that had been the core of the Rikna burrow had been blocked, filling the cavity with a calm pool. There was a waterfall at the outflow.

"Look at the waterfall," he said. "How many channels do you see?"

"Um. Three, no ... four I guess. There's a little one on the far side."

He led her on, down the valley below the waterfall.

"Look at the little tree next to the round boulder. Position your right and left arms at exactly the same position as the two biggest branches of the tree."

She frowned, her eyes closing. "The two biggest branches." Hesitantly, she held out her arms, shifting them into the correct angles.

He spent another thirty minutes mentally walking her through the landscape, testing the precision with which she could see the scene across the ocean.

Then, finally, he said. "That's enough for now. You have a good distance *sight*."

Holana opened her eyes and gave a wistful smile. "Mom never could understand this. Now, she could could count the individual fibers in the threads between her fingers as she worked them into cloth, but she couldn't really *see* the next room. It was frustrating to her that I couldn't work as precisely as she could."

Joshua quietly commented, "Your *ineda* is good. I've been checking. It's better than most of the people here at New Home use. Do you find it hard to keep it going?"

She shook her head. "Not really. I had a friend, back before... back when I was little. He was a *tenner,* and he bragged that no one really needed telepathy; that it was a crutch. I didn't believe him at the time, but I had a teacher who kept her mind blocked all the time. She could read me, but I couldn't read her and it irritated me. I think I trained in *ineda* just to get back at her."

Joshua scratched at his neck. "I grew up at Base, where everyone lived with constant *ineda.* The only thoughts I could sense were those of the children in the nursery and the distant churn of all the other people in the world. When you can't sense the emotions of those around you directly, you learn to rely on other cues—the pauses in speech, the facial expressions, the tone of the voices. I guess it's like the original humans, back on Earth. You can tell a lot more about what people are thinking than just the details that the words give you. For example, from the way you talk about her, I know there's a story about your mother that you haven't explained yet."

Holana looked down at her hands. "I suppose so. Is it important?"

"I don't know. Should I know about it?"

She hesitated. "Maybe. I guess there's no reason you shouldn't."

She raised her eyes and said, "Mom was... attached."

Joshua sighed. "I'm sorry." It had to be painful, having her mother's mind absorbed.

Holana began fiddling with her hands, picking at her fingernails.

"Dad was sold early. He was one of the first workers taken when Elehadi decided to sell off all the Rikna workers. Mom took it hard. She got very clingy. Kelly, my little sister, had to be by her side all the time. Mom wanted me to stay close too, but... I didn't want to. I wanted to find a place to get away from it all—a place to hide, I guess.

"But there was no place to hide. As workers began leaving, one by one, it was plain that those of us who were left were just going to be killed. The depression was so thick I could barely breathe."

Joshua whispered, "I know. It was my job to monitor the situation. It was unbearable."

She managed a faint smile. "I wish I'd known." She shook her head, and looked away. "I hid out at the bath. There were chambers there, you know. It was just a place to be."

She took a deep breath. "And then, the news came out that workers could take their wives with them. Mom couldn't take it. If Dad had just been sold later, maybe they could have stayed together. She tried to find me, tried to get me to come back. I clamped down my *ineda* tight, hiding my thoughts. And then after a bit, I could sense that she'd changed. Her panic went away, and her thoughts were even stronger, but... it was like she wasn't the same person.

"The whispers spread through the Home. Every thought was about the attachment. It had happened. More and more people were becoming part of a hive mind. I could sense Kelly was one of the first, and she was attached even more firmly to Mom. I hid in the darkness and put all my effort into the *ineda*. They'd track me down, I knew it. They'd make me part of them. I'd be swallowed up."

Her eyes were wet. She looked at Joshua, pleading to be understood, "But they were my *family*. Mom and Kelly, and I abandoned them."

He realized he'd been holding his breath and let it out in a long sigh. "You survived. Your mother, even attached, would have wanted that. You made the best choice."

He gave her a moment and then pulled out a chart of semaphore positions. "I hope your memory is good, because you're going to have to memorize all of these, and quickly."

Semaphore Practice

"Hugo!" Joshua shook the man's hand. "How's it going, being a New Home man?"

"Great. It's good to see you, kid."

Hugo's smile was broad and genuine, but he looked a little thinner and a little older than Joshua remembered. He wondered if it was the New Home diet—but the light was dim down in the depths of the New Home burrow. It could just be that. But the gray hair was definitely more pronounced.

"How are things back at Base? We've been missing you."

Joshua spread his hands. "Constant Cerik overflights. We couldn't even get the sub out in the bay most of the time. I was on messenger duty, swimming back and forth."

Hugo punched him lightly on the arm. "I can tell. You've filled out great. Having to fight off the girls?"

Joshua smiled and looked around the room. "Hey, you've got all the girls here."

Hugo looked embarrassed. "Oh, yeah. Let me introduce you."

He had three women with him. Betty, Jenta, and Lacruse all looked to be in their twenties. They were certainly cousins, although you might mistake them for sisters.

Jenta stepped closer. "Good to meet you; Hugo has talked about you."

Joshua frowned. "Sorry about that." Lacruse laughed. She was slightly shorter than the others. Behind her, Betty seemed to be trying to stay out of his line of sight.

These four made up the crew digging deep into the abandoned machinery, hoping to discover wonders the Delense had left.

Jenta pointed over at a blank console. "This probably controls this section." She cranked on a lantern and the light increased. "It looks a lot like the machinery we had back at Rikna."

Hugo sighed. "But it's cold. We just don't have the power to bring it back to life."

Joshua frowned, "I thought you had hydroelectricity, like at Factory."

Hugo shook his head. "It's just like that hand-crank lantern. Not the same thing at all. Base has a whole lake at the top of the mountain feeding water down hundreds of feet of drop into a turbine. Here, we had to dam the creek and run it past a paddlewheel. It's just enough to light the passages, and we have to constantly fight with the kitchen crew. They want electric skillets to cook indoors in the clean air, so they don't have to work outside in breathers. If you notice, the lights get much dimmer around meal preparation time. There'd be a revolt if we dimmed out the whole place to try to activate the machines. We even have to refresh the breather filters at night, when we can spare the power."

Joshua asked, "How did the Delense operate this place?"

Lacruse took his hand, "Let me show you."

Joshua fell in behind her, but he removed his hand from her grasp as soon as politely possible. They went down the dark passage then turned left. After a moment, there was a hint of outdoor light. He sniffed the air.

"Is there an opening?"

"It's a glass window. This is right next to the outer wall."

They entered a wide and relatively well-lit chamber, complete with the promised window to the outside. The illuminated machinery looked familiar.

Joshua asked, "Are those ... power cells?"

Lacruse nodded. "Bigger ones than I've ever seen before. Three huge power cells, right next to a boat landing pad outside."

"Then this place has to be a lot more recent than Factory."

Hugo said to the others, "I told you he'd get it. Yeah, Joshua, this place was built after the change-over to power cell technology. They never needed a hydroelectric power source because it was powered like everything today—from power cells ferried in via boat. I suppose the Delense did all that themselves. Today, everybody but us gets all their power from the Tenthonad clan."

Joshua said, "Other than Factory."

"Right, other than Factory—which probably has the only working hydroelectric plant on Ko."

Joshua's mind churned. If the Delense built this place, they must have been manufacturing something, and it was probably more current technology. Factory had been largely restored back to the capabilities it had when it was abandoned, but that was metal fabrication, chemical processing, and some electrical machinery, like lights, motors and generators. None of the more advanced devices could be built, like power cells or the boats' pushing devices. They could never build a boat, for example. That was why the three salvaged ones they had were so valuable.

Joshua looked at the window. "In theory, if I understand it, one of our boats could land right out there and push a charge into these big cells."

Hugo nodded. "A partial charge, of course. It would take many runs to fully charge this monster. We've been siphoning off a little electricity during the dead of night, running it through a converter and feeding it into these cells. It still doesn't even register."

Jenta said, "We know it works because we can tap the power back off the cells, but it's just not enough to do more than light up the control panels. For real progress, we'll need to feed power from a boat's cell into here. I'd love to see that. We could bring the equipment back on line, I'm sure."

Joshua saw their eyes, all shiny with anticipation.

"I guess it all depends on what can be made here. Factory's power can barely keep up with its existing demands. Keeping all the boats charged is an on-going effort in itself."

He asked, "Can you tell what's been manufactured here?"

. . .

Carson looked to be in heaven. His task, while waiting for the order to return to Factory, was to interview people who wanted to leave New Home and join Factory or Base. They were all girls. He talked to them one at a time, getting them to talk about what they were good at and what they wanted in life. He'd set up a table and had the candidates for migration arrive in groups of three.

Joshua paused in the corridor, just out of sight, listening.

The girl leaned forward. "I mean, I was scheduled for Festival anyway. If Rikna hadn't been conquered, I'd have been traded off to another Home by now. New Home isn't really 'home' to me. I've got a few friends, but with too few men around, it can get *competitive* here."

Carson smiled as he wrote down a couple of lines on his sheet of paper and asked, "What are your daily chores here?"

Joshua took a step in. "Excuse me. I need a word with Carson."

The female eyes on him were a little dazzling. He smiled back. "I promise I won't keep him long."

Carson picked up his paper. "Sorry, Linda. I'll be right back."

They stepped out into the hallway.

Joshua asked, "Enjoying the chat?"

Carson grinned. "Yes, actually. The hardest part is looking stern and staying on topic. If it was up to me, I'd bring them all back."

"Okay, I won't keep you. What's the charge level on Boat B?"

He frowned, thinking back. "We started off at about half-charge. It took about a tenth-charge to get here. I'd prefer to top it up, but you know how stingy Patrick is with the power budget."

"Okay, that's all I needed to know."

Carson went back into the room. Joshua waited just a little longer, listening.

One of the other girls said, "Carson? What did you mean about being the pilot of Boat B? Is that its name?"

"Um, yes. That's what we call it."

"That's stupid. Why don't you give it a real name, like Cloudsplitter, or Dragon, or Angel?"

Carson hesitated, "Well, it's just a machine."

"Oh, I know that! But I name all my machines. I have one cart named Squeaky, because of the wheel, you see. And the other one's named Wayward, because he always wants to drift of to the left while I'm pushing him. I named all of Polly's knives in the kitchen for her, and she likes them. Do you want me to name your boat for you?"

Joshua moved on, grinning. He hoped Carson chose that one to bring back. He'd never thought of naming all their vehicles. But she was right. Suppose they built another submarine, or even some new kind of craft.

Boat A, B, and C did nothing to help him visualize which was which. They needed someone with a different way of looking at things.

He arrived back at the semaphore room. Holana was sitting at the table, eating from a bowl of small round things and studying the chart.

"Hi. Do you have them all memorized yet?"

She straightened up, her hair swaying behind her. "Oh. Yes. I'm good at that. I was just wondering at who drew all these figures. They're all so ..." She sighed. "They all look the same. I could never draw a man twice and have him look the same both times."

He looked down at the chart. "That looks like Ash's work. He's about three years younger than me, but he draws all the time."

She fingered the sheet. "And the paper is so smooth. We can't make paper that good here."

He nodded. "That may be a problem. You'll be using a lot of it."

She looked nervous. "Okay."

He gestured with his fingers, and she got up out of the chair.

"Are you ready to practice?"

"Okay."

Joshua said, "To start a message, you face the person you wish to talk to, and then put your hands on your head, like this."

He rested one palm over the other, his elbows pointing out from his head like giant ears.

She smiled. "What do I do?"

"When you're ready to copy the message, spread your arms out wide."

"Like the T symbol?"

"Exactly."

She stretched out her arms. "For how long?"

"Until I start to send. For this practice, just speak each symbol out loud as you receive it."

He began moving his arms into different positions.

She spoke. "W H A T A R E T H O S E T H I N G S Y O U A R E E A T I N G question."

He paused. She hesitated, then asked, "Are you done?"

"When someone sends the 'question' symbol, it means reply to the question."

"Oh." She looked puzzled.

He asked, "Did you remember all the symbols?"

"Oh, yes. No problem. I'm just trying to fit them into words."

"It may have been too slight for you to notice, but I paused a little longer between words. If it's a longer message, there'll be a longer pause between sentences."

Her eyes suddenly widened. "Oh! I got it! They're—"

He held up his hand. "Reply via semaphore."

She nodded, and then hesitantly began to move her arms. "B O W L O F T O S T D S L U G S D O Y O U W A N T S O M question."

Joshua smiled and then signaled, "message understood B U T T H E R E W E R E E R R O R S end of message."

She frowned. "What did I do? Did I mess up the thing in the middle when there were two letters nearly the same, one after the other?"

"No. It was spelling, I think. Spell the word 'some'."

"Uh. S-O-M-E."

"And 'toasted'."

"T-O-S-T-E-D."

"Well it's a little bit spelling, but you occasionally drop a letter."

"Really?"

He nodded. "It's just a practice thing. It's all new stuff, so you're trying to keep a lot of fresh information in your head. If we had more paper, I'd advise writing the message out first, so your eyes could just follow along on the line instead of having to compose and signal at the same time."

They worked some more, and she grimaced every time he sent: "error back up 1 word."

It was a couple of hours later when he noticed Bernard at Factory facing his way with his hands on his head.

"Holana, take a break. I've got a live message coming in."

She watched him in fascination as he signaled his intent to receive and then began lettering out the new message on a piece of paper.

Then he began moving his arms.

When he was done, she shook her head. "I didn't understand that."

"How much of it didn't you understand?"

Holana frowned. "I caught all the symbols, I think. But after 'code follows', it was just random letters."

"That's right." He sat down across the table from her. "Holana, I think we need to talk about secrets."

"Joshua!" came a familiar voice from down the corridor.

They looked up from their conversation just as she walked in.

"Sally!" he said, pushing back from the table and standing.

Secrets

Sally looked at him and then at her. "Holana. Hi."

"You're back," Joshua said. "People told me you were on the other side of the island."

She came in closer, hesitantly.

Joshua turned the paper face down and smiled. "I've got to hear about your expedition."

Holana looked from her face to his and settled back on her bench, just watching.

Joshua and Sally both reached out and held each other's hand. She said, "We heard the echoes of a boat coming in for a landing. It was faint, but my best clairvoyant checked it out. It took me a while to make the trek back, but once I was sure you had come along, I had to make the effort. How long will you be here?"

He shrugged, his eyes locked on her face, remembering again every curve in her smile and the directness of her gaze. "I don't know. Days yet. I'm training Holana here in semaphore."

Sally looked down and gave her a nod. But her focus was on him. "So. I was wondering if I'd ever see you again. You promised to visit. But then ... nothing. We could see your flags, but we didn't know if you'd just abandoned us or not."

He squeezed her hand. "I could *see* you. I checked on you every time I could." He chuckled. "You were plucking slugs from the seaweed a few days ago." He sighed. "But Elehadi started search flights along the shoreline. We were bottled up."

"But..." she started, then shook the thought away. "So you'll be here later tonight? I'll take the time to wash the sweat away, then. I'll find you at the evening meal?"

"Of course."

Sally nodded again at Holana and her hand slipped free from Joshua's.

When her footsteps couldn't be heard anymore, Joshua sighed and sat back down at the table.

"What were we talking about?" he asked.

"Secrets."

He tried to clear his thoughts. He turned to face Holana. "Do you have any questions?"

She grinned, "Why did you hide the message from Sally? Don't you trust her?"

He looked over at the paper as if it had mysteriously appeared on its own. "Um. No. I didn't mean that. It was just automatic." He picked up the sheet and reread it. "There's nothing here that's sensitive anyway. It's just that the message wasn't intended for her."

He realized he sounded defensive. He paused, then continued. "That's part of your duty, Holana. Messages only go to the person they were sent to. They're *all* important. Don't show it to anyone else, even if you trust them. And don't delay a message, either.

"I can guarantee that you'll see messages that you disagree with. Everyone has opinions. There will come a time when a message you copy will seem stupid and idiotic, and you'll be tempted to make everything better by *redirecting* it. Maybe if you're an elder, then you can make that call. But until then, you're being trained to be the eyes and ears of the elders. The messages you send out are the elder's commands, either directly or indirectly."

Her lower lip was slightly extended. "I guess you're right. But if I saw something really wrong, I could tell Otto, right?"

Joshua said, "He's your elder. But you shouldn't tell me, or Sally, or anyone else. Can you live with that?"

She nodded.

Joshua looked up at the ceiling. "When I was little, I thought that Cerik were the bad guys, and U'tanse, all U'tanse, were the good guys. I would have trusted *anyone*. But then I monitored Samson and got into his thoughts. I thought of him as a good guy—"

"Really? The guy who blew up Rikna?"

Joshua nodded. "Yeah. The guy who stopped the spread of attachment. He gave his life for the greater good. I still respect him. But the thing is, he worked on the side of Elehadi against the people at Rikna Home. He had his reasons, and I fear there are people like him, who would betray the people of New Home if their master asked."

Holana's thoughts were ripples of expression on her face. He could tell she was trying to get her head around the idea.

Joshua said, "And more personally, there are good people at New Home and good people at Base and Factory that will try to solve our problems in different ways. My father Cyclops and your elder Otto disagree on a number of things, but they'll have to work out those differences by talking to each other. The messages you send and copy are how they're going to be talking, for the most part. Every little word, every confusing code symbol—they're all very important. Your job is very important."

She nodded, her face solemn. Then she said, "So the codes. They're secrets, too."

"Right. Secrets come in layers. An untrained U'tanse worker with no *ineda* has no secrets—any thought can be read by anyone. All U'tanse elders, and for that matter, Cerik Names, are trained in *ineda* to keep their thoughts private. All Free U'tanse, from Base and Factory or New Home, have been declared rogue. All Cerik Names want us killed. All it takes is a single unprotected thought, picked up by a Cerik telepath, and boats full of warriors would be on their way. My grandmother had her head cut off by a Cerik warrior, and I don't wish that fate on anyone."

He picked up the piece of paper. "Messages like this will give the schedule and location of our boats, the numbers of our people, and our plans for the future. Suppose the page is lost and picked up by accident by a child or one of the people who've just never learned good *ineda*. Without those codes, critical information could be plucked from their minds and used to kill us all.

"Even among people that are all *ineda* trained, coded messages are important. I was part of the Rikna rescue attempt, but I knew nothing about the plan to salvage damaged boats. I didn't need to know, so that secret was kept from me. I know secrets that most people at Factory and Base do not know. And I'm sure Cyclops knows secrets that are still kept from me."

She nodded. "Layers of secrets."

He patted her hand. "So don't take all these codes personally. Sometimes it's important for even trustworthy people to stay in the dark."

. . .

There was no large common area for meals in New Home, but they'd reserved a half dozen of the smaller chambers near the kitchen for groups of up to a dozen to eat together around a table. Carson and Joshua walked up together.

"Better hide that scowl," Joshua said.

"Okay, but I still don't like it." Carson shifted the borrowed tunic on his shoulders. It wasn't quite large enough for him. Joshua had the same problem. With the population mostly female, any spare clothes weren't a very good fit for the men.

"You're a pilot, I wouldn't expect you to. By the way, did you decide on a name for Boat B?"

He tried to scowl again, but halfway through, it turned into a grin. "Not yet, but Stella tracks me down in the hallway every few hours with a new suggestion."

Joshua suggested, "Bring it up at dinner and get some feedback."

Carson looked at him with one eye half-closed. "You're really taking this seriously?"

"Possibly. What can it hurt? Even if it stays Boat B on Patrick's roster, you can call it anything you want. If New Home feels like part of the process, so much the better."

Joshua felt a little strange in his role as the senior member of the party. Carson was at least five years older than he was. A year ago, Cyclops had explained nepotism to him and apologized for the stress his position would put on his friendships. He'd wondered if Hugo's decision to migrate to New Home had been triggered by his father's decision to name his son as his main assistant. There'd been several older, more experienced men who could have taken that role.

But the decision was made, and considering some of the secrets that had been revealed to him, like their partnership with the Ba, it would be difficult to change the assignment now.

Otto waved his hand as they approached. "Come on in, boys. It's *jenna* with *ooro* in white sauce tonight. The cooks decided to splurge."

It was nearly the same group of four as the day before. Joshua hadn't asked, but these were probably the elders of New Home, even if only Otto and Lonna had the gray hair that usually went with the title. Ruth and Derry were quietly chuckling about something at the other end of the table.

Joshua mentioned, "I'd planned to meet up with Sally this evening."

Lonna nodded, "We have a seat for her. We've been wanting to hear about her hike."

They dug into the first bowl when Otto wasn't willing to wait any longer.

Carson said, "Hey, this is good. What's in the sauce?"

Three voices said in unison, "Don't ask." Then everyone laughed.

Lonna said, "I really don't know. We've had our trials getting a healthy diet here, and it's our standard joke. Better to laugh than fume about it."

Joshua said, "Carson's got a point, though. New seasonings, even new recipes, can be worth something at Festival. Anything you invent here, even if it just seems like a temporary workaround, might be an extra resource at the right time."

Lonna looked thoughtful. "I'll talk to the cooks and see if they have any secrets they'd like to write down for us."

Hugo entered the chamber. "Hey, that smells good. Is this a private party?"

Otto pointed at one of the empty places on a bench. "We've got room. Have a seat."

Hugo scooped a portion, and only when his eyes skipped past the guests from Base and Factory did Joshua sense that something was off.

Otto asked, "Joshua, I understand how important it'll be for New Home to have a presence at Festival. And the sooner we could get some trade goods, the better. But how do you manage the process—I mean how do you manage to show up at an event surrounded by Cerik guards? Each Home's party is ferried there by boat, piloted by a Rear Talon Cerik. I remember from the times I attended, the pilots all stayed outside by their boats, occasionally growling at each other. They ignored everyone inside the Festival hall, of course, but I can't imagine a boat landing there from an unknown clan, with a U'tanse pilot, would go unchallenged more than a few seconds."

Joshua nodded between scoops. "You're right. Sometimes, when Festival is held somewhere close, we take a watercraft as close as possible and hike overland. Walking in has never been a problem. The pilots pointedly ignore the other parties of U'tanse. They know all the U'tanse are from other Homes. What's more, the bulk of the parties are female, and no Cerik warrior can imagine that those would have any plans or thoughts of their own.

"I know it took me a long time to accept that Cerik females weren't just prisoners in their pens. They really are like another species—no hunting claws, legs not designed to leap. When I tried to read their thoughts, I realized there was no language, just their limited patterns, ruled by instinct only.

"Our party at Festival, for as long as I can remember, has consisted of my mother and a couple of women to assist her. They don't carry any bulk cargo. Even when we have machinery to trade, she negotiates the deal, and then later the goods are dropped off at staging huts. When Cerik pilots arrive to pick them up, our boats and people are long gone."

Otto listened carefully. "Interesting." He turned to Lonna. "So it might be up to you to play that role."

She visibly shivered. "I think I'd be more comfortable coaching someone like Meredith. Besides, I've been to Festival before. People might recognize me."

Otto took another scoop of the food, thinking. Then he glanced up and smiled. "Joshua, she's here."

Sally hesitated at the doorway. Her tunic was decorated with blue and yellow stitches, and she'd combed out her hair into a smooth wave. She smiled as Joshua stood up and invited her to sit beside him.

They held hands for an instant, and he knew that something was up. She was nervous.

It's Otto. I can tell. He's planning something.

Joshua whispered to Sally, "I'm glad you're here."

Otto looked pleased. He cleared his throat. "Hugo, you were part of the Rikna rescue. I've heard parts of that tale. Tell us what you were doing then."

The whole party around the table were attentive, but Joshua could tell they were really watching him, not Hugo.

Dinner

Hugo looked uncomfortable chewing his last bite. He shrugged, "I'm sure most everyone knows what happened. We were all there. Joshua, Sally and I went into Rikna, trying to collect all the survivors that had escaped being attached. At the same time, Samson was arriving at the main entrance, preparing to overload the main power cell and destroy the whole place."

He hunched his shoulders. "It was a frantic effort. We had to split up to gather the different groups. I'm sure we all have our nightmares of that time."

Otto asked, in a low, even voice. "I know I do. You had to fight, didn't you?"

Hugo hesitated, then said, "Yes. Little kids and people who looked like my grandparents. They *knew* they looked like my grandparents. The hivers reached into my mind, plucked out my favorite memories of Bill and Neda, and then they pretended to be on my side." He growled. "I hate that about the hivers. Even through your *ineda*, they could crawl into your head and use your own memories against you."

Otto gestured with his hand. "But you pushed past that. You brought us out. We escaped the Home and made it over the ridge before the whole place exploded. We're all grateful. But one thing I've always wanted to hear; what did you do after that? You vanished."

Hugo nodded. "It was part of the plan. Getting the survivors out was our first priority, but we had an opportunity that couldn't be missed. We had a very short time to salvage the boats that had crashed during the battle between Elehadi and Rikna's Name."

Otto said, "This was your plan, I understand."

"It was. I was listening to Cyclops narrate the crash as it happened, and from his description, and some detailed investigation with his *sight* later, it appeared that repairs could be done that would get two of the three boats back into the air. Patrick had some repair modules in our original boat, Boat A. He ferried our electrical expert Terry, Sally's brother Jack, and myself over to the crash site.

"The place was deserted because the word was out that Rikna Home was being *flicked* and all the Cerik had tried to get as far away as they could." Hugo chuckled. "It was a smart move. When the blast wave hit, the boats rocked hard. One of them—the one we just gutted for parts—flipped over upside down."

Otto said, "But you succeeded."

Hugo grinned, "Mostly. We got the large transport, Boat B, repaired enough to fly, although it took a lot of work later to fix the hull and get it to hold air properly. I flew it back to pick up the survivors and you know the rest. Patrick and Terry got the other crashed boat to fly as well, and got it out before the braver of the Cerik came back to check on the burning landscape and see what the damage looked like. But by then, we were all gone. I don't think anyone even noticed that the two crashed boats were missing."

Otto leaned back. "That's wonderful. So the boat that brought us all here is the same one that Carson brought. The one outside right now?"

Hugo nodded. "That's right."

"And it was all due to your planning and execution that the boat was even salvaged."

Sally spoke up. "Hugo rescued the boat. He knows how to fly it. It ought to be his. The boat should stay here at New Home so we won't be cut off from the world again, like we have been these past few months. It's only fair."

Joshua had expected this. He gave Sally's hand a little squeeze.

All the faces turned to him. He said, "I knew part of the story, but at the time, it was a surprise to me."

Carson's face was tense and sullen. Hugo looked embarrassed. Joshua understood.

This was Otto's plan for this evening. Surround me and make me feel obligated to turn the boat over to them. Hugo was told to be here and play his part. I knew Sally felt that way. Did Otto tell her to dress up for me?

Regardless, Joshua had known something like this was coming. He knew what Cyclops would have said. Timing was important.

When Joshua said nothing more, Otto spoke, thoughtfully, "One thing I've been forced to worry about, with all this talk about participating in the Festival, is just how dependent we at New Home are on the direction of Cyclops. With no transportation of our own, we'd have to be ferried to and from the Festival site. Perhaps Sally's suggestion has some merit, unless, perhaps, New Home is really just a Home in name only, and my job as elder is to be a subordinate to Base's leadership."

Joshua shook his head. He knew the answer to this one. "Trying to run New Home from across the ocean is a bad idea."

Every eye was on him and he had to phrase it carefully, or everyone around the table would join into a big, unproductive argument.

Derry, seated right next to Otto, growled. "You certainly don't act like you think that! You decided to move us here. You brought us supplies, yes, but at your whim, not when we need them the most!"

Joshua felt his heart beating faster. It was a struggle to slow down his reply, to pace out the words. He couldn't let everything blow up now.

"Historically," he began, "Base and Factory grew together as one group. There's no Base Home, no Factory Home. We're physically close, and before the recent change, people moved back and forth between the two locations all the time. We grew slowly, with a few births, but mainly by collecting survivors—one abandoned worker here, a handful of people trapped by a quake there—people given up for dead by their Names as too much trouble to rescue.

"Survivors joined the group and learned the new rules. Some lived in Base, some in Factory, but we were all the Free U'tanse. We never even adopted the standard way of living that is common to all Homes. There's no Name, of course. But we don't even have any formal elders. My parents lead, but no one calls them elders. I suppose we could adopt even stranger ways to live if the need arose."

Joshua pointed at Otto, "When we rescued the survivors of Rikna, you were too many. We couldn't absorb you all like we did with the others. There was no time for all of you to learn the new rules, the new way of living. We had to make a different choice, and quickly.

"Cyclops had discovered this island, but we never used it. We didn't have the time to explore places like this. But we gave it to you to make what you could of it. You're short on resources, but you have no demands from a Name, either. Cyclops and the team of specialists that make all our decisions had hopes New Home. With our help, you could quickly become independent, and a partner among Free U'tanse."

Ruth, who had been quiet up until now, said, "But then you abandoned us! We nearly starved."

He winced, seeing the anger on many of the faces. He raised his voice, "That was never the plan!

"It was *painful* to watch you at a distance, not being able to come to your aid. But even though New Home has put us all in danger of being wiped out, we still want, even more, for you to be independent!"

Derry leaned forward, "What do you mean by that? We didn't do anything to you!"

There was a pause, just a couple of seconds, before Joshua looked him straight in the eyes. "Not you personally, Derry. You have a good *ineda*, and you use it. But among your people, there are a number who don't. Right now, can't you feel all the thoughts spilling out all around us?"

It was true. The *ineda*-clamped people around the table were an island of quiet among the chattering thoughts all through the dining area.

Joshua waited until that point registered.

"Months ago," he began, "one of your people working outdoors on the shoreline thought about living free of the Cerik. They did nothing to hide their thoughts. Some telepath across the ocean, perhaps U'tanse, perhaps Cerik, told their Name. And from that moment, the secret was out. Free U'tanse were living on the coastline."

Joshua shook his head, his face solemn. "Every Name, at least those on the west coast, started actively hunting for these rogue U'tanse living by the seashore. Before this, a Cerik boat might fly overhead once a month. Now, we are constantly in danger of warriors overhead. It's a major operation—a major risk—just to take the submarine from Factory to Base. Our boats are kept hidden in caves or protected ravines. All it will take is one observant warrior, and Base and Factory will be overrun or *flicked*.

"I'm sorry you had to struggle to find adequate food. But I'm overjoyed that you succeeded. Elehadi just recently increased our risk by raising the stakes, offering access to the females for any warrior who brings back the head of a Free U'tanse. This change in the search tactics gave us a brief opening to send you this resupply mission, but our danger has multiplied."

Sally gripped his arm, "Then you should stay here!"

He turned to her. "For my safety?"

She nodded. "Yes!"

"Then why don't you come with me, back to Base? Because it's too dangerous here!"

She leaned back, her eyes widening. "What do you mean?"

"The Cerik are searching the coastline of the mainland because that's what they thought when they picked up the loose thoughts. But once *one* of your people starts thinking about living on an island—once that piece of information gets out, the whole search changes.

"The first thing I noticed when landing here this time is your croplands. It's very distinctive, even from the air. All it'll take is a boat flying by within a couple of miles of this place make it a target."

Joshua looked around at the faces at the table. "An island doesn't make you safe. The Cerik are committed to wiping out any rogue U'tanse. None of the promises and pledges between U'tanse and Cerik apply to us. We're free game. What's more, as potential Ferreer, we're active threats. The Cerik are the masters of Ko. They always have been, even back when their best technology was stacking logs to make a perch. They can't imagine anything else."

He looked down at his scoop, still streaked with the remnants of his dinner. "Secrecy keeps New Home safe, but there are still many people here untrained to preserve that secret. Nor can Otto order people to stop thinking about living on an island—that'd just make it impossible *not* to think about it."

Ruth asked, "But what can we do?"

He gave her a weak smile. "We do what we've always done; plan for the worst, but keep living as if our future is bright. As far as what that means for New Home, ask your elders."

Ruth may have been one of those elders, but she turned to Otto.

The man sighed. "It's been easy, these past months, to imagine that the Cerik were gone—as if the ocean was a barrier that they'd never cross. But Elehadi made his reputation by loading up his warriors into boats and flying off to where they weren't expected, and the water isn't really a barrier to boats."

He leaned back. Shooting a frown at Joshua, he said, "*Ineda* is important. You told us that from the first, but training our cuties and the people who look down at *me* as a brash youngster is not easily done. We'll try harder, but we have to assume that the idea that we're living on an island will leak out. Doesn't that *demand* that we have the boat stationed here, so that if the worst happens, we'll be able to escape?"

Joshua toyed with the scoop, rocking it on the table. "I think it was two weeks ago that my father and I had a long talk about stationing one or two of the boats here. The overflights have been very trying, limiting many of the things we've been used to doing. But, a boat hiding in a cave is as useless as a rock. So one of my tasks for this visit was to check out if it was possible to do just that—move a boat here, as its permanent base of operation."

He could feel Sally's hand. It was something she'd been advocating since the new boats had first been rescued. New Home was her family, a fraction of what Rikna had been, but still every face was familiar to her. She had friends at Base, but her heart was here.

He let out a sigh. "So it's very difficult for me to say this, but it's impossible. There's no way New Home can currently support the operations of its own boat."

Impossible

Otto asked, sharply, "What do you mean *impossible?*"

Joshua tuned to Carson, "How much charge remains in the boat's power cell?"

Carson repeated what he'd said before.

Joshua then said, "So, the boat has only two flights left, maybe three, before it needs to be charged again. And New Home doesn't have that power."

He focused again on Otto. "A boat is just a dusty storage shed if it has no power to lift it. Back at Rikna Home, you had a power cell that kept the lights on, that allowed you to circulate filtered air, and to run other systems like the kitchen stoves. You can remember how it ran down eventually and your Name had to bring in a new power cell to keep the Home livable. Just like a Home needs power, a boat needs power, and that power needs to be replaced."

"We have power. Hugo, tell him."

Hugo straightened a bit. "I'm sorry, but we have no power to charge a boat."

"What?"

"I'm sad to say it, but Joshua is correct. Our paddlewheel generator produces enough electricity to keep our lights on at half power, to recharge our air filtration system, with just a little left over to cook our food. We're occupying a Delense facility here that may be more extensive and have more capabilities than Base and Factory can boast, but we can't make enough electricity to turn on the controls—certainly not to run the machinery. We tried to charge the main power cell, and had to give up because we weren't making any headway. This place was meant to be powered up by boats. It has no capability to charge the boats themselves."

Otto's face was stern.

Joshua sighed, "It's hard to get a picture of the problem in your head. Think of the massive destruction that happened when Rikna Home's power cell was overloaded. All of the burrow was destroyed, the shockwave through the atmosphere flattened trees and overturned boats. The ground was turned to lava. That was enough power to charge several boats, but certainly just a few. Compare that to the power you're struggling to come up with to cook this dinner. There's a massive difference.

"At Factory, there's a lake feeding a water turbine generator. It was a power system designed to run a metal forging operation. Both Base and Factory can run comfortably off that power. But even that generator struggles when it's time to charge the boats and the power cells on the watercraft. Without that water power system, none of the Free U'tanse would be able to survive. We've been very lucky to have it. Certainly the Tenthonad clan isn't about to trade any power cells to rogue U'tanse."

Otto asked, "Hugo, isn't there any other way we can generate power?"

He scratched his chin. "I've actually been thinking about this since the day Elehadi decided to shut down Rikna Home by threatening to starve it of power. I checked the records. There's one story about Hakla Home in the central mountains. Their Name wasn't rich enough to buy more power, and they had to survive without a charged power cell for more than two years. To keep their air filtered, their engineers built a boiler that turned water to steam, and then used that to drive a paddlewheel, much like the one we have in our river. But they had metal-working capabilities we don't, and even then it took a big crew to cut down trees to keep the fire burning under the boiler.

"When I look at our island, we just don't have a forest to burn. We'd have to convert much of our farmland to trees, and that wouldn't last. Nor do we have the machinery or talented workers to build the boiler system. Even then, it's not enough to charge a boat."

Derry asked, "Isn't there any other way to make power?"

Hugo said, "The Book talks about solar power, but no one has ever understood that technology. With effort, we could possibly make windmills powered by the sea breeze, but again, we don't have the ability to build enough of them to drive a power cell. Our mountains aren't tall enough and our river doesn't have the volume for a water system on the scale of the one at Factory.

"All the other power on the planet comes through Tenthonad. Somehow they get power from space, and it's been enough for all the clans' needs since the time of the Delense. They set up the process and Tenthonad has the only way to access it."

Joshua said, "If I had a solution, I'd share. I'd stay and help you build it. But I don't. The Free U'tanse need every boat active and ready to use. We need them to rescue abandoned workers. We need to salvage the machines the Cerik are too impatient to fix themselves. And we need to discover more places like this island—places were U'tanse can live out of the reach of the Cerik."

He looked at Otto. "I have been talking with Cyclops via semaphore, and I have an alternate suggestion I'd like to propose."

...

Joshua and Sally walked shoulder to shoulder, close enough he could feel her when she brushed his arm.

She grumbled, "I can't believe you talked them out of it. We *need* the boat. You don't know how it is to be trapped here on the island."

"Hey, I was open to suggestions. If you have a way to keep the boat charged, you should have said so."

"You know I don't. The science isn't my thing. We still need a boat."

He took her hand and sighed. "I wasn't sure Otto would understand. Good relations with New Home is my first priority. We can't afford to be squabbling between ourselves, not when Elehadi could come down on us at any time."

She gripped his hand. "Is it really as dangerous as you say? Are we just one leak away from being discovered here?"

He nodded. "But it still might take them some time to discover the location of the island. In the Tales, there's really only one island mentioned, Far Island, and that's a couple of hundred miles north of here. Cerik don't really have any maps either, but several of the U'tanse Homes have compiled map information over their history. I've seen maps with the location of Far

Island filled in, the result of some clairvoyant exploration, I'm sure. That's how Cyclops discovered this place. He *saw* it."

She sighed, "So we might have a warning period, once they start to send boats to search Far Island?"

"I guess. It's all guesswork, really. But it really doesn't make me feel any better about the situation. The Cerik won't give up. When the Delense made their big escape effort, it took time, but the Cerik warriors tracked down every fleeing spaceship and destroyed every Delense. Once they realize the rogue U'tanse have fled to an island, they'll send boats all over the ocean until they find them. You don't realize how much effort they've already put into the search for the U'tanse 'living on the shoreline'.

"Elehadi is hurting. During the last Face, he was penalized for letting the Rikna Home situation breed 'Ferreer'. Part of the penalty is limitations on how much power he can buy from Tenthonad. Now, part of that penalty might have just been from the fear his neighbors were feeling about his invasions, but he hasn't been able to recharge his boats as rapidly as he has been before—and yet he's still putting boats in the sky every day, hunting for us. His reserves must be low."

Sally nodded, "So you don't think he'll stop."

Joshua shook his head, "Not unless there's a new battle that puts other demands on his fleet."

She leaned against him. "Then maybe we should pray for war."

They walked together in silence, until the corridor branched.

He paused, "I'm sure Hugo will be ready to start charging New Home's power cell at dawn. I *should* go to bed."

She clutched his hand, "Can't we spend a little more time together? I've missed you."

He chuckled, "I'd love to share some bath time with you, but I'd hate to keep the whole Home up."

She blushed, "Slurking?"

"I wouldn't put it past them. I feel like Jinger's *chitchit* in his pen. I feel eyes everywhere. Far too many people have expressed interest in how well I'm getting along with you."

She sighed, "I've been getting that, too. But I thought it was just girl talk."

He nodded toward the entrance. "Would you care for a walk outside? The moon is up."

"Um. My breather is back at my chamber. And I don't have leathers."

"You've been hiking across the island without leathers? You had them when you left Base."

She shrugged. "The gardening crew needed them more than I did, and I've gotten pretty good at healing. I've got an outdoor suit as well—a head-to-toe cloth one, with fat rubbed into the fabric to keep it from breathing. Not as good as leather, but we make do here at New Home."

He smiled, "I've been doing pretty good at healing myself. I've been swimming a lot lately—messenger duty."

She felt the muscles on his arm. "It shows. But I'd better check you myself. Guys never do a thorough job of healing."

"Then come for a walk, just a few minutes, and then I'll let you check out my body to your heart's content."

She let go of his arm, ending with a pinch. "Okay, but just a short one."

They left through the airlock and walked one of the paths through a garden of broadleaf bushes.

When they paused at a bench, they spent a few minutes sharing breath.

He took a deep breath of the unfiltered air, so deadly if left untreated. "What is that scent?"

She shrugged. "Maybe the sack-peas over there. They're in bloom. I don't really know. Gardening isn't my thing."

He pulled her closer. "Maybe it's you. I've missed you." The crescent moon was just coming over the hills. The sight of her shining eyes in the faint light brought a peace he'd been hungry for.

A little later, when he coughed, she pulled free and said, "Back indoors, now. We've breathed too much of this stuff."

They went back in, and Sally walked him to her chamber. "I'm kicking you out before too long, but after I check you out."

She undressed him, but shut him down when he tried for another kiss. "Face down on the bed. Just relax and close your eyes."

Her hands on his back brought back memories. It was her preferred position when she scanned his body, healing what had gone bad. The times they had been in the bath together, he rested his forearms on the rocks and felt in harmony with the water, and her warmth on his back.

In spite of the whispers it would cause, he wouldn't mind spending the night. He'd dreamed of it often enough.

"Joshua? Have you been scratching at the back of your neck long?"

"Ummm. A while, I guess."

"There's a skin cancer there. I'm killing it out, but it'll be tender for a couple of days. I told you, guys don't heal themselves properly!"

He muttered, sleepily, "I'll let you do it, then."

Sally slapped a palm down on his back hard enough to sting. "You'd better."

She kicked him out a few minutes later, as promised. The last stolen kiss kept him smiling all the way back to his chamber.

Charging New Home

The boat kicked up dust and pebbles, rattling the windows as it settled down on the landing pad. The girls clustered by the entrance shrieked.

Joshua was a little worried about the windows himself, but as the engines shut down and the silence began to be heard, he could see no damage.

Hugo yelled out, "I've got the system set to charge!"

Joshua waved his right arm in a big circle. Inside, he could *see* Carson nod and start the charging operation on his end.

Hugo, half hidden in the machinery, shouted, "I can see it coming."

The air had a texture to it, a tension. Joshua could feel the effects as he moved his hand. It was hard to define, but the edges of the charging beam from the boat to the New Home power cell was spilling out in some way. Carson worked carefully, intent on his control display.

Then in less than a minute, the pilot waved his hand up and down in a chopping motion.

Joshua yelled, "He's cutting power."

Hugo said, "I see it."

Joshua walked closer to where Hugo stood, peering down at the control panel designed for the Delense, who walked comfortably on all fours. Hugo had a thoughtful frown.

"Well?" Joshua asked, "What does it look like?"

"I won't really know until I try some things, but the status display is up, and I can see readings from all over the place. There are more levels to this facility than I knew existed."

Joshua tried to make sense of the display. There were diagrams, but it wasn't like a map—more abstract. "I wish I could read Delense."

"Me, too. I can make out some of the more common words, but it's going to take some trial and error to work this out."

"How are the power levels?"

Hugo shook his head and sighed. "Barely reading, actually. I'm sure it's a lot of power, but this place was designed to operate at a much higher level. I can get some things running, but I'm going to have to be cautious."

He turned his head. "Jenta, have we blocked the feed to the other cells?"

She nodded. "Yes. Hardly any shift. I'll need most of the day to check the remote power centers."

"There's more of them than we knew about. Come here and look."

Joshua backed away as the New Home crew focused on their task. Right now, he could do nothing more than get in their way.

Carson was coming in through the utility door, moving quickly, since it wasn't fitted with an airlock. He was grumpy.

"How did it go?" asked Joshua.

"Smooth. But I hate giving up that much power. I've got enough to get back to Factory, with reserve to turn around and come back here if there's trouble. But if that happens, we'll be stuck. I can't do it twice."

Joshua nodded toward the girls. "But at least you'll have someone to talk to on the trip."

Carson's frown threatened to crack at the edges of his mouth. "I said I'd be leaving today, but I didn't know the time. All four showed up at first light. Do you have a schedule for me?"

"I'll check again. All I know is that they're expecting one overflight daily, with Elehadi's new plan."

He found a place out of sight of the others, faced Base, and put his hands on his head.

After a couple of minutes, his father noticed: *"How is it going?"*

Joshua gave him a summary: *"Energy transferred with no problem. Four girls returning."*

Cyclops told him to monitor Base's secondary flag. The instant a blue square was shown, the boat should leave, and Carson should monitor Factory's flags for any warning that Cerik were in the area.

Joshua composed another question: *"Status of ground searches?"*

"Too many to monitor. Twenty to thirty groups, various sizes. Most to the far north. Five cutting through Graddik-controlled mountains to get closest to Rikna lands. Two parties abandoned normal work assignments to head for Rikna territory. I'd assign you to watch them if you weren't already busy."

Joshua signed off. His father hadn't asked, but he knew he'd have to add yet another task to his day.

When he went back to notify Carson, he found even more people. The girls leaving for Factory were having tearful goodbyes with their friends. Just like Festival, a change like this was likely forever. Sally was the only girl of New Home who had left and come back.

Carson, being a pilot, had good clairvoyant skills. It was a necessity to avoid meeting up with Cerik in the skies. While they talked, Carson checked the two flags and went back to the boat to avoid all the wash of emotion. Part of the requirements for the girls leaving was skill with *ineda*, but that didn't mean their friends were able or willing to block their feelings. Telepathy was often a matter of focus. The thoughts of a person crying within your line of sight were much more vivid than from someone out of sight across the continent.

Lonna arrived and Joshua was glad someone was there to manage the process when it came time for the girls to leave.

He gave Hugo a wave and walked back toward the living areas.

Sally met him in the hallway. "The boat is leaving?"

"Yes, although we haven't been given the final notice. Base has to make sure Carson will have a clear flight, with no chance of being detected."

"And you're not going with them?"

He smiled, "No, not this flight. I have work to do here at New Home before I can leave."

She moved closer, "How long do we have?"

"Just a few days, at most. I have to finish training Holana to handle the semaphore duties, and I'll be checking to see what Hugo's crew can do with the power. The next boat will bring another charge, but unless New Home's machinery can produce something valuable, we can't commit to draining Factory's resources more than that."

Sally nodded. "I bet there's something here. My crew found a whole new burrow to the west and it looks like a factory, too."

He gave her a sour look, "Don't expect me to argue for power charges for two locations. We can't really afford the drain we're supplying this time."

She gave him a nudge. "Oh, pretty please?"

He grumbled. "Be happy with what you're getting."

She turned and walked with him. "Why did you choose Holana? Why not me?"

He spread his hands. "It wasn't my choice. Otto and his people chose her. Besides, I wouldn't have chosen you in the first place."

Sally frowned, "And why is that?"

He rubbed his nose with a finger, puzzled at why she looked upset. "It's just that your skills don't match. Semaphore operators have to have excellent *sight*—the distance kind. You have to easily see how people's arms are positioned when they're far away. You're good at healing and that close-range stuff, but I didn't think you'd be good at semaphore."

"Not that you ever gave me the chance."

Joshua asked, "Do you want to spend all day sitting in an empty room, looking across the ocean at a couple of other people sitting in empty rooms?"

"That's not the point."

"What is the point, then?"

She sighed, "I just wish ... I wish we could work together on something again. We're always on opposite sides these days."

He took her hand. "I don't think we're on opposite sides."

She tilted her head. "Maybe. But you're always the son of Cyclops, and you'll do whatever he says. And these people, here on this island, are my family, my first priority."

He said quietly, "I just want us all to survive."

She didn't reply. They walked to the next branch point in the corridor and she stopped. "You know, I'm going to have to go back to join my group. I just came here to see you."

"When do you leave?"

She hesitated. "What will you be doing today?"

"I've got a few hours with Holana, training. Then a few chores for my father, and then I'll need to check with Hugo to see how he's coming."

"And then more chores for your father, right?"

He gave a slight smile, "Well ... yes."

She nodded. "I like Cyclops, really, I do. But he's just focused on one thing, and he expects everyone around him to do what he says. That's why I had to leave Base. I could feel myself being pulled into that whirlpool and I couldn't breathe."

Joshua couldn't reply. Not without replaying an argument they'd had several times before. She was torn between her family at New Home and him. He had to choose between staying with her or following his father.

Cyclops wants us all to survive, and he's probably the only man on the planet with all the facts. If he needs me to work long hours, every day, then that's what I'll do. He's doing no less.

She sighed, "I'll be leaving in a couple of hours, as soon as I collect some supplies and repack my bag."

He frowned. "I've *got* to go attend to the semaphore training."

She nodded stiffly. "I'm sure Holana is looking forward to spending the quality time with you."

"It's not like that."

She turned and walked off.

He kept his churning thoughts to himself and went the other way.

. . .

Holana looked up with a worried frown as he came into the room.

"Joshua! I tried to check the flags at Base and Factory, like you told me. I found them, but what does a yellow flag with a white triangle in the middle mean?"

He stopped dead, closed his eyes and turned toward Base. There it was, the emergency warning flag just like she'd said. But ... the blue square secondary flag was also up!

A quick look showed that Carson had seen it, the order to take off. People were bringing their bags into the boat, getting ready to depart.

What was going on? Should he stop Carson? Could he stop him in time?

Taking of the Survivors

Joshua sought out his father. Cyclops wasn't at his usual place at his table in his private chamber. Joshua scanned the layers of Base and found him a few seconds later standing alone in a corridor near the nursery.

Joshua put his hands on his head. The wait was only about two minutes, but it seemed like an hour.

"Cerik ground search found small U'tanse group. Rikna survivors probably. Mountain pass west of old Rikna Home. Continue with Carson's return."

Joshua let out a sigh and opened his eyes. Holana had her hand to her mouth. "Other Rikna survivors?"

"You copied that?"

She nodded, her eyes haunted. "He was fast, and I missed some letters, but none of it was in code."

"Then run—tell Otto directly. I'll see if I can find them."

She ran out.

Joshua sighed. Another group of Rikna survivors. They'd kept their existence quiet all this time, and somehow managed to keep breathing filtered air.

It wasn't surprising that another group had fled the doomed Home, but how could they have survived for so long?

His *sight* zoomed in on the blast crater where Rikna Home had been and then he shifted his focus to the west, hunting for activity.

A few minutes later, he found them. Three men and one woman were fleeing down a gorge, just dressed in tunics with no breathers. Two Cerik warriors were chasing them. It was obviously just a game to them. They leapt from one side of the gorge to the other, just fast enough to keep the U'tanse running.

Then, one of the men tripped. A Cerik was down on him in a flash, smashing his face with a claw, then taking his time to sever the head and stow it in his bag.

Joshua could still get no thoughts from the remaining three, in spite of the fact that they were in blind panic and their lungs must have been aflame from breathing raw air. He followed them for another five minutes, until the last one was cut down and butchered. The warriors spent a few moments together boasting of their kills.

Joshua plucked enough from their surface thoughts to follow the headless bodies back up to a cave. It had been sealed and draped with a camouflaged cloth, but the door was now hanging loosely from the hinges and the cloth was loose on the ground. Inside was one more headless body and the bare necessities. There were two breathers, still attached to some kind of pedal-wheel apparatus, probably designed to refresh the active chemicals in the filter. A pipe showed that the survivors had somehow managed to feed air through a personal breather to keep the air inside the chamber usable.

Five people had lived in a cave not much larger than the room he was in now. They'd cobbled together the necessities of surviving on Ko, and now, the searchers had ended their struggle.

He wished he'd known about them. There were dozens of people at Base and Factory who would have jumped at the chance to rescue them.

When he dropped his focus and opened his eyes back in the semaphore room, he found Otto and Derry there with Holana. Otto's face was white.

"Did you *see*?" Joshua asked.

Otto nodded, "Just the last couple of minutes. Those were Jim and Perry, sons of Matt bar Keith. They managed a herd of *sendt* to the west of Home. I'd heard there was a place they could rest in overnight."

Joshua nodded. "I found it. There were at least five people, two of them women."

Otto slumped a little more. "Maybe the whole family. Could you tell?"

"No. Even to the last, they kept their *ineda*, and I didn't know any of them by sight."

Otto jerked, as a thought hit him. "The boat! Did they leave yet?"

Joshua nodded. Quickly, he checked their progress and the flags. "Everything is still on course for them. Sad as the deaths were, it might make Carson's return that much safer. Everyone will be thinking about this."

"Will they give up the search now?" asked Holana.

Joshua shook his head. "I doubt it. They were hiding out in the mountains, far from the coastline. Elehadi will realize that his warriors still haven't killed the rogues that started the search in the first place."

Otto said, "Us. That's us."

Joshua wasn't about to point any blame—not right now. "If there were two groups of survivors from the fall of Rikna Home, there could be others. Are there any other things, like that herders' cave, that might give us a clue?"

Otto was silent. "I'll ask around. But keep that idea quiet. If there are clues, then we need to keep them to ourselves and not let a stray thought leak to the Cerik."

...

By the time he thought to check, Sally had already left. He saw her, doubled over with an extra large pack of supplies, making her way along the coastline.

Stupid. I should have checked earlier. If she knew those people, I should have been the one to break the news.

He shook his head. Maybe that made no sense, but it was how he felt. They needed to face everything, the good and the bad, together.

...

Holana was solemn and intent on catching every signal he sent her in training. She was still weak in her spellings, and he had no idea how to correct that. As long as the message got through, he guessed it was a minor issue.

He had her monitor his next check-in with Base, both what Cyclops sent him and his reply. She copied everything in her over-large handwriting. He then read her copy for errors.

Cyclops had asked, in code, for a detailed report of what he'd *seen*. He sent his reply, also in code. There was no need to force Holana to relive the gory deaths. He'd told her everything he'd seen already.

Cyclops then asked: *"Did you have any hint that they were hivers?"*

He replied: *"No. I did notice that their* ineda *was solid, right to the last, but whether that's the result of being hivers or the practice of living in a hole in the ground right next to the Cerik, I can't tell."*

It was a valid question. Was there any chance that hivers had survived the explosion that had been meant to vaporize them all? It wouldn't make any difference with the dead family, but there could be another group, a fragment of the Rikna hive, that had survived.

Joshua felt a shiver. He'd faced them before, and he didn't want to repeat the experience. Dying was one thing; getting absorbed and losing your self into a hive mind was another.

"Here's your next task," he handed a paper to Holana. "Lonna has this message for the girls that left. Make contact with Factory and send it."

Hesitantly, she looked over the words. *"Although you are gone from us now, you will always be in our hearts and memories. Find a new life and make us proud. We will be watching."*

Holana said, "Okay. Um. How do I start?"

"You already know that."

She nodded. She put the sheet of paper down on the table before her, faced across the ocean and held her hands over her head. There was a wait, and then, she started moving her arms.

Joshua nodded, watching. She'd added the preface, addressed to the New Home girls from Lonna, and then copied the message with no errors.

Holana signaled, *"My arms are tired."* Then, she giggled.

"What?" Joshua asked.

Holana smiled down at the floor, "I think that guy is flirting with me."

"His name is Bernard, and he probably was."

. . .

New Home was under a cloud of depression. He could see it in the faces he passed in the corridors and feel it in the unblocked emotions all around him. All U'tanse across Ko felt the shock of the brutal killings as well, but it was worse when you knew the people. Joshua decided to put off questioning Hugo about his progress for another day. Instead, after sneaking a quick dinner alone, he investigated the baths.

This burrow proved to be designed similarly to what he remembered of Rikna Home. The stream that flowed through the complex was lined with a number of chambers open to the water. The major difference was that Rikna had been inhabited for a long time and the people there had roofed over the water in order to keep out the contaminated air. In New Home's design, half the place had been built open to the outside. To seal off the air for U'tanse, the people had been forced to put up barricades on many of the openings. Rather than being a long common bath, this one was now several isolated areas. Swimmers could move under the walls to reach other areas, but only by swimming through the common open area.

It was fine by him. He searched out an empty chamber and settled into the darkness, finding a place where he could rest in the shallows without drifting and bumping his head against a rock.

Across the waters and to the northeast, Kakil was lit by a hundred torches, and a crowd of warriors and workers from all the *dances* had come out to see the spectacle. Elehadi had sent a boat to ferry the two lucky searchers from Rikna territory and they were surrounded by envious workers, and several *sendt* were chased through the yelling predators to the pen before the High Perch. Elehadi shouted his encouragement down to the two, and they chased down the runners just as they had chased down the U'tanse—only this time, the prey were devoured on the spot.

Bloody human heads were piled on an elevated rock platform, barely recognizable as the people they had been.

Joshua crept into the thoughts of the victorious warriors.

One was already dulled with his full stomach and distracted by thoughts of tomorrow's visit to the breeding pens.

The other's mind was sharp, relishing the blood and the meat, and thinking far beyond tomorrow, still feeling old angers fed by the lesser-name of the herder's dance.

<He cannot ignore me any more. I've proven myself. He'll call me his right-eye, or there'll be more blood spilled.>

Elehadi from his perch was plainly in a good mood, although his mind was as tightly shut as ever. Joshua could imagine this was a great victory for him as well. At the next Face, he'd be able to point to his pile of skulls as proof that he was cleaning up the last of the rogue U'tanse and well able to take care of his own territory.

The other Names could only approve of his actions. Of course, across the planet, the U'tanse were horrified, but they had no ground to complain.

Rogues were not protected by the covenants made between Tenthonad and the original U'tanse captives. It made no difference that Elehadi had caused the problem in the first place, forcing them to run. If they weren't obedient to their Name, then they weren't protected from being chased down and beheaded.

Joshua could take only a little of the celebration. He moved his mind's eye to the coastline, starting in Kakil territory and scanning southward, hunting for Cerik on the move. It was a harder job than he'd anticipated, especially with the darkness and the predators' natural stealth. He supposed he could track Cerik on the move, but he'd have to find them first. He could track them even in blackness with his *sight*, but his human brain was confounded by the dark, even when his eyes weren't involved. Instinctively, he *knew* the darkness concealed them, so they were harder to *see*.

Then, he heard a splash of water on rocks. It knocked him out of his focus on the mainland. Someone had entered the dark chamber where he bathed.

Betty's Pump

"Hello?"

There was laughter, at least a couple of voices.

No, three of them. His sight showed two of them approaching, one holding back.

"Hi," one of the girls said, "you're the guy from the mainland, aren't you?"

"Yes. I'm Joshua."

They swam up, and he felt one on either side of him. The other asked, "You're Sally's boyfriend, aren't you?"

He didn't hesitate. "Yes, I am."

The one to his right asked, "Why isn't she here with you?"

The one on his left took his arm. "Yes, why not?"

Sight was good enough in this darkness, and touch told him quite a bit. The two by his side appeared to be a couple of years younger than he. The one swimming lazily just out of reach was maybe his age. He didn't recognize any of them.

He said, "Sally has her job to do. *As do I!* I'm trying to monitor some Cerik on the mainland. It's very hard to do with naked girls clinging to me."

"Oh," said the one to his right, sadly. "We were hoping to spend some time with you. We don't have any boys around here. All the good ones are already taken." Her free hand was feeling up his leg.

He grabbed the wayward hand and moved it aside. Tensely, he said, "Then you should consider moving to Base and Factory. There will be more boats visiting, and there are a lot more boys there—all of them happy to see more pretty faces."

The girl keeping her distance said, "Are you going to stay at New Home?"

"Certainly not if it's going to be this hard to take a nice quiet bath!"

In his right ear came a whisper, "You're not that upset with us. I can tell."

He knew she was right. It wasn't a situation where he could hold out forever. He was weakening by the second.

"Please leave, or I will." He pushed aside some soft flesh and started to stand up in the shallows.

In chorus, they said, "Awww!"

"I mean it. Have you ever seen Sally when she's really, really angry? I have. I don't want to see that again. You don't either."

Reluctantly, they detached. He said, as they moved out into the deeper water, "If you want to talk, catch me at a meal. But really, I'm trying to work now."

"Bye," said one, and then ducked under the water to leave the chamber.

The last one, the older one said, "I did ask my mentor if it was okay if I got pregnant. There really aren't any available guys here."

"I understand, really, but I can't help you. Practice your *ineda* and have a skill you can brag about the next time a boat arrives. You'll find your guy."

With a splash, she was gone. His heart was racing. Part of him very much wanted to get them all pregnant, but he couldn't let himself be led along like a tame pet. If he couldn't do what he wanted with Sally, then he definitely wasn't going to have sex with every random girl that floated by!

He monitored them as they swam away, and then got out of the water himself, taking a different route.

I'm going to have to find a sleeping chamber with a door, or else get the elders to pass the word that I'm off-limits.

He was angry all the way back to his room. Not really at the girls—he'd dreamed of such opportunities before—but at the fact that there was so much going on that he didn't have any *time* for cuddling with available girls.

It would be so much nicer if I could share a bed with Sally. Why did things have to get so complicated?

It took him a while to settle down and get back to his search for roving warriors.

. . .

Jenta sat down across from Joshua at the worktable the next morning and spread out her papers. She gave him a cautious look, and Joshua was afraid she'd say something about the girls that visited the bath. Surely every gossip in New Home knew all about it.

Instead, she was all business. "Hugo and the others are tracking down another power drain, but they'll be here soon."

"That's fine. I certainly don't want to slow you down. What do you have here?"

She rotated one of the sheets. "This is a list of the various sections we've identified so far. I think we've got about half of them."

Joshua read down the list. "I wish I understood more of these. I've never been trained in Delense technology. What's a 'power-slip'?"

"Oh, that's nothing more than a very small power cell. Some devices operate independently of the power-cell distribution feed, for example, hand-held tools. Sometimes control panels for larger devices like boats will have their own smaller power-slip so that the main power cell can be swapped out without losing control."

"So there's a place here that makes power-slips?"

"Partly. I think they're assembled here, but there's a large bin of the parts used to make them, and I don't know if those are built here or in some other factory. And you have to know—the power-slips are made, but not charged."

He chuckled. "You anticipated me. It'd be great if there was a machine that made fully charged power cells, even if they were little ones."

"No luck there."

He gestured at the list. "Tell me more, and remember that I'm not trained. I *do* have to go back to Base and Factory and tell the smart guys there why it's so vitally important that we keep shipping you power, though."

When Hugo, Betty, and Lacruise arrived, they went over the list again. Hugo's big hands tried to describe what the machines did.

"It's not like tiny people assembling the parts with tiny hands, it's more like a garden in some ways. Various parts and some raw materials that are like powder are fed together and the system grows a bigger part. There's a view inside, and it's fascinating. It's just like watching a flower grow in superfast motion."

Lacruse had been nodding. She added, "And there's several bays of the growth machines. Once we figure out how to make a particular part, we can have several growing at a time."

Hugo gestured, "There's different sizes. Small, medium, large, like that. I guess the same process works in all of them, but for making different-size devices."

Jenta pointed to the papers. "We're starting to map out which bays have which features. But the hardest problem will be giving the instructions to the growth machine. It's all in Delense code. I guess they didn't bother adding the picture interface like they did in the factories on the mainland."

Joshua asked, "So this factory is different? I know there are a variety of different factories under control of the Names."

Hugo nodded, "Right. They trade each other for the parts fabricated by their factories, then trained U'tanse can keep the boats and the other machines working by replacing parts when needed. Back when I was at Dalla Home, I worked in shifts at the three factories Dalla maintained." He smiled, "Before an eruption destroyed one of them and I was rescued by Cyclops and your mother.

"But back then, where I worked, there was a simplified system. You chose the part from a picture on the display, and then the factory machine would make that kind until you stopped it or chose another setting. A factory might support a dozen closely related devices.

"Our setup here looks much more flexible. There's a library of parts, hundreds of them, but all listed in Delense symbols."

Lacruse leaned forward and added, "And it looks like you can customize a part, too. I've toyed with the controls, but I've hesitated to make any changes because I'm not sure what all the adjustments do yet."

Joshua could see why they all had that look of having worked all night, fired up on the excitement of discovery. Hugo, in particular, was showing his age. How old was he, anyway? Older than Cyclops, Joshua was sure, but Hugo had always been an active and muscular man.

Betty stood up and walked out. Everyone looked her way. She hadn't yet spoken a word in Joshua's presence, but if she was part of Hugo's crew, there had to be a reason.

Jenta rubbed her forehead, frowning. "We've been wondering what extras we should be looking for. It seems like the Delense built this place out of sight of the Cerik, with more capabilities than a typical mainland factory. It's less … dumbed down than the ones U'tanse have been used to working with. From the level of technology here, it seems to be as modern as anything we've seen. It was probably in use when the Delense were planning their great escape. If there's anything you can think of that we should be looking for, let us know."

Joshua shrugged. "Weapons, maybe. Cerik fight with their claws. It's primitive but they're born that way. They can also *flick* places they don't want to touch, but that's overwhelmingly powerful. They don't seem to use anything in between."

Hugo chuckled, "I've wondered whether Rikna's Name deliberately rammed those boats, or whether it was just a crash landing. You're right, though. The Book tells of human weapons of many kinds, many types of knives, projectile weapons, even powerful beams of light. I'd love to have a device that would allow us to keep a boat from coming close to the island. If they can't land, or can't fly overhead to drop a power cell on us, they'd be helpless."

Joshua nodded. It was a nice thought. Unfortunately, it'd be up to people like Ace or the people at this table to come up with it.

Betty came back in the room, carrying a two-foot-long metal tube as wide as her forearm in both hands. She had a big smile on her face.

Hugo asked, "Betty, what do you have there?"

"Pump."

She set it on the table. She pressed a symbol on the side and air started blasting out of one end. The papers swirled as Jenta jumped up to catch them. There was no fan sound, or any noise other than the whoosh of the air.

Hugo asked, "Where did you get this?"

"Made it."

"When?"

"Just now."

Joshua put his hand in the air flow. It was a stiff wind, and showed no sign of slowing down. Betty touched it again and it stopped. They all examined it. It was cold, looking nothing more than a simple section of pipe. You could look all the way through, and there were no fan blades or anything like that.

"What powers this?" Joshua asked.

Betty looked anxious, but when Hugo asked the same thing, she tapped the sheet of paper in Jenta's hand.

Hugo said, "It uses a built-in power-slip."

Joshua asked, "So, is there a power converter to operate the invisible fan, or whatever it's using?"

Betty shook her head. Hugo translated. "No, I'd expect it's just like the way a boat flies by grabbing the air and pulling it around itself. Only it's all in a self-contained assembly."

He looked at the girl. "You charged it with one of the tall stations?"

She nodded.

Hugo said, "That's it, then. The tiny power cell in the tube uses the same pushing technology the boats use, only to push the air down the center of the pipe. I can think of a lot of uses for this—assuming it's easy enough to recharge."

He asked, "Betty, was this in the standard lists?"

She waved her hand in a rocking motion.

"So, you modified the plan?"

She nodded, moving both palms together indicating that she shrunk the original down to this size.

Jenta sighed. "Betty's usually ahead of us on this kind of stuff. She knows a few of the Delense symbols, but she'd pretty intuitive about machines in general, too."

Joshua nodded. "Thank you, Betty. This is very informative."

Betty tensed, hunching her shoulders slightly, but then she relaxed and gave him a slight nod.

Jenta put the collected papers back on the table. She tapped a list. "This is how fast we're losing the charge that we got from the boat. It's not too bad, but I'm anxious to see what the new readings are, now that Betty grew the pump."

Hugo apologized. "There's still a number of unexplained power drains I just have not been able to track down yet."

Joshua looked at the pump again. "We'll get you some more power. I'm starting to see just how useful this place can be."

Looking Homeward

With the boat gone, Joshua felt the pressure ease up. Every meal was no longer a conference with the elders. Although a couple of days later, when a girl sat down across from him at the table, dressed in the full-length tunic and leggings that the outdoor gardeners wore, he wondered if Otto wouldn't be a less-stressful lunch companion. She pushed back her hood, and he saw she'd braided her light brown hair into a tight cap. She smiled at him.

Something about her felt familiar, but he couldn't place her face. In this place, where everyone was closely related, with the same eyes, nearly the same hair, and about the same height, he'd had to rely on mannerisms and voice to help him avoid embarrassing himself when greeting people. It had been easier back home, where people were rescued from a wide variety of places.

The girl at the bath? Maybe.

"Hello," he said, then concentrated on the mush. It had bits of bug parts, but its most unfortunate aspect was the clumps of fiber that he had to just chew and spit out.

She poked at her bowl, as well. "I just wondered …," she started. "Um. What kind of things are the people on the mainland wanting … in a girl?"

He nodded. It *was* the girl from the bath.

"There's too many guys at Factory. Everyone wants a more even balance, both here and there, but skills are important. You'll want to find a place where people value you for more than just your gender. What's your name? What are you good at? You're a gardener?"

"I'm Kaeli. Mom wanted Mary, but my father said there were too many Marys around already. I'm a fair gardener, but I can heal myself quickly. They need that here. But gardening is nothing special. There's a lot of us."

When she didn't offer anything more, Joshua nodded. "Factory can be a dangerous place. Are you good at healing others?"

She thought a moment. "Maybe. I've done it a few times."

"That's a valued skill. How about reading and writing? There's a need for people who are fast at copying books."

She frowned. "Not so much. There's nothing to read here. We didn't come away with any books."

He made a mental note about that.

They talked for a few more minutes as Joshua fumbled for leading questions to get her to talk about herself. Talking to girls wasn't in his toolkit. He could talk to people he knew, about the tasks at hand, and of course, he could talk to Sally, but random girls bothered him a little. When they were done, Kaeli finished her meal, tucked her hood back in place and headed out.

He supposed this might not be as easy-going a place as he'd thought. Looking around, everyone was hard at work at some chore. Heading away to Factory, a place full of men, might seem like a trip to paradise.

When he finished, he visited Holana. She was hunting through a stack of papers.

"What are you looking for?"

She frowned at him. "A clean sheet of paper! I just know Bernard is going to send me another message, and I don't have anything to write it on."

He helped her, and she was right. The home-made pages were useless. The ink bled right through and made the back-side a mess of blotches. There were just a few sheets he'd brought from Base and Factory, but she'd already made use of available space on them.

She could memorize the messages easily enough, but except in special cases, she would need to hand them over to the person addressed, and nothing but paper would do.

He hurried down to pester Derry about finding more paper, and he made a mental note of the sad state of New Home's paper production.

. . .

Joshua waved his arms in the relative privacy of his sleeping chamber.

"Dad, how do you keep at this? Everywhere I turn, there is another problem that desperately needs attention, and I don't have the power to fix it."

Cyclops gestured back. *"I don't try to fix everything. Factory is constantly in need. More power, more raw materials, more trained people. They complain to me as if I could do anything. But there are experienced leaders there to make the real decisions. I listen and nod. It's the same with the nursery here, or your mother's garden. They say there's a problem and they bring it to me, but they already have the answers.*

"I would think Otto is in the same position at New Home. You're really not in charge. You can make observations, but you can't control them. You need to talk with the elders there, and the people who are making real progress. Talk a lot, mention the problems. Let them bring up the solutions. If you do know something critical, keep them talking until they notice it for themselves.

"As an outsider, it's natural they will be resistant to anything you tell them to do."

Joshua could tell that his father's arms were *really* tired even before he sent the sign-off code. He'd had to guess at a few letters where the arms drooped.

The day had turned to night again. He was making progress, even if it was nothing more than sending the list of items New Home could really use on the next boat. But he couldn't rest, and he wasn't about to spend a lot of time in the baths again. Maybe New Home did need more pregnancies, but he wasn't ready to help with that—not until Sally brought it up.

He scanned the island until he found her. Their party was sitting around a campfire, roasting some fish. They were talking, hands gesturing and then suddenly, everyone broke into laughter.

He sighed. Sally was doing okay. She was building a team of her own. He'd like to meet them sometime—under circumstances where his presence wouldn't cause her any trouble.

Maybe the wandering Cerik search parties needed his attention, but for now, he wanted to see his family and his friends.

Back at Base, his mother Debbie had entered Cyclops's office, carrying a food tray. Joshua wondered if she had been waiting out in the hallway until he'd finished with his semaphore talk. He was glad she was always watching out for his father. In spite of the advice he'd just given, the man was the undisputed leader of Base and Factory. He'd been leader of all the Free U'tanse until the rescue of Rikna had created New Home. People jumped when he gave an order, and he knew it. It was a weight on his shoulder that drove him to work long hours to keep everything running smoothly. Without Debbie, he'd probably forget to eat, and work until he collapsed.

Joshua looked down into the nursery. Veronica, his sister, was probably skilled enough in her *ineda* that, if she pushed, she might move out and gain free access to Base. She'd actually escaped it once before, so she knew that Base was a larger world than just the nursery.

However, from what he'd seen, she seemed to be content to stay with the other cuties in the nursery. It was the only collection of people close to her age, but Joshua thought she might be frightened of going outside. Her growing psychic skills were giving her nightmares, and she might suspect that there was more to it than just bad dreams.

Tonight, he saw her sitting on her bed, her draperies closed, slowly sketching her drawings. Joshua wished his clairvoyance was clear enough to see her work, but that was a skill only Cyclops had.

But she seemed okay, not fretful or worried. He was glad, in a sense, that she'd blocked her thoughts. It was an adult skill, and she was growing up.

He looked around. Ash had already dozed off. Joshua would like to have a nice private talk with him one of these days. Ash was probably Very's closest friend. He probably knew more than anyone how she was coping.

Joshua scanned the rest of the nursery, but nothing seemed too much out of the ordinary. Jinger, a Rikna survivor and a girl who had been touched by the hivers, was playing with her *chitchit*. She looked like a normal cutie, one getting more grown up every day. He attempted to read her thoughts. There didn't seem to be anything sinister going on. She was feeling offended by one of the other girls and irritated that one of the babies needed changing. The feel of the *chitchit's* vibrating skin under her fingers was soothing.

There was no hint of hiver influence in her thoughts. He was glad of that. Fear that people's minds could be gobbled up and that they'd never get them back plagued U'tanse and Cerik alike. But the destruction of the hive mind at Rikna, although traumatic for her, had released that grip.

Joshua's virtual visit home shifted across the water to Factory. Ace was his primary interest. The *tenner* was hard at work on some project, but since

Joshua couldn't read his diagrams nor make sense of his adjustments to the metal fabricator's controls, he just had to be content with a quick peek.

All his closest people were safe, and either sleeping or content. The flags at Base and Factory were showing all clear.

Joshua started up his monitoring of the Cerik search parties on the mainland, but probably because his bed was just comfortable enough, he dozed off quickly.

...

When he woke early the next morning, he realized he'd thrown off his schedule a bit. He was wide awake, but the people he needed to talk to next were still asleep. His bag containing his underwater breather caught his attention.

That was an idea. If he couldn't hit the baths in the evening, why not early in the morning? He hurried down the quiet corridors and found an entrance to the baths. He slipped on his breather and ducked under the partition and out into the unroofed center area. There was the glow of early dawn, just enough to let him see. He swam downstream until he reached the low dam that kept the fresh water at an even level, despite the tides. He was tempted to climb over and check out the ocean, but maybe he'd save that for another day. Now that it was getting lighter, he turned back and swam upstream, keeping his goggles under the water, looking at the rocks and rubble that had collected there over the years.

He was surprised to see a few freshwater *janji* fish in among the others. He liked the taste of those and was surprised they weren't fished out. There were signs of the Delense construction there, too. Several places, the bottom of the creek was smooth, not natural rock at all.

Hugo had mentioned lower levels to the complex. Did those extend below the creek as well?

The idea intrigued him. It was still early. He had time. Hurriedly, he turned back again, swimming rapidly to the dam. There was an easy way to crawl over it. Once in the cooler water of the ocean, he swam straight out, searching the bottom for any sign of Delense construction.

Knowing how Base had been constructed, he wasn't surprised to see a circular underwater entrance carved in the bedrock even larger than the one at Base. Partially blocked by rubble from quakes or tides, it was still plenty large enough to swim through.

It was pitch dark, with only the morning light leaking through the entrance. Joshua extended his *sight*. The tunnel stretched hundreds of feet, and he didn't sense any air pockets close enough to use.

Not the time to test how long I can hold my breath.

He went back out for another breath and then paused there at the opening, checking to see just how much he could discover by *sight* alone.

...

Hugo found him hunched over papers when he arrived to start work for the day. Lacruse was helping him.

Joshua looked up and asked, "Do you have a more complete map of the facility?"

Hugo looked to see which papers he was looking at.

"What kind of detail are you looking for?"

Once Joshua explained, they found a room layout.

Joshua carefully added the tunnel's position with light dotted lines. "It was what you said. There's another level below, with access to the ocean via this tunnel. It's wide enough to bring the submarine inside, if it came to that, and the sub was originally a Delense design. They probably used something similar when shipping large components by water. Or maybe it was just to avoid the Cerik observing them, like we do today. Who knows?"

Hugo said, "Even if we just leave it sealed off, we need to get down there so we can shut off the power leak. Is this position accurate?"

Joshua nodded. "Now that I know it's there, I can *see* it. Come with me. I think I know where the access hatch is."

Underfoot

Joshua stamped his foot. "It's under here." They were in a wide, vacant room, about fifty feet in each direction, well lit by an external window. Outside there was the glint of water, as the creek was visible just beyond a flat section of ground.

Hugo looked around. "This would be a good place to unload cargo. There's room outside for a boat if things were to be transferred. But I don't see any hatchway."

Betty joined the group. Hugo told her they suspected a passage down to the lower level, and they were looking for access.

Joshua could feel something, but he couldn't make sense of it.

Lacruse was searching the walls, hunting for hidden controls. Hugo was using his own clairvoyance, confirming that the tunnel was near here.

Joshua whispered, "What's Betty doing?"

Hugo looked. The girl was dancing. It was a slow hop and a step much like the little cuties in the nursery played. She was making a slow pace across the floor. When she reached the wall, she shifted over a dozen feet and began dancing back, with the same steps. Half-way across, she stopped and knelt down to examine the floor.

Joshua moved closer, aware that he might spook the timid girl. She put her lips down to the floor and blew.

Hugo came closer, too. "What is it? What did you find?"

Betty pointed. Joshua could see a faint line in the floor. He dropped to his belly and looked closely. "There's a crack, but it's slanted. I can get a fingernail in there, but I'm not sure...."

He looked over, and Betty had both hands, the nails of her hands, tugging upward. Hugo waved, "Lacruse, get over on this side of the room."

Hugo joined with Joshua and just when Lacruse knelt down to help, it started to move.

Half of the floor began to rise. Hugo said, "Keep it moving."

As the gap widened, Joshua shifted his hands to grip it better. And quickly, the floor began moving on its own.

Hugo said, "Stay back!"

A huge, wedge-shaped section of the floor rose smoothly until it was vertical, exposing a matching ramp down into the darkness.

Hugo said, "It was counterweighted, and the narrow edge has to be built of something less dense."

Joshua looked at Betty, "You could sense that, with your steps, couldn't you?"

She nodded, just slightly.

Lacruse asked, "Was there any power-assist, or was it just balanced that well?"

Joshua had no answer for her. He cautiously began walking down the ramp.

"This reminds me of Base," he said. "The Delense liked their ramps."

The air was cool and damp. At the base of the incline, Lacruse found a standard control panel and tapped the familiar dots. Lights came on.

The vast lower level was open wide, with very few supporting pillars. They could see hundreds of feet in all directions. The reddish illumination was bright enough.

Betty started running.

Hugo said, "Wait!" But she didn't pause, not until she reached the row of machines parked up against the wall.

Betty was climbing up and through the machinery, and Hugo just sighed.

"She'll come back when she's through looking. I guess I shouldn't even try to stop her."

Joshua pointed to one of the machines near the end. "That's one of those burrowing machines. It's not exactly like the ones back home, but I can see the resemblance."

Hugo nodded. "And that one is for hauling dirt or rocks. That one appears to be a sander, although larger than any I've seen before. It's all the machinery needed to build an underground place like this. Once they were done, they just parked them here."

Joshua asked, "Do you think they'd still work?"

"The growth machines above us still work. But I don't know. The air is damp here. If they were protected against corrosion, maybe. And we don't know how they're powered."

Betty yelled back, her voice echoing. "Power cells!"

Joshua shared a pained smile with Hugo. It was familiar tech, but once again, they were critically short of power.

Joshua didn't say it out loud, but his heart beat faster. The idea was ringing in his head; with these machines, could they be in a position to make a new Base? Could they make a place where people could live that was totally hidden from above? How about a dozen hidden bases, spread out all over Ko, where a lucky Cerik search couldn't wipe them out, no matter what!

Hugo called, "Over here!"

They found the dock at the tunnel entrance. The tide was low and there were signs that various creepers and plants had populated the lower part of the ramp, but the width was just right for the heavy machines. They had probably unloaded here.

Hugo said, "They could ship those machines by water. Some are too large to get on a boat, but watercraft are different. I can remember moving some things on the tub that the boat wouldn't handle. But this is a dock for underwater craft only. It would take *big* submarines." He sighed. "It would be nice to have one of those fat submarines. We could ship supplies directly from Base and Factory, all the way under the surface. We know they have to exist. It's just bad luck they didn't leave one docked here for us."

Joshua nodded. "But our existing submarine could make it here. We didn't consider it before because there was no dock. Your seashore is just shallows and no sign of a place to unload. It's one more option."

Hugo sighed, "And one more need for charged power cells."

. . .

Otto was taken down for a tour a few hours later. "It's big. Sparse, but plenty of floor space."

Hugo asked, "You want to use it for something?"

"Maybe. Joshua's prediction of doom has had me worried about what to do, should a Cerik boat find us here. Maybe we could all hide down here and close that massive door."

Lacruse said, "I'd hate to be trapped down here. All the time we've been down here exploring, I've been nervous the hatch would close on us."

Otto said, "It'd be better than facing bloodthirsty warriors. If we stockpiled some food and basic supplies here, we could hold out for a long time."

Joshua said, "And don't forget, the submarine could evacuate everyone, even if it took several trips. The real threat, if the Cerik come here, is hiding the door from them, and keeping people's fears from leaking to their telepaths."

Otto frowned. "How many people know about this place?"

Hugo said, "My team and Joshua. We've all been under *ineda* as a matter of habit."

Otto said, "Okay, it goes no further. Put barricades on the exterior doors up at ground level and make sure no one randomly walks in on your team. We'll need more people to build the stockpile of supplies, and those people will have to be told. But everyone has to be trained."

Joshua waited until Otto was done with his tour. They walked out together.

Then he asked, "Otto, I would like your permission to share this with certain people at Base and Factory. I use special codes to transfer information that should not go out to the general population. However, we need to make sure that the submarine can handle a round-trip visit on one charge, and make sure that it can indeed navigate the tunnel in from the ocean."

Otto stared straight ahead, a frown on his face. "That's true, but if we're in danger because of idle thoughts, then I want our only place of safety kept quiet." He frowned, then nodded. "Okay. But only the people who really need to know about it."

...

Holana listened intently.

"The layers of secrets includes layers of codes." Joshua had scrounged a small stack of fresh paper, nearly depleting all of New Home's stock. But he needed the paper for her training.

"There is a code shared by all of the semaphore operators—the semaphore symbols themselves. But that means any sufficiently talented clairvoyant with a copy of this sheet could understand any message from any source."

Holana nodded. She had already experienced this, looking in on messages between Base and Factory, and messages between Cyclops and Joshua. "But there are other codes," she said.

"Right. My father and I share a code that hopefully no one else on the planet understands. He also has a code that he shares with the top people in charge at Factory that I don't understand. I'm not even sure if it's just one code or several.

"What I'm leading up to is that there needs to be at least two special codes you'll have to deal with. The first will be a code between Cyclops and Otto. You won't be able to understand it, but you'll have to be able to send and receive the letters exactly, with no errors."

She nodded. With her memory, she was confident she could handle that.

Joshua said, "Now there'll be another. It will be for important information New Home won't want to share with anyone but the person on the other side of the conversation, but this isn't elder-level stuff. It's like a message between Hugo and Carson, or between Ellen and Debbie about gardening stuff. It's private, but you are going to have to translate the codes for the people you're helping."

She shook her head, "I'm not sure what you mean."

"Okay, here is an example. The head cook at New Home needs to find out information about a new crop that may or may not be poisonous. She knows Debbie at Base might know the answer, but for whatever reason, she wants to keep the question private. She'd come to you and ask to send the secret message to Debbie. You'd take her words, translate it into New Home's private code, and then send it to whomever is on semaphore duty at Base. When the answer comes back, also in code, you'd have to convert it back to words and then take it privately to the head cook."

Holana nodded. "Okay, so I'm in the know on this one?"

"Yes, but it's a secret you have to keep to yourself."

"Okay, I get it. But what is the code? How do I convert it to and from words?"

He smiled. "There's a trick to it." He held out a sheet of paper which had the formula and a counting circle of letters. "Since there are many codes, part of the message, the first few letters, identifies which code follows."

Holana struggled a bit with the math, at first. But then they practiced, until she got the hang of it.

"This code here identifies New Home's code, so you'll have to recognize it every time it arrives, and some time after I've left, the elders may decide to change it to something I don't know. But for now, since I'm teaching you, I'm temporarily in the loop."

"And Otto has a different one?" she asked.

"Right. A different code number and a different formula. As far as you'll be concerned, it'll just be a stream of nonsense letters."

She carefully stowed the translation sheet in a drawer. "And all the semaphore operators know how to do this stuff?"

"Yes. That's why only certain people can do the job. Part of it is native skills: the *sight*, the perfect memory, the ability to work rapidly and understand the translation job. But a person in your position has to be trustworthy. You learn things about people that you might not want to know, but it all has to stay secret. People have to trust you—or they won't send the message. It's tough, but Otto thought you were the perfect person for New Home's semaphore operator."

Gifts

Joshua placed the sketch on the table. Everyone who knew about the tunnel to the sea was there, and the doorway was barricaded to prevent casual onlookers.

"This is what the entrance looks like. We'll have to remove all those rocks."

People stood to get a closer look. "That swimmer is you?"

"Yes, I tried to give you something to imagine the scale. A single swimmer will never be able to move those larger boulders, but unless we clear the entrance, a submarine won't be able to pass through."

Otto said, "I wonder if a crew of swimmers would have any better luck. It's hard to get leverage on anything when you're in the water."

Hugo said, "If we had a block and tackle, we could place a sling around a rock and anchor the other end. I don't know how to brace ourselves to pull the rope, however. It would all be underwater work. How many strong swimmers do we have?"

Joshua said, "I suspect a new boat will arrive in a couple of days. Factory can make a number of tools."

Hugo said, "That's right! They could make us pry bars and a ratchet pulley. There are some smart people there. Just tell them what we need to do, and they'll come up with something."

Otto said, "But we still need to keep the underground level a secret."

Joshua said, "We could still tell them we need to move an underwater pile of rocks, and I'll verify that it is important. There's some advantage in being Cyclops's kid at times."

"Won't they guess why the pile of rocks has to be moved?"

Joshua shook his head. "Both the tub and the submarine were originally discovered on the bottom of the ocean. They expect that there are Delense artifacts still hidden under the waves. But this request won't give away your secret. And anyway, New Home has to work together with them on this project. The more information you share with the engineers at Factory now, the faster you'll have your escape plan."

...

Joshua had another coded handwaving conversation with his father later that day.

Cyclops said, *"Ace intrigued by your latest request. Expect tools on the next boat. Happy to see Otto becoming more secrecy-minded. Shipping power to New Home causing complaints here. Hope it is worth it."*

Joshua replied, *"It will be. Imagine Factory if it had been built with power-cell technology. But no solution for the power drain in sight."*

"How soon can you return? Need your insight on Elehadi. May need to talk to Ba again. Two more one-on-one visits with Names to discuss our extermination. He shows off the human skulls and it gives him more credibility."

"I can return after moving the rocks. Semaphore training going well."

"Bernard likes her."

...

They paddled out into the surf, the three of them, towing a wooden raft they'd borrowed from the seaweed crew. Joshua was surprised at how fit Hugo looked for his age. And he noticed how Jenta's eyes followed the old man, too. The two of them worked as well together in the water as they had among the machines.

Hugo brushed aside his long gray hair and said, "I'm jealous of that breather of yours. Who built it?"

"It was a joint effort. The first couple of them leaked badly. I almost drowned. Ford had to measure every detail of my head, but it saves me quite a bit of healing time."

Jenta chuckled. "Don't worry, Hugo, I'll take care of you."

He nodded. They were nearly over the entrance to the tunnel.

Joshua picked up the metal anchor from the raft and took a deep breath. He swam down and secured the claw among the rocks next to the opening.

Back at the raft, he said, "The water is very clear today. Take a look."

Hugo and Jenta let go of the raft and they swam down to make a first-hand assessment. The old man had the shortest breath, but he was persistent, swimming up to the surface regularly. He toured the full extent of the rockslide, making sure he didn't miss anything important.

Joshua and Jenta both tried moving some of the smaller rocks. It was difficult. The best that they could do was to dislodge smaller boulders and let them tumble lower on their own. They moved a dozen, but it was just a fraction of the work that needed to be done before anything as large as the submarine could enter the tunnel.

They retreated to the raft, panting from the effort.

"Get your breathers back on."

Jenta nodded, and she and Hugo climbed up on the raft and dug into the bag for their masks.

Joshua held his hand up above the water, feeling the breeze chill one side of his arm. "Let me pull you back. The wind is in the right direction. I can handle it."

Hugo objected, but Jenta overrode him. She put her hands on his shoulders. probably checking his lungs for damage. Joshua ducked down below to free the anchor and once that was taken care of, began the process of towing the raft.

It felt good—a good, hard swim, towing a load. He'd gotten used to it on his messenger runs. He was happy to be the muscle. Hugo and Jenta weren't used to this kind of work.

Dried off and dressed, they went back behind the closed door of Hugo's work chamber. They turned Joshua's original sketch of the rockslide into a more detailed diagram, with much better estimates of where the largest boulders were.

"It's going to take much more than simple muscle power to move these." Hugo tapped a series of huge rocks. "Pulleys and ratchet hoists might work, but I think we should consider bringing an electric motor out on a raft to drive the cable spools."

Joshua asked, "Do you have the equipment?"

Hugo frowned. "No. But we might be able to grow it."

There was a knock on the door.

Hugo stood and checked. "Yes?"

It was Holana. She smiled and handed him a slip of paper, raggedly cut from a larger sheet. "There is a message for you."

She saw Joshua, "And I have one for you, too."

He took his slip of paper. It was just code letters—the Factory code, he noted. From the ease of practice, he converted it in his head: *"Boat C will be arriving shortly. Notify elders."*

He stood. "The boat's coming, I need to warn Otto."

Hugo nodded. "Mine says there's tools arriving. I guess we'll postpone the rest of this meeting until later."

Joshua walked out with Holana. "Any other messages?"

She grinned. "Does privacy of messages imply that the existence of a message is secret?"

He chuckled. "Probably. I shouldn't have asked."

"It's okay. The only other message in this group was to me."

"Oh?"

She smiled timidly. "Bernard said he sent me something, but he didn't say what."

· · ·

No one could hide the arrival of a boat, they made so much noise, so no one tried. The word spread quickly, and there was a much larger crowd watching when Patrick's boat, a smaller transport than the one that brought Joshua, settled down in front of the airlock. Most of the people were just there to see it arrive, so once the engines quit and the dust settled, they headed back inside.

Joshua grinned at the sight. The boat had changed color to a pale reddish gray since the last time he'd seen it. Maybe Patrick was experimenting with camouflaging the boats, too.

He walked up beside Otto and was there when the hatchway opened. Patrick looked out and nodded his way with a smile. But he gave a deeper nod to Otto. "Greetings. It's been a while."

Otto held out his hand. "Yes, it has."

Derry was there, moving inside to check what supplies had arrived. Joshua heard a familiar voice.

He went in, too. "Ace? What prompted you to make the trip?"

"How could I not, after what…" He looked at Derry. "After what I heard about New Home?"

Derry wasn't paying attention to him. He was looking over the bags of supplies. He pointed, "Those are the tools you're going to use to work on the rocks?"

Ace said, "Yes."

"Then we'll leave those. I'll tell the others so that only the bags are to be unloaded. I suppose you'll get the tools when you move the boat?"

Joshua nodded.

Derry called for his work crew. He and Lonna took a peek inside each bag before handing it off to the string of girls, who hauled them out to the waiting carts. There were more food supplies, but a lot of the bags contained items Joshua had requested for New Home during his stay.

"What's this one?" asked Derry.

Joshua took a look. "Books. There's a copy of the Book, of course, but I've also asked for a number of references that are critical for any new Home."

Lonna said, "Oh, that will be wonderful! I wonder where we should put them."

Joshua said, "If I may make a suggestion, perhaps next to the semaphore room. Holana needs to be reading more to improve her spelling, and since her job consists of a lot of waiting, it would be particularly convenient for her."

Lonna nodded and gave that instruction to the next worker in line.

There were more gardening supplies: cuttings, soil microbe enrichment bags, and more kinds of seeds. There was also a bank of blue lights to emulate Earth's sunshine. There were bolts of cloth, and some of tanned leather as well. There was also a bag containing twenty breather masks.

Otto looked at everything as it was carried out. He sighed.

Joshua asked, "Problem?"

"I keep wondering—when is Cyclops going to start asking for things in return? Not that I wouldn't pay him back, if I could, but I worry about when that time will come."

Joshua chuckled, "Think up a way to generate power and we'll be in debt to you! But for now, I think everyone is just trying to keep every Free U'tanse alive. Hey, if those search parties get too close, we may have to have a place for our own people to evacuate. It makes sense to build up New Home."

Lonna picked up a small bag, tied with a pale blue ribbon that was labeled with a string of nonsense letters. "What's this?"

Joshua chuckled, "I bet that's for Holana from the Factory semaphore operator. They've been ... talking. I'll take it to her."

Joshua smiled as he looked around outside. Ace, Hugo and Patrick were talking off to one side. The more those guys talked with each other, the better.

Different groups of workers were hauling their bags of goodies off to their destination, most not waiting for the carts to come back from their first trips. He was reminded of one of the Earth legends written about in the Book. He couldn't remember the name, but there was a magical being, dressed in red, who traveled the world giving gifts to everyone. Joshua thought it might be something like this.

When he reached Holana's room, she was already busy unpacking the books. She held up a scroll, "Did you see these? So many books. Is one of them the Book?"

He looked over the stack. About half of them were rolled-up scrolls. There were a couple of metal scrolls in sealed tubes, and the rest were stacks of sheets, bound on one side with twine worked through holes in the paper. He sorted the stacks, then piled five of them together. "This is the Book. It's actually several—all written by Abe the Father over the course of his life. When he realized that the only record of human culture was in his head, he spent years writing down everything he remembered. My parents made sure I read it all. I'd recommend you do the same. And pay attention to the spelling! The only way you'll get better is to read."

He gestured. "I had them bring all the books here so they'll be handy when you have time between messages."

"Thank you, but it's a bit overwhelming."

"Take your time. Oh, by the way, I think this is yours."

He handed her the small bag.

Hesitantly, she took it. Plucking at the ribbon, she paused and carefully puzzled out the code.

She chuckled.

"What is it?" he asked. "Something you can share?"

She took the blue ribbon and carefully bound up her long hair with it. "Bernard said this is to keep my hair from swaying and messing up my codes." Her face was bright red, and he wondered exactly how Bernard had phrased it. The code wasn't one he was familiar with.

Opening the bag, she found a large stack of excellent quality blank paper, as well as a pen and inkwell. She reverently found a place for them in the room's drawers.

Mechanics

Joshua handed Hugo the metal scroll. "This is for your team."

His eyes lit up. "The Delense dictionary!"

Jenta asked, "Where did this come from?"

Hugo unsealed the cylinder and carefully unrolled the shiny bright copper sheet part way. "This is one of the most important projects the Free U'tanse created. As we puzzled out what a Delense symbol meant, we added it to the list of others that had been discovered over the years. There's a machine at Factory that remembers it all, and can make a fresh scroll at any time. We've traded them to other Homes over the years, and they've proved very valuable."

She asked, "Why a copper scroll?"

He shrugged. "That's what the machine produces. It's a Delense process. But when a copy of the dictionary gets out of date because symbols are understood better, or because too many new ones are added, then we can just toss the copper back into the melt and create a fresh one with all the changes. Believe me, at Factory, copper is much more common than paper."

Ace added, "But be careful, the edge of the copper is like a knife edge. I've sliced my fingers a couple of times on it."

Betty slipped in between the others and peered closely at the symbols. They were organized by shape, with the circular ones first and then the lines, increasing in complexity as the scroll unrolled.

Her finger stabbed at a particular four-sided figure with a cross bar and she read its meaning. Without a word, she turned and ran.

Ace asked, "What's that about?"

Joshua said, "Betty's the Delense expert here, I think. She's on the track of something."

Ace nodded. "I want to see this." He headed off after her.

Patrick sighed, "Looks like we'll need to do the power transfer without him. Once Ace gets distracted by a puzzle, he's useless until he solves it."

Hugo looked off in the direction the two had gone. "I hope they get along. Betty's shy."

Then he looked to Patrick with a smile. "More power, you said?"

Boat C had delivered the latest shipment because, in spite of the Boat B's larger size, Patrick's boat had larger power cells.

"I topped up the power before I came," said Patrick. "There's no guarantee we can do that again, because it leaves Base and Factory with minimal power. Elehadi's search flights have worked in your favor, actually. Since we've been unable to use the boats for much of anything, we've actually built up a larger-than-normal reserve. We've brought a lot of that here."

Hugo said, "We appreciate it. We're not wasting it, I assure you."

Joshua rode with Patrick as they moved the boat to the transfer point. "I'd like to watch."

Patrick nodded as they settled down next to the windows. He smiled. "I like the windows. Base and Factory are all underground. It'd be nice having a workplace where you could look outside and share the light.

Joshua looked over through the window where Hugo was preparing to receive the power. "New Home needs the sunlight. Their paddlewheel can't ever get the internal lights over half brightness. Walking the corridors is like hiking after sunset."

He saw Hugo wave at them. "He's ready for power transfer."

Patrick waved his hands in front of the control panel, shifting from flight mode to the power utilities. Joshua could almost imagine a Cerik doing the same with his claws. The boat controls had been designed by the Delense to allow their masters, who had no dextrous fingers able to push buttons, to control everything by simply slashing the air.

The panel showed clusters of bubbles.

Patrick said, "On the left is the boat's power. The system has already detected the presence of the New Home cells over there. See the wavy lines? That means we're close enough to transfer power."

Patrick moved his hands, pretending to push one of the ship's bubbles to the other power cell. The system showed it moving, then quivering as it was absorbed. When the bubble winked out of existence, Patrick repeated the process with another bubble of power.

Joshua said, "We need more power, all of us. I wish I understood how Tenthonad makes it."

Patrick shrugged. "The Tales say it comes from the sky, and we've watched Tenthonad boats fly all the way above the atmosphere, and then return with charged power cells. There's something up there that they're tapping. It must be inexhaustible, because all the power needs of Ko have been supplied that way since before U'tanse came here."

"We need our own access to that power."

Patrick sighed, moving another bubble, "I agree, but I don't know how. It might be easier to find a stockpile of power here on the ground that we could sneak in and tap."

Joshua remembered an encounter between Elehadi and Samson. "You know, Elehadi planned to tap the space power himself several years ago. I don't now whether it was a bluff or not, but the Name of Tenthonad bought him off with an important relic. I wonder how widespread the information is. Did Elehadi know the trick?"

Patrick shook his head. "I doubt it. Tenthonad is the exclusive supplier of power to the other clans and has been all my life. That clan also been flexing its muscle lately. Part of Kakil's punishment was restricted power shipments. If Elehadi really knew how to get around Tenthonad's restrictions, he'd have done it already."

He sighed. "Well, that's done. That's all the power I can afford to drain out of Candy."

Joshua snorted, "Candy?"

Patrick looked embarrassed. "Yeah, one of the new girls has been pushing us to name the boats. It was getting to be a popular meal-time discussion. I said the pilots had the final say, and I'm still sticking to Boat C in my reports, but Candy struck me as a better choice than Cloudhopper, or Cynic, or even Cancer. Maybe I should have taken more time to declare, but really, people's choices were getting pretty ridiculous."

"And the other boats?"

"Carson is holding out, still thinking about it. I think he's just doing that to keep the girl pestering him. Den was happy with Angel."

"So when we acquire another boat, it'll have a D name?"

Patrick shrugged. "Probably." He sighed. "I'd love a few more boats. Then we could afford to keep one here at New Home, even if it was never used except for emergencies."

They unloaded all the tools Factory had sent; sturdy cables and winches, ten-foot-long iron pry-bars, and some nets and slings built out of metal mesh sturdy enough to wrap around the boulders. There were also a number of metal tanks.

"Ace knows what those are." Patrick said. "Where did he run off to?"

Hugo said, "I bet I know. How would you like a tour of the lower level?"

Patrick was suitably impressed at the ease with which the massive floor hatchway raised with just a tug of Jenta's hand.

She said, "Once we cleaned out all the collected dust, we found that it's almost perfectly balanced."

They went down the ramp and then Jenta pushed the counterweight and the hatchway began to slowly close. It was so precisely fitted that the air squeezed out from between the hatch and the ramp cushioned it. There was barely a noise as it settled back in place.

As their eyes adjusted to the dimmer red light below, Patrick gasped at the row of machinery. As they walked closer, there was motion visible there as well, coming from one of the large-wheeled transports.

Ace and Betty were only half-visible, like a four-legged monster trapped and thrashing. Only the banging of metal on metal gave credibility to the idea that they were working on the machine, rather than doing other things.

Hugo cleared his throat. "Betty? Is that you?"

The legs thrashed and first Ace and then Betty wiggled out from the cavity into the interior of the machine. Ace was holding a device about as long as his arm. Betty held onto his other arm for stability as she got to her feet and then brushed her hair back out of her eyes.

"Hey, Patrick, you've got to see this thing! Betty's found a way to fish a small charging cell into the harness." He turned his eyes to her. "Want to show them?"

She nodded and climbed the ramp up the side. Ace backed away, and then with a grumble, the large wheels began to turn. Slowly, the device nearly as large as a boat began creeping forward from where it had rested for ages.

Betty moved it out a full length, and then she did something else and it turned sideways.

Ace yelled up to her. "I think that's all we should do. It sounds like it needs lubrication."

The machine noise ended, and he helped her climb down. They were flushed and happy. Joshua noticed how they held hands, even when she didn't need his support anymore.

There was a frown on Hugo's face before he could hide it, then he smiled and said, "That's amazing! I wasn't sure we'd be able to do anything with those machines."

Ace said, "It was all Betty's idea. I bet there's something useful you could do with a machine like that."

A little later, when they met with Otto, he was enthused, as well. "Yes, of course. A machine that could haul dozens of carts' worth of supplies all at once would be a great asset in making use of this island. There are perfect flat meadows part way around the island that would make good cropland, but we've never considered using them because the problems of moving people and the crops back to New Home were too overwhelming."

Then he frowned, "But that's not our first priority, is it? We need to clear the tunnel entrance. Until we have a way to protect our people, everything else is a distraction."

He nodded to Ace, "Not that your discovery isn't valuable, but everything in its time."

Ace pulled Betty's arm, pulling her from her hiding place behind him. "It was Betty's discovery. I just helped."

The girl looked flustered and embarrassed. Ace gave her a reassuring smile. Changing the subject, he asked Hugo, "What's the schedule for this rock pile? Have we got diagrams? A plan of attack?"

Clearing the Rock Pile

Joshua was surprised that they didn't head out to the tunnel entrance with the new tools immediately.

Ace shook his head. "No. Without a plan, we'll just be wasting our time. When dealing with rocks that can crush an unwary worker, you don't jump in and hope trial and error will pull you through. If the Cerik boats were on their way and the submarine was already parked in the waters off the island, then yes, we'd try anything, but we have time to do it right and make sure no one gets hurt."

Joshua was impressed. Ace had always been the *tenner* who had the wildest ideas and left him with greater ideas of what was possible. This cautious side of him was new.

They spent hours poring over the sketches of the rockslide. Ace tested the local rocks and estimated just how heavy the largest of the boulders was likely to be.

"We're going to need an eight-times power multiplier here, just to tip it, and we'll need to double-strand the cables. Patrick, just how stable is your boat? Could you tug at the cables while in flight?"

Patrick didn't like that plan. "Boats were never meant for that. There's no place to secure the cable, not without ripping off the hatchway or punching a hole in the hull. We can't risk a boat for this."

A few hours into the planning session, Betty came in and handed Ace the pump she'd made. She whispered something.

"Really?" Ace took a closer look at the tube. "Where can we test this?"

An hour later, down at the dock below, they powered up the test rig.

Once the button was pressed, the submerged pump began spewing seawater. Held in place with a metal mesh net and cables running up the ramp to a sledge piled high with rocks, they tested how much pull the pump produced in reaction to the water flow. They ran tests for two hours, with differing weights of rocks, until Ace was satisfied he understood how well it worked.

"Normally, you clamp a water pump to a building and never see it move, but one of the laws of physics, right out of the Book, is that every action has an equal but opposite reaction. It's just like a boat blowing air down to lift the boat up, this pump is blowing water one way, and pushing itself in the opposite direction.

"Now, this sample pump isn't powerful enough to move the larger boulders, but Betty assures me we can make a cluster of larger ones. We'll hook the cable to our pumps, run it through a block-and-tackle to magnify the force, and pull the boulders aside with that."

Hugo had to look over Ace's figures to prove to himself that it would work, and then gave the go-ahead to grow the necessary pumps.

"It'll take another day, but this is our safest solution. We don't risk divers being crushed by rolling boulders and we don't risk damage to the boat."

Joshua was content with the delay. While Ace, Betty, and the others worked out all the details of making the pumps, he took the time to update Cyclops with their progress.

Cyclops was a little more worried about events on the mainland.

I need you back here as soon as you can. Return with Patrick. Elehadi's plan is advancing, and I think we're going to need to contact the Ba and see if they can help.

Joshua knew what he meant. The Ba were their allies, but only he and his father knew of their arrangement, and communicating with them was difficult. The Ba were off-worlders, and so alien that about the only thing they had in common with humans was the ability to listen to sounds. They weren't telepathic, either. Joshua and Cyclops could listen in to some of their thoughts, but only with difficulty and because of their familiarity with the creatures.

The only way to talk to the Ba was to walk out to a particular meadow a ways up the slope from Factory, when one was there to listen. And they had to talk out loud together in the Cerik language. The treaty that Aaron,

Cyclops's mentor, had forged with the Ba allowed only him and his successor to know of it. The Ba would only recognize father or son, and if anyone else tried to make contact, then it might just break that tenuous understanding. As much as the Free U'tanse held tightly to the secrets of their existence, the Ba were even more secretive. Cyclops had no idea of how many there were, and the Ba weren't inclined to share that information.

To talk to the Ba and to see if they would be willing to help in additional ways, Cyclops or Joshua would have to hike out from Factory and ask. And Joshua couldn't imagine anyone letting blind Cyclops walk out there alone. It would be hard enough for the both of them together to make that hike without someone raising a fuss.

But this secret alliance was too valuable to risk. Reading the sounds the Ba heard in Elehadi's secret place was the most valuable information source they had, and people were already curious how Cyclops was managing it.

. . .

The next day, Otto called in everyone at New Home for an important meeting at the noon meal.

Joshua would have liked to listen in, but he was with the engineering party hauling their tools through the empty corridors all the way out to the raft. There were still plenty of people with no *ineda*, so he listened to their thoughts when he wasn't fully focused on getting the raft loaded and listening to Ace go over the instructions on how to use the tanks and the weird pump contraption that he and Betty had created.

The thoughts he picked up were scattered. Otto had started the meeting with a mourning for the family of Matt bar Keith and then he shifted to news about the Cerik that found them, and how there were others, now searching intently for any rogue U'tanse they could find.

The speech was initially just a distraction so they could move their gear through the burrows without being observed, but Otto seemed to be taking advantage of the moment to make a point.

He was succeeding, too. The fear levels were rising. Joshua was glad he wasn't the one trying to scare his people into using *ineda*, while at the same time avoiding attracting the notice of far-off telepaths.

. . .

Ace gripped the edge of the raft tightly, the hose in his hand.

"Only Joshua has a breather that can couple to this, the rest of you will just have to stick the tube in your mouth and breathe in when you need to. It's all filtered air, so there's no problem there. We should be able to stay underwater for a long time to get our work done."

Jenta held her tube, looking at it and the tank contraption it was connected to suspiciously. "It looks like a monster nobbly." Hesitantly, she breathed in. "Tastes okay."

Ace, Joshua, Jenta, and Betty all sank down into the water, each one testing the breathing device. Joshua was happy as he sank down ten feet deep and still had no problem breathing in. The tanks were the result of his conversations with Ace. A high-pressure tank, filled with filtered air, fed through a valve to a lower-pressure tank, regulated to stay at just the right pressure to supply air to the fragile lungs of the swimmers.

Once they all waved their readiness, tools were lowered off the side of the raft on cables. Jenta and Joshua, already experienced with the rockslide, took pry bars and began loosening boulders they hadn't been able to budge the last time. She had her breathing hose tied to her wrist, and frequently, she let bubbles of old air escape her mouth, then suck in a new breath from her monster nobbly.

Joshua certainly had it easiest. He didn't even have to think about the hose or breathing. He could just concentrate on the work.

Ace and Betty constructed their strange harness. The seven large pumps were bundled into a circular cluster and chained to a flexible hook. It took the both of them together to support the weight of it. Ace looked like he was having the time of his life as he and Betty looped a metal web around a larger boulder and attached it via cable to the pump's tow hook.

They gestured for everyone to stay back. Ace tapped a button on the side and all seven pumps began sucking water, kicking up silt from the bottom of the sea. The cable strained, and slowly the boulder began grinding free of its resting place.

Ten seconds in, the pumps stopped and Ace hurriedly tapped the button again. It took three of the timed cycles to draw the boulder to a safe place to the side of the tunnel opening.

Ace and Betty bulled aside their breathing hoses and gave each other a celebratory kiss that gave Joshua a few tingles of his own. He looked at Jenta and she grinned back at him. Betty was definitely loosening up around Ace.

After a few seconds of congratulations, they were all business again. They moved the web to the next large boulder and repeated the process.

Two of the boulders were so large that even the pumps couldn't move them directly without help. They anchored a block and tackle, using a much longer cable with the pumps again providing the power.

Occasionally they would scare up one of the seabed creatures, but for the most part, the water seemed free of fish. Maybe the noises they were making had scared them away.

It was a long, hard workday, with a couple of breaks on the raft to rest and eat.

Joshua remarked, "That thing was frightening. What if the cable broke? I'd hate to be hanging on to those pumps if it came free."

Ace shrugged. "It was a risk. The way we held it, it'd just rip free of our grip and go sailing off on its own. That's one of the reasons it shuts down after ten seconds—so we'd be able to find it again. The real danger would be the cable, slicing through the water after being under so much tension. That's what could kill us."

Betty nodded, agreeing with the assessment, but neither of them seemed overly worried. Joshua just had to trust they knew more about such things than he did.

When the light began to fade, there was nothing left but a few smaller boulders. It was certainly clear enough for the submarine to get in and out safely.

Hoisting the pumps back onto the raft was the hardest part, but they had many hands. Joshua chuckled, "Why don't we just strap it below and push the button? We could get back to shore fast that way!"

Ace looked at him with a patient shake of his head. "More likely to swamp us and leave the raft stranded off in the ocean." But they had succeeded in their task, and everyone was happy. Joshua had help towing the raft back, and as tired as he was, he was grateful.

Wrapping Up

"Patrick," Joshua said as they met at Hugo's workroom, "I've reported the task completed to Cyclops and he's ordered me to come back with you as soon as we're ready."

The pilot nodded. He waved at the glass windows. "But we're not flying at night. I'll check the status flags and we'll probably leave sometime in the morning. Otto has told me there are a few girls wishing to move to Base and Factory as well, but I haven't had time to talk with them. I guess I'd better start with that now."

Ace had been listening. He frowned. "Um. I'm not done here yet. There's much more of the Delense operations that I need to examine. Maybe I should stay a while longer."

Patrick asked, "Would you say the same if you hadn't met Betty?"

Ace didn't quite meet his eye. He took a deep breath. "Yes. I . . . admit I've been distracted, but the technically advanced capabilities here haven't been mapped out yet, and I *need* to get started on that!"

Patrick sighed, "Ford and Jason will skin me if I don't bring you back like I promised. Don't you have projects you left back at Factory?"

"Well, yes. But this is more important! Nothing I left back there can't be handled by the others. This stuff is new! Besides, I'm not asking to stay here permanently. I just need more time."

Patrick looked over at Joshua. "What do you think?"

He shrugged. "We don't have any official rules, and nobody's a slave." He looked at Ace, "You're probably right. These new capabilities are important. I'll need a report I can take back when we leave. Make it as detailed as

133

possible. And remember, we may need to hop on the boat and head out on a moment's notice when the skies are clear. I'll need it in my hand before then."

Ace nodded. "I'll get right on it." He ducked down the corridor.

Patrick sighed, "I bet he's going to meet that girl."

"Probably. But, you know, you didn't see Betty before Ace arrived. She's like a different person when he's around. I don't think we could have separated them. They're kindred spirits, both in love with machines, and ... all the *new* things are here."

Patrick pushed his fingers through his graying hair. "They're kids. I hope that girl has women's training."

Joshua chuckled. "Don't talk to me about romance. I've got my own problems. And don't you have your own pretty girls to talk to? Take my advice and watch out. Some of them are pretty desperate, and old sperm still works, or so I've heard."

Patrick gave him a swipe that just brushed his hair as he ducked. "You're no better than Ace." He sighed and chuckled. "I think I'll blame this gray hair on you."

...

Joshua paused in a vacant room to look across the island, hunting for Sally. After a moment, he found her huddled around a campfire. It was a party of six. Five of them, including Sally, were dozing. Everyone wore breathers. The lookout stirred the coals and put on another branch.

I never asked. Are there dangerous animals on the island? They said there wasn't anything to harvest for leather, but there are always lulurs *and biting creepers of all kinds.*

He checked Sally's location. It was an easy walk to the burrows they'd discovered, but for some reason, they chose to sleep outdoors.

There's no way she can come here, or I can go there, in the time I have left.

So close in his *sight*, he wanted to reach her. From easy familiarity, he focused on her mind. He didn't try to read any organized thoughts. The habits of *ineda* sometimes carried over into the dreamworld and sometime not, but dreams were hardly the place to mine for data, as chaotic as they were. Still, all he really wanted was that soft hint of who she was—a touch of her soul.

134

There had been times, before it had gone bad, when they had spent hours at a time together, talking about nothing—just the little things of life. He missed that. There was nothing to replace it.

He nodded quietly to himself, then shook it off and slipped back into the corridor. He had some last minute things to talk about with Holana. It'd be his last chance to give her any training.

. . .

"I'm glad you've come. There's a message for you." Holana was braiding a long, but thin lock of her hair into a tight cable. She seemed subdued as she nodded at a sheet of paper.

It was from Cyclops, a coded string.

"Things speeding up here. Ba at Elehadi's meadow is gone and I've missed monitoring a strategy session with his telepath. We're going to need a cover story for a personal visit. Return as soon as possible."

Holana was watching his face. "I thought so."

Joshua asked, "What do you mean?"

She shrugged. "Sometimes you can tell things about a message from the way people move. Your father was worried when he sent that."

He nodded. "I'll be leaving when morning comes. Do you have any last questions before you're really on your own here?"

She looked up at the curve of the ceiling, still working the strands of her hair into a tight braid. "I think I've got it covered—at least until my paper runs out. I've started asking Bernard when I have questions."

"Good." He noticed the ribbon in her hair. "I'm glad you have someone you can talk to about this. I wish we had more people trained—two or three per location—but we're just starting out."

"I guess that's a question, then. How much of this can I tell other people? Should I try to train someone to help me here?"

Joshua thought a minute. "If you do find someone with the right talents, sure, train them in semaphore. But it should be up to your elders who knows the codes for private messages. Still, someone who could write down the codes, even if they couldn't translate them, would be valuable. Be sure you don't lose the chart of the semaphore positions."

She smiled, "That's good. I was starting to worry that I'd talked myself into living in this room for the rest of my life."

He shook his head. "I move around a lot. The only reason to have a particular location for the operator is so that the others will be able to find you easily—other operators, and the people here who need to send messages, too."

She nodded with a slight smile, "But I couldn't . . . travel, like you do."

He grinned, "Where would you like to visit?"

"Factory sounds interesting. But I know that's out of the question, for now."

He nodded, "For now."

She looked him in the eyes. "How do you and Sally handle it—living in different places?"

"It's not ideal. It's rotten, actually. But we have other issues."

She declined to press for details. "Help me with this."

She held out a knife and pointed to the place on her scalp where the thin braid ended.

"Cut it?"

She nodded. "But don't let it unravel."

Carefully, he sliced the hairs and held the braid tightly between his fingers. The short stub vanished among the rest of her long hair. She took the long braid from him, knotted the ends and wound it into a wrist-band.

"Can you give this to Bernard for me?"

"I'm sure he'll love it."

. . .

There were only two girls carrying all their possessions in little bags this time, waiting for the sun to get all the way above the horizon. Kaeli, who claimed to be a healer, was one of them. They looked a little nervous. Lonna was with them, chatting quietly.

Joshua found Patrick talking with Ace. The *tenner* looked a little rough around the edges, as if he hadn't managed to catch any sleep.

He looked up as Joshua entered the room. "Ah, there you are. I've got to show you what I'm sending back."

They entered the boat and checked the storage hold.

"These are the pumps we used before. If we need more, we can make them here. I think Factory would like to see these." Ace tapped the sheets of paper he had rolled up inside the pump. "And here are the operating instructions and specifications. Make sure Ford gets these before anyone tries to activate them."

There were also five other gadgets that Ace and Betty had made overnight. Joshua nodded as Ace explained the details, but much of it wasn't likely to stick in his memory. He was content to remember that it was all written down in Ace's report.

Hugo and Otto brought written messages to be hand delivered to Cyclops. Patrick's boat was still the fastest way to pass detailed information, in spite of Holana's growing skill with semaphore.

Patrick held up his hand. "Sorry to cut the talk short, but the flag has gone up. It's time to leave."

Joshua helped the girls to find a secure place to sit while Patrick did his last-minute checks. The boats were never fitted with seats.

Joshua smiled. "Look out the windows as you travel. I enjoy it. But remember—you'll be living with your *ineda* from now on."

They nodded seriously.

Joshua walked over to where Patrick was waving his hands in the air, activating the boat. "Do you think we could make a pass over the island before we head to the mainland?"

Patrick nodded. "Fine. But I'll have to be fast."

"I understand."

Joshua went to a side window and held onto a railing. The boat named Candy began blowing up the dust and rattling the windows, and then they lifted. The girls held hands tightly. He gave them a reassuring nod.

The fields of New Home began spreading out as the dimpled domes of the burrows shrank. To one side, the shallows of the sea deepened into the darker colors as the depth increased. Now that he knew what he was looking for, he could see what was clearly a channel that the Delense probably carved to let in the submarines.

On the other side, small hills rose in bands, blocking the interior from easy access. There were no true mountains, by his definition, but it was uneven land, carved with several narrow creeks, each heading to its own part of the beach.

"Patrick, could you head that way?" He pointed, and the man nodded.

The place was easy to notice from the air. The burrows were centered in a large circular crater, just like the one that had been formed when Rikna

Home had been *flicked*. The only difference was a notch through the rim that let the rainwater drain out of this one.

It only took a minute, but he could see the tiny figures spilling out of a burrow. The place looked overgrown and weathered, and it was far from the seashore. It was hardly a typical location for a Delense site, and the crater was disturbing. Why did they *flick* the place and then build a burrow in the middle?

Down on the ground, he could see the one girl who had come out first and fastest. He wasn't surprised it was Sally.

Patrick said, "We can't stay any longer."

Joshua sighed. "I understand."

The noise of the engine increased and the craft tilted slightly. They sped up, heading toward the mainland.

Joshua could still *see* Sally watching. She waved. He waved back, although he doubted that she could *see* him.

Next time. Next time, we'll… He shook his head.

Back to Work

On the flight back, Joshua talked more with the girl who had intruded on his bath time. Kaeli had taken his suggestion and had concentrated on improving her healing skills. Her friend Jaesel was experienced with fabrics and weaving and had been frustrated by the limited materials available to her at New Home.

Patrick interrupted their chat. "We're approaching Factory. I'd appreciate a little quiet while I land."

Joshua pointed at the windows. They all watched as the bay appeared. Joshua could see the landing raft sitting in the water.

Jaesel giggled. Joshua didn't understand why, at first—not until he saw the workers swimming near the raft and realized the girls were appreciating the men's bodies.

They landed in a spray of water and then the towing began, bringing the raft in through the tall draperies.

Through the window, the docks looked very crowded to Joshua. The submarine was here. So was the tub and Boat B. It was resting on a wooden raft that he'd never seen before. The dock workers were taking their time easing Candy into place.

But there was a cluster of people waiting for them. He turned to the girls.

"The moment we exit, someone will hand you a breather. This dock area doesn't have filtered air, and they want to make it easier for you." He slipped his own breather on and confirmed the valve was in the right place.

He led them to the door, going through the motions of being a good host. But his mind was elsewhere. Cyclops was with the greeting party. The visit to New Home was over. It was time to get down to business.

. . .

Ciara and Anra were in the greeting party and took the girls off to the airlock. A lot of the workers were sad to see them leave. A bold spirit yelled out instructions on where to meet at mealtime.

Cyclops waited while Joshua handed Ace's report off to Ford, with instructions about the new toys he'd sent. Ford was still a little grumpy that Ace hadn't returned on schedule.

But finally, father and son headed through the airlock and walked briskly toward one of the less-frequented passageways where they could have a reasonably private talk.

Cyclops asked, "The girls have been coached about maintaining their *ineda*?"

Joshua nodded. "Patrick did the interviews, but that was really the only thing that mattered to him. I remembered Debbie's stories about when she was a girl and went off to Festival and sort of told them the same thing—that they needed a skill—but I guess that isn't really the point now."

"Right. Getting a good male/female ratio at both sites is more important than all that."

They talked about his assessment of New Home, Otto's new appreciation of *ineda*, and the potential of the new technologies the island held.

"Sally is the leader of the exploration group?"

"Yes. They're younger girls, but from what I've observed, they take care of each other and make a good team."

Cyclops nodded to himself. Joshua wished for the thousandth time that he could see his father's eyes. The mask he wore did more than just protect the sensibilities of the people he interacted with. It also reinforced the fact that it was hard to read the man's emotions.

"And she says the new burrow is different than the original?"

"That's what she said, but I haven't had time to probe the corridors myself. From the air, it looked overgrown, and it was much farther from shore than the New Home complex. It was also built in the center of a crater."

Cyclops said, "The Delense wouldn't have put a *residence* that far from the ocean or a large river—not without a good reason."

"From the few seconds I had to look, it didn't look like there was a residence there, just a factory of some kind. There is no significant creek there either, just a little outflow from the crater. But on the island, there are no large rivers. Everything drains to the shoreline through small creeks."

"Tell me about the fabricators Hugo and Ace are working on."

"Include Betty in that party. I've never seen a girl like her before. It's no wonder Ace was smitten."

After Joshua had given him a rundown on her, Cyclops rubbed his forehead. "Keep me on track like this. I've lived all my life with the women being experts in some things and the men in others. I'd never heard of a woman with machine skills."

"Maybe Betty learned machines out of necessity. I don't know. But she has the kind of genius skills you'd expect only from *tenners*."

Cyclops laughed, and Joshua was startled. It had been years since his father had laughed. "What?"

"You say Ace and Betty are emotionally attached?"

Joshua couldn't help his grin. "Ah, yes. I'd say so."

"Then we should encourage them to have lots of kids."

...

It was late in the day when Joshua broke free of his duties. He headed for the kitchen to see what Ciara was cooking, but he took a side trip to Bernard's chamber.

The man was filing papers by rolling them up in tight bundles and stuffing them in a tall, dark-wood cabinet made of hundreds of square cavities.

Joshua chuckled. "I've been meaning to ask you. There're no labels. How can you find old papers?"

Bernard looked up with a smile. "Hey, Joshua. I was wondering if I'd get a chance to see you before you ran off to Base. How did your trip go?"

"Hectic. But you probably know that. You're at the center of everything here."

Bernard hesitated. Joshua handed over a paper folded into a little box. "And this is for you."

He carefully unfolded the box and examined the arm band it contained. "This is hers?"

"Holana's? Yes. She was thrilled by what you sent her. She wears that ribbon all the time now."

Bernard nodded, "I know." He slipped her hair braid over his wrist, holding it up in the air. He faced off to the west and smiled.

Joshua asked, "She's watching?"

He nodded.

"Looks like you two have a good working relationship."

Bernard sighed. "The only real girlfriend I have, and she's so far away." He held his wrist up to his face and sniffed.

Joshua didn't mention all the other girls Bernard had tried to get closer to in the past. He was right. None of them had ever really been girlfriends.

"Well, I'll tell you what I told her. Train someone to be your assistant, or your replacement."

"Yeah, that's an idea. Thanks."

...

It was early the next morning when Joshua walked out on the dock. The sky, from what he could see of it through gaps in the drapery, was at half-light. Workers were already busy. The fishing crew were stripping down and unwrapping their nets from frame where they'd been left to dry. There was a pair of workers on ropes, climbing the draperies. It appeared that they were preparing to fix a tear in the fabric.

But the most unusual thing was the ringing of hammers on steel. He walked to the far end, where three men were driving spikes into the rock face.

"What's going on?"

The man holding the plumb bob nodded. "You're the kid, Cyclops's boy, right?"

"Yeah. Joshua. What're you building?"

"A new exit. I'm Ewan. Burke is on hammer..."

The guy kneeling down on the ground interrupted. "And the guy trusting Burke to hit the drill and not my hands is Leon. Keep back while he swings."

Burke was by far the strongest of them, stripped to the waist and holding a big hammer. He grunted. "It's a ladder." Leon, braced and holding a steel rod to the rock, looked aside as the hammer struck. Rock chips flew.

Leon twisted the rod a quarter turn and the hammer struck again. After a few rounds, they extracted the rod and replaced it with one of the spikes.

Joshua watched the process. The position for the next hole was measured and marked.

"Are you going to go all the way up?"

Leon nodded. "Yeah. Building an alternate way to get in and out of Factory, one the Cerik can't use."

Joshua saw it then. The old passage from the dock, a walkway the Delense had created to carry carts up to the ground above, was the most vulnerable point should the Cerik locate Factory and attack. But the human body could climb a ladder, even carrying loads. A Cerik couldn't.

One of the alien races that had been brought to Ko as slaves were the Uuaa, natural climbers—captured solely for their ability to climb trees that the Cerik couldn't.

Cerik were natural jumpers, easily moving over boulder fields and across open terrain, but their claws would be useless on a rock face, even with a ladder. Nor could they approach from the water. Cerik had no water vessels.

Joshua looked over at the old walkway. It had to go. Someone was planning its destruction, he was sure. Would they carve it away, or build an unscalable wall to make it unusable?

Nothing could stop a *flick* attack, but even the blast that leveled Rikna Home wouldn't totally destroy Factory, built as it was deep into the granite.

He asked, "What happens when you can't reach the next rung level?"

Ewan, holding his measuring tools, paced his words between the ringing of the steel. "We'll build a platform ... once we get another couple of ... feet higher. We'll stand ... on it to put in the ... next level."

Joshua looked up the rock face. "That's a long way to go."

"Yeah. It'll take us a while."

Ba

Cyclops grumbled as he noted details on the paper, "I wish Lincy was here."

Patrick said, "Hey, if you've got writer's cramp, let one of us take the notes. Not that I'm volunteering... but you know, most of us can write."

The blind man shrugged. "Oh, I'll do it."

Joshua wasn't surprised. Cyclops was a little out of his element, holding a status meeting at Factory with his most-familiar assistants back at Base. But he was the one who always insisted on good notes, and if Lincy wasn't available, he wouldn't force the task on anyone else.

When it was Joshua's turn in the circle, he asked, "I've been trying to monitor the search parties, but there was so much going on at New Home that I barely had a chance to watch a few hours at a time. What's the big picture?"

Cyclops replied, "There were twenty-two ground parties, originally, but more than half of them have given up. At first, many were inspired to go hunting on their own, but after a few days, many of them realized it was more trouble than it was worth and went back to their jobs. When heads were taken, there was a resurgence of enthusiasm, in spite of the fact that one of the hunters was promptly killed in a duel. Another four parties headed out then, all in the direction of the Graddik border mountains."

Patrick added, "The overflights have eased off a little, and we now know when they are scheduled, so it's easier to avoid them, but there's a regular flight to the Rikna grounds to rotate Kakil warriors. There appears to be some worry that the remaining Cerik in Rikna will decide they've been abandoned by Elehadi and try to set up their own clan."

Joshua asked, "Is that even possible? I thought the Rikna females were either killed or brought to the Kakil breeding pits. I know that some Rikna Cerik went nomadic. We heard some during the rescue. Surely there aren't many of them?"

Cyclops said, "But there's definitely a lack of control there. Elehadi's plans were upended when the Faces turned against him. The former Rikna lands with free ranging runners and few herders trying to round them up is an attractive prize to any of the surrounding clans. I know for sure that Graddik has warriors in part of those lands. Elehadi wants to keep that to a minimum."

Joshua said, "So ... there's maybe fourteen parties? How many of them are close?"

"There's one to the south, but heading away from us. The closest one searching the coastline coming our way is still about five days out. We're doing our best to hide all evidence of our presence before they get here."

"Is that why the dock is so crowded?"

Robert nodded, "Yes, but I'll be moving the submarine back to Base in a couple of days."

Patrick added, "And I'll have Candy back at New Home during the days when they're closest. We'd probably take both of the big boats if we had them charged. Right up to the last, we'll keep them at the dock where we can haul charged cells up from the converter into recharging range."

Joshua asked, "And the walkway? I saw workmen putting up a ladder."

Ford, who had been mostly quiet until then said, "Yeah. We're going to detonate a little power cell to cover the walkway entrance. Hopefully, we can make it look like a normal quake-triggered rockslide. It'll cut us off from easy access to the shoreline, but we can't afford to have the Cerik find the dock."

Cyclops asked, "When does that happen?"

Ford shook his head, "Tomorrow, and I'm sweating it. I've gone over those rocks myself, and I've found a good fracture. It's just I've never set off a *flick* before, even if this is just a baby one. I wish we had planned for a chemical explosion, but it's too late now to try to cook one up and the smell of a chemicals would linger and attract the Cerik."

Joshua knew what Ford was thinking. He wished Ace was there to help. The crew at Factory were talented, but they were all cast-offs rescued from thoughtless Cerik masters. Ace was their only real genius at engineering tasks.

Joshua asked, "So we're giving up the walkway forever?"

Ford nodded. "I think we have to. If we had a year to disguise it and build a wall that couldn't be jumped or battered down, then maybe we could have converted it into a hidden tunnel, but there's no time. We have to unmake it. And even if the Cerik stop looking for us, repair would take a long time. We'll have to live with the ladder and rafting over to the shoreline."

Cyclops agreed, "It's a sad choice, but I think it's the only one." He sighed. "You know I have fond memories of hiking up that hillside. Joshua, do you think you could accompany me for one last walk?"

Patrick said, "Isn't that too risky?"

Cyclops shook his head. "Oh, we've done it before. The search party is still quite a distance away, and we could be out and back well before the next overflight is due."

There were other objections, but Cyclops got his way. The meeting went on for another hour, and then Joshua and his father walked out to the docks.

Their trip to visit the Ba had been planned out before the meeting had been scheduled, and Joshua's leading questions had done their task.

The ladder construction was twenty feet up, but it was still a long time before it would be completed.

Joshua said, "New Home could never cut itself off from the outside like this. They're dependent on their croplands."

"No indoor gardens?"

"Not like we have at Base. They have the space, but no power to run the lights."

Cyclops shook his head. "With all we're giving them, we're running low ourselves. All the big fabrication jobs have been shut down until we have power enough to heat up the foundries again."

"Has Patrick told you about his scheme to find power-storage places and tap them?"

Cyclops nodded. "But that would be very risky. I've searched Tenthonad's lands, looking for some kind of storage house of power cells, but I haven't found one."

"How close does a boat have to get to a storage cell to tap it?"

"I think that depends on what's in the way. I know boats can't just hover over a Home's storage cells and beam power into them. Nor can our boats beam power through the metal hull of the submarine. But in open air, boats can exchange power several feet away. Patrick is the expert there. Ask him."

Joshua had a strange feeling, walking the path that would soon be nothing but rubble. How long had it been there? He could see vegetation that had managed to edge out an existence in the cracks. All that would be gone in another day.

As they reached the entrance, where the walkway opened up to stone paths that looked like nothing more than animal traces, he looked up at the cliff above. Somewhere up there was where they'd place the explosive.

They were halfway up the trail to Ba's meadow when Cyclops said, "Joshua, if something should happen to me, you're going to need to take special care of your sister."

He looked at his father, trying to read his bandaged face. "She's having more dreams?"

Cyclops nodded. "She hasn't been sharing them with anyone, but I took a look at her sketchbook. There are some things there that are ... disturbing."

He wouldn't say more, but they reached the meadow and had to concentrate on the Ba.

Cyclops said, <We wish to speak with you.>

Joshua straightened up suddenly as a plume of dust erupted from the ground a few feet away.

In a deep voice resonating from the ground, sounding much more like a Cerik than any U'tanse could manage, the Ba replied, <You wish to speak of the walkers?>

Cyclops nodded, although that gesture was probably lost on the flat creature below the ground who had no concept of visual sight. <Yes, the Cerik are searching the coastlines and other places, looking for U'tanse that have no Name. But we are also worried about the Ba who listens.>

<All Ba listen. But the one who listens in Elehadi's meadow is well.>

Cyclops sighed. <We were worried because that Ba moved and we feared the Cerik had detected it.>

The Ba was silent for two minutes. Then, <There was an event, and that Ba took care of it. It will not happen again.>

<May the U'tanse know what happened?>

The Ba was clearly reluctant to explain. <Certain things about the Ba must be kept from the Cerik.>

Cyclops replied, <Many things must be kept secret. The U'tanse understand. However, although you can know all about the creatures who are standing on your back, we cannot sense you in the same way. This silence creates worry where there should be none.>

Joshua puzzled out what his father was saying. From previous discussions, he knew the Ba could see them, even the details of their bodies, using sound pulses and reflections that he couldn't hear. The Ba were limited to their sense of hearing, but they could do much with it.

He could *see* the Ba, but to his clairvoyance only major features were clear. It was a huge, round, flat beast, with many feet, like flippers. He couldn't resolve much of anything else.

The Ba replied, <The foot of a Ba can sometimes become a new Ba, but patience and silence can only be learned.>

Cyclops nodded. <The U'tanse understand. No more explanation is needed.>

Joshua thought he understood the Ba's cryptic answer. Ba had babies, too. Perhaps the listener in Elehadi's meadow had one, and it was making noises that Elehadi had detected. He could understand that the Ba wanted that kind of information kept secret.

Cyclops's questions shifted to the possibility of more special listeners, but the Ba was reluctant to commit to anything like that. Cyclops didn't press the issue. He ended the meeting with the gratitude the U'tanse felt for the Ba's help and a promise of a better future for them both.

Joshua thought the meeting was over, but then the Ba said, <Take care when you return. The walkers are close.>

Cyclops turned his face to Joshua, and even with the bandage across his eyes, Joshua could read his fear.

He whispered, "Nomads. Just over the hill."

U'tanse-That-Swims

Joshua gripped his father's hand and hurriedly led them back along the trail. They'd neglected the Cerik nomads in their monitoring, more concerned with the Kakil search parties, but they were no less lethal than the warriors of the bigger clans. No one knew how many of the Rikna Cerik had abandoned their clan affiliation and fled to the mountains during the conquest. At least some of them had raided the breeding pens and come away with females, but surely there were smaller groups or single hunters as well.

"He's smelled us," Cyclops whispered. He was the better clairvoyant, and Joshua left the lookout task to him. Horrible memories of the tracking and slaughter of the family of Matt bar Keith came back to haunt him.

What had Very seen in her dreams? What disturbed Cyclops? What is in her sketchbook?

Joshua kept a firm grip on his father's hand. The Free U'tanse could not lose him. Cyclops was too valuable.

"One of them is following us. The others are moving off into a gully."

Joshua asked, "Can we outrun him? How far is he?"

"No. He's fast. And we can't lead him to the entrance."

Joshua stumbled slightly. It was true. They couldn't lead a Cerik hunter right into the docks, no matter what.

Joshua scanned the terrain ahead with his *sight*. "This way."

The Ba meadow was just a place where the stream had widened out. If they couldn't retrace their path down the stream trail, then the best course was over the ridge. He had to help his father manage the steep incline. The nomad covered the same distance in two easy leaps.

Cyclops panted hard, overtaxing his breather. He'd sat at a table day in and day out. The hiking had been hard enough; the chase was too much. Joshua pulled his hand harder, and glanced back.

The Cerik leapt from place to place at a leisurely rate. It was running them down, possibly with an eye to finding their home.

There were thoughts, simple hunting tactics, spilling out of the hunter. There was no deep strategy, nor concern for Elehadi's rewards. It was a nomad. It might not have any idea about the big search for rogue U'tanse.

They crested the ridgeline, and then it was a struggle to keep from stumbling as they raced downhill.

Joshua tugged his father's hand, running them right up to the edge of the cliff. Only when it came into sight did Cyclops tug back. "What are you doing?" he asked, fearfully.

"Get to the water."

"No!" Cyclops pulled back.

Joshua knew of his father's fear of the water. Even a submarine trip from Base to Factory was a trial for him, which was why he rarely did it. For years, he lived every day inside the stone caverns, roaming the world with his *sight*.

But Joshua had no doubt. Unless they swam out of reach of the Cerik, they would be dead. He tugged his father off balance and they stumbled down the rocky face, on the verge of falling. Waves crashed against the boulders below.

The Cerik reached the edge and paused. He didn't like the water any more than Cyclops did.

But the hunter saw that his prey were making their escape. He leapt, landing close by on a larger slab.

No more time! Joshua gripped his father's arm and threw them both off into the air. The Cerik slashed, catching Cyclops by the leg.

Cyclops screamed as they tumbled, and Joshua could only grip his father closer.

And then they hit; the shock of the water drove breath from his lungs and turned the world into swirling chaos.

The arm slipped in his grip and for one panicky instant, he struggled to find his father. But then he found him, limp and lifeless.

Then, there was a heave as Cyclops tried to pull in a breath through a water-clogged breather. Joshua hurriedly wrestled it from his face, holding the man afloat, face up. The standard breather was useless in the water, and when the waves stripped it from his grip he concentrated only on keeping his father from drowning.

They were only a dozen feet from where the waves churned to foam among the rocks.

The Cerik stood just above the high water mark, watching them. There was no chance they could climb ashore safely. *I've got to distract him, or he'll keep watching us from shore.*

Joshua put a few more feet between them. He shouted, <Nomad, it is useless to try to catch us. We live in the water now.>

There was an impatient growl in response.

Joshua could feel some uncertainty leaking through the hunter's thoughts.

There was one of the Tales of the Cerik that Joshua remembered. It was a lot like this. Maybe he could use it.

<Nomad, remember in the Tales of the Prey, the story of the Hunter who decided to help a Builder repair his home, so that the Builders wouldn't die out?>

The Cerik shifted his position on the rock. <Perhaps I do, U'tanse. What does that mean to me?>

Joshua shifted the weight of Cyclops slightly. He was still breathing, but he looked unconscious.

But he had to get the nomads out of the area.

<There is no meat to be gained when a prey is lost, but talking together can bring meat in the future. I know things you would like to hear.>

The hunter grumbled. <What should I hear, U'tanse-that-swims?>

<I know that a party of Kakil warriors will arrive here from the north in five days.>

A wave of fear surged from the nomad. He'd guessed correctly. The nomads had to remain hidden from the established clans or they'd be killed.

Joshua shouted out, <There are five runners in the gully past the ridge to the south. Take your prey and move to safer ground. Then remember that talking with the U'tanse-that-swim will bring meat to your claws.>

He had made his point. He began swimming to deeper water. A moment later the Cerik began jumping from slab to slab, making his way back up to the top of the cliff.

That was no guarantee that Joshua could make it safely back to land. Perhaps it would be best to swim around the point and get closer to the hidden docks.

He swam, concentrating on what he could tell about his father's condition.

The cut on his left leg was shallow and still bleeding. The salt water was helping some, but it would need to be bandaged soon. His breathing was mostly regular, coughing up water sometimes.

His father's thoughts were confusing. His *ineda* had been knocked down, but there was nothing but the swirl of pain and fear of drowning. If he'd been conscious, Joshua would have had to deal with a man struggling for his life. He could hardly be grateful for the passive body since he didn't know when he'd wake up.

When he first caught a glimpse of the draperies concealing the dock, he was shocked to see them open. But it was barely a minute later when the waters started swirling around him, and his knee struck metal.

The submarine surfaced and the hatchway came open instantly, even before the waters had drained off the top of the hull. Robert was out and helped him move Cyclops.

Inside, white-haired Anra was waiting, helping move the unresponsive body to the floor. She worked quickly. "Be careful, his spine is damaged."

They cut his leathers free, and she stopped the bleeding with a cloth bandage wound about his leg.

Joshua sat back, letting the experienced healer work. He looked over at Robert.

"What do you know?"

The submarine pilot shrugged. "Not much. A couple of us were watching your hike. Suddenly, the both of you started running and a Cerik appeared out of nowhere. When I saw you turn toward the cliff, I didn't even wait. Anra saw me running and came along. I got the sub loose from the moorings as fast as I could manage and I was grateful you made it into the water."

He looked over at the unconscious man. "Cyclops always hated the water."

Joshua nodded. "I didn't ask him." He sighed. "Maybe I should have."

"Don't say that. You'd been gutted for sure."

Joshua asked Anra, "How bad is it?"

She shook her head. "I won't know for a while. He'll need lots of healing."

Joshua said, "Robert, take us to Base."

"Right."

Shortly, they were under the surface again.

Joshua asked, "Who's on semaphore duty?"

"At Base? Paul, I think."

Joshua scanned Base and saw Paul in the map room. He put his hands over his head and waited, but Paul never looked his way. After a minute or so, he turned to Factory and signaled Bernard, who was watching. Shortly, Bernard flagged Paul, and the word was sent. People would be ready for them when they arrived.

...

Cyclops had three healers standing beside his bed. Debbie stepped quietly around the room, aching to put her hands and healing skills to work as well, but her skills couldn't match those of Anra, Sylvia, and Comfort.

Debbie looked over at Joshua, who stood in the doorway, watching helplessly. She stalked over and pulled him out of the room.

"Tell me what happened."

His mother could not be denied. He said, "Cyclops and I were hiking—it was a secret thing we had to do. We'd made sure none of the Kakil search parties were in range, but there was a nomad we hadn't seen and he chased us. The only way we could escape was to jump into the sea."

She breathed in sharply. "He... your father... he has a problem with water."

"I know! I knew then! But we just barely escaped his claws. Cyclops got cut as it was. It was a long drop. I don't think we hit any of the rocks, but he was unconscious from the moment we hit the water."

She looked back at the doorway. "Sometimes, great fear can cause people to lose consciousness. I don't know if it's that or the damage from the fall. I just hope he will be okay."

Joshua took her hand and held it. She clutched it gratefully, but two minutes away from Cyclops was too long and she went back in.

Joshua moved to a different room and scanned the land for the nomad. It took a bit, but he found him with two runners in a *dul*, carrying them back to his group. The nomadic clan looked to be five males and two females. They had a crude hut up in the mountains, but if they were wise, they'd be gone soon.

He'd need to check on them regularly, just to make sure that they avoided the Kakil searchers.

Then, Joshua tracked down Robert. He was in the kitchen, chatting quietly with one of the cooks. The cook gave them a smile as Joshua sat down and went back to her chores.

"Robert, I need to ask, when Cyclops is out of action, who is in charge? There's some things we need to take care of."

He looked uneasy. "I don't think it's ever been decided. We all knew he was training you for the job."

"Yeah, training is one thing, but all of you at the status meetings; you, Patrick, Ford, my mother—you all have years of experience that I can't match. I was just his messenger, really."

Robert frowned, "Is he... will he recover?"

"None of the healers are talking. It might be days yet, and we don't have days. The Cerik are coming and we have to be ready."

Robert frowned, "You're right. But we don't really have anyone ready to step into his shoes. Then you take the lead, at least for now."

Joshua shook his head. "I don't know what do to, and I'm just 'the kid' over there."

"No, you're *his kid*. We're all at a loss. No one expected this. Somebody needs to step up and keep things running. You've spoken for Cyclops before. We'll all listen to you. Get us past this."

In the Garden

Joshua retired to the map room, pulled out a stack of paper and began writing.

"Cyclops is unconscious and surrounded by our best healers. Hovering around them are people waiting anxiously for him to wake up. I'm sure you'd like to be there too, but we can't afford to wait.

"The Cerik searchers are still coming. Everything has changed, but nothing has changed. All the projects decided in Cyclops's last status meeting are still on and must proceed with our best efforts."

He wrote a summary of what happened on the hike, admitting that it was more than just an idle whim on his father's part, but keeping all mention of the Ba secret.

Then he composed separate messages to the team leaders. Patrick still had to make plans for moving the boats to New Home during the most dangerous days, and Joshua emphasized that all the decisions about boats were Patrick's to make, even if there were no more status meeting updates.

Ford was given a similar message, as leader of the Factory engineering team.

He then took the pages to Robert.

"Get these to the team leaders. I'd have written one for you if you were back at Factory, but face to face is better anyway.

"I'm going to pretend like I'm a leader for now, just like you suggested. So, I want you to know that just like Patrick is the team leader for the boats, you're the team leader for the sub."

Robert chuckled, "A team of one?"

Joshua shook his head, no smile showing. "No. We're not going to be stuck with a submarine no one can drive if you get hit on the head. You're a team leader. Train at least one replacement. Explain everything. Maybe before too long, we'll build more submarines and your team will be even larger. But get started now.

"Now, I know you'll be coming back to Base a few days from now, but while you're at Factory, be sure to talk with the others that attend the status meetings. The status meeting group is the real leadership of the Free U'tanse, and you all need to work together. Even if Cyclops wakes up before you leave, he's going to be recuperating for a long time. There're some tough decisions to make, like how we really decide who's going to be in charge. The status meeting team will have to make those decisions eventually."

Robert nodded. "You're not coming back to Factory?"

"Not yet. I've got things to do here. But remember, I can swim back if necessary. Our semaphore operators are going to be getting a workout until then."

. . .

He checked on his father, but refrained from walking in there personally. He'd only be a distraction. The instant his father could talk, there was much he had to ask, but not now.

Instead, he went to the second level and checked the nursery.

"Joshua!" Ash was there waiting for him.

The young man's enthusiasm brought a smile to Joshua, and it was a strange feeling to have his face bend that way.

"What are you up to, Ash?"

The boy looked to his side, just to see who was listening. "Oh, things."

Joshua nodded. Ash was developing his sight, and he probably was aware of something bad going on. "Go get Very. We'll take a little walk."

Ash nodded seriously and hurried to find her.

Joshua took a quick tour through the five rooms that made up the whole world for those babies and cuties who hadn't yet learned *ineda*. It didn't matter if their thoughts could be read, because they didn't know anything that could compromise Base. As far as they knew, it could be any nursery in any of the Cerik-owned Homes spread across the continent. Only those like his sister and Ash, who had expanded their talents and learned how to block their thoughts, could be allowed to move about the Base.

He waved to some of the cuties. But he'd been gone so much lately that he was a stranger to some of them. This was where he was born and raised, but it was hardly his home anymore.

Veronica came up and gave him a big hug, burying her face in his chest. "I'm so glad you're back."

He returned the hug, feeling her shoulders shiver a bit. "Let's go for a walk."

She looked up with a worried smile. "Okay."

He said, "Bring your sketch book."

She frowned, "My dream book?"

He nodded.

She hesitated, "Okay. And I've got to tell Rachael that I'm going. She asked me to help with the babies when Comfort didn't show up."

Soon, they went through the locked door. Both the youngsters tightened down their *ineda*, he was pleased to notice.

"Let's go sit in the garden."

The large rooms, brightly lit by overhead banks of bluish-tinted lights, provided a number of benches where they could sit and talk with no one around. Cornstalks stood in quiet array before them. A potato field with low green leaves was behind them.

"Cyclops has been injured."

Veronica put her hand to her mouth and her *ineda* shivered just an instant, but she firmed it back up. Ash looked like he knew already.

"We were outside, working together, when a Cerik discovered us. We ran to the water and escaped, but Cyclops's back was hurt when we hit the water. The healers don't know how bad it is yet."

He gave them as much information as he thought they could take, and told them it was like so many other things—they couldn't share this with the cuties. You can't know secrets without a good *ineda*.

When Veronica asked about her mother, he said, "Debbie is there with the healers. I don't think she's likely to leave his side until they know more. That's why I'm here telling you, instead."

He turned to Ash. "The both of you are going to have to take on more duties now. I'd love to let you stay in the nursery for as long as you wanted. I know you're comfortable there, but with both Cyclops, Debbie, and several of the healers unavailable, I need you."

"Ash, how has your *sight* developed?"

"It's getting better. People have been coaching me. I knew that Cyclops was hurt. I *saw* when the submarine returned."

Joshua smiled. "That's good. There's a job, an adult job you need to start. I'll tell you more, but you need to go back and tell Rachael that you'll be gone for several hours. Do you need the code for the door lock?"

He grinned, "No. I can handle it." He jumped up and hurried back the way they came.

Veronica looked worried. "I don't know if there's anything I can do, other than work in the nursery. I like helping the babies."

He sighed. They were alone together and now was the time to bring it up. "Very, you have a skill that no one else has. We've all—Debbie, Cyclops, and I—we've all known about your dreams, and we've kept quiet. We didn't want you to worry."

Her forehead crinkled up. "My nightmares."

He nodded. "We pretended it was nothing. But you know, don't you?"

She stared down at her sketchbook. She looked up at his eyes, and then opened up to a sheet. It was hardly artwork of Ash's quality, but it was plain enough. There was a sketch of a man lying down on a bed. He had a bandage over his eyes, and three women were surrounding him, holding their hands on his body.

Joshua gasped, "When did you dream this?"

"Last week. I worried about it, but Ash always told me to take the nightmares that worried me and put them away in my dream book. It sort of works."

He tapped the sketch. "That's exactly what's going on right now. Sometimes you dream things before they happen. Nobody in all the world can do that."

Veronica shook her head, tears welling in her eyes. "I don't want that. The nightmares are hard enough, without knowing they are real."

He took her hands. "Very, I don't know why this is happening to you, but it's something we can't ignore. Maybe our parents will get mad at me for telling you this, but *if* there are things in your dreams that can help us survive the Cerik, then we have to know. I'm asking you to take on this adult task. You have to share your dreams with us."

She held her eyes together tightly, looking down at the sheet. "But bad things happen! They're nightmares. If bad things are coming and I can't do anything to stop them, it just makes it worse!"

He tried to be comforting. "It's not always useless. Remember when I got burned?"

She nodded.

"You dreamed that. You mentioned something about burn ointments before it happened, and because of that, Sally had medicine for me when I needed it."

She frowned. "Even back then, you knew?"

He shook his head. "No. Things like that gave us the idea. All we knew at first was that you had bad dreams. Only in afterthought did we realize what was happening. And we worried that you were too weak to bear it. I don't think that's true anymore."

"Why? I know I'm weak."

"They trouble you, your dreams. It would trouble anyone. But you've learned how to cope." He nodded toward the sketchbook. "You have your tools. And guess what? Right now, when you're having to face the truth, you haven't fallen apart. I suspect you already knew."

Hesitantly, she nodded. "It was the little things, not the horrible ones. When little Timmy fell and broke his finger, I wasn't even surprised, because I'd already known about it. There was a spill when one of the babies knocked over the poopie pot, and I had been avoiding that place for two days. Sometimes I have an idea when it's going to happen, most times not. But it was a little too much to ignore."

He gave her another hug. Just because. "Even if you can't stop bad things, maybe you can avoid being in the path of the spill, right?"

She nodded with a half-smile. "I guess."

"Now, show me your sketches, please."

Reassignments

Joshua escorted Ash and Veronica up to visit Debbie and to see how Cyclops was doing.

Comfort was resting in a chair, looking even smaller than she usually did. She gave them an update. "He's resting. The spinal injury will take some time to heal. We've never dealt with this much nerve damage, and none of us are really confident we can get everything back the way it was." She sighed, "It might be like his eyes. Some things we can heal, but no one had the skills to re-grow his eyes."

Veronica held Debbie's arms. "He'll smile at you again. I know it."

When Debbie looked at her daughter in a strange, serious way, Veronica blinked and said, "Hey, not like a dream. I just have a feeling."

Debbie looked at her son, "You told her?"

Joshua nodded. "She knew already. She can handle it."

Veronica gripped her mother tighter. "Don't worry about me. Take care of my father, okay?"

...

After they took her back to the nursery, Joshua walked with Ash up the ramps to the fourth level.

"You drew the semaphore chart, didn't you?"

"Yes."

"I thought I recognized your style. So ... you're familiar with the arm-waving code?"

163

Ash gave him a timid grin. "I listen in from time to time, but a lot of it is nonsense."

"Great! Base needs another semaphore operator, and I think you're the right candidate. Besides, you'll make a good partner with Very. She trusts you."

"Partner? Explain."

"Very's nightmares sometimes tell the future. You're aware of that, right?"

He nodded.

"Well, she's agreed to share her dreams with us, just in case we can find something useful in them. We still have to keep this mostly secret, so if she had a trusted partner, someone who she could talk openly with, then they could pass the results on to me, or whoever else is in charge. Very would get someone who could sympathize with what she's going through, and she could describe her visions to you. You're the right person, if you're well trained in semaphore."

He frowned. "I could just tell Debbie, or Cyclops when he's healed, couldn't I?"

Joshua nodded. "Yes. But until then, the fewer people in the chain of communication, the better. If Very knew semaphore and could describe things clearly, I'd have her signal me directly, but those aren't her talents. You're the one who can talk to her and make sure she's describing her nightmare clearly."

Ash's frowned at the ground as they walked. "I guess I understand."

Joshua put his hand on the younger guy's shoulder. "You're an artist. You know how to tease out the minimum lines to get the truth across. I've seen it in your work. Too many scribbles, and it can hide what you're trying to draw. Very has a confusing dream, and there's a truth hidden there. She saw Cyclops reclining on a bed with people around him. The truth was that he was injured and people were healing him. She might have thought that she was seeing him dead, surrounded by mourners, but that would have been speculation.

"What we'll need is the purest vision, with no wild interpretation. She saw a man with bandaged eyes, surrounded by three females with their hands on him. You're going to have to talk her through it, and find that pure vision, and then clearly send it on. Can you do that?"

Ash looked worried, but he nodded.

Joshua explained a bit more, particularly how semaphore would fit in with his other duties.

And then they reached the room where Paul sat, staring off toward Factory, scribbling text. They waited patiently until he was done.

Paul frowned at him. "More messages?"

Joshua chuckled. "Keeping you busy?"

He sighed. "I can barely get them delivered before Bernard flags me with another one."

"Are you the only one on duty?"

Paul growled. "You used to help, but now you're always off somewhere else. Cyclops used to handle a lot of it himself. Robert helped when the submarine was docked here."

Joshua nodded. "I thought that must be the case. Well, I've got another task for you."

Paul sagged. "What is it?"

"Ash here is your new trainee. He's familiar with the codes, but you're going to have to turn him into a first-class semaphore operator." Joshua grinned at Ash. "He also gets to run errands. So, if you've got a message to deliver, give it to him."

Paul looked the boy over. "I don't think I've ever seen you out of the nursery. Are you up to it?"

Ash nodded. "I think so. And I can tell Timothy that I'm working with his daddy."

Paul smiled. "Okay, then." He picked up a paper and handed it over. "Take this to Hoop, down at the docks. Then come back here as soon as possible. We'll check and see how good your signs are."

Ash hesitated, glancing at Joshua. "Um, which one is Hoop? I've only been to the docks once before."

Joshua smiled. "He looks wider than most guys and he'll likely be yelling at someone. Ask someone there; they'll point him out." Ash nodded, then hurried off, paper in hand.

Paul asked, "Do you think he has the skills?"

"Probably. I think he's as ready to take on adult tasks as he'll ever be. I've already given him other jobs as well. But you do agree we need another operator on duty, don't you?"

Paul sighed. "Yes. And I guess I'm the only one to train him?"

Joshua nodded. "Not only him. All the locations need more people skilled in semaphore. And I think there needs to be someone in charge of communications—someone to take care of finding and training new people. That person would make sure that each location has someone on duty at all hours of the day, and show up at the status meetings to make sure everyone knows what you can do and what your needs are. You and Bernard are the only candidates. What do you think?"

Paul shook his head. "Dump that on Bernard. I only took on this job to help out. I didn't realize it'd take over my life. Sylvia has been nagging at me to come by and help with Timothy, and I haven't been able to get free lately. Now she's helping with Cyclops."

"Then go, take a break. I'll handle messages for a while."

Paul didn't put up any argument, hurrying off before Joshua changed his mind.

Joshua tapped the table, thinking. Then he turned to face Bernard over at Factory. He put his hands over his head and soon sent a message, addressed to Ford.

"If you had an opportunity to look at the report Ace sent, I need your opinion on whether a small utility sub could be constructed using egg tanks and the pump assembly that was created at New Home. Very soon, we may need to send the existing submarine on a long trip, and having something to haul limited cargo and a person or two between Base and Factory would be extremely useful."

Joshua could see how it would look—just as Veronica had sketched in her dream book. He suspected she didn't even know what she had drawn, but with the pump tubes arranged around an egg tank, it could only be one thing. If Ace hadn't already invented it and sent instructions in his report, surely Ford could work it out once someone described it. It existed in the future, so as soon as possible, he wanted it available.

In spite of Cyclops's injury, New Home had to feel that they wouldn't be abandoned the instant troubles arose. He needed them to know that Factory was actively working to insure New Home's escape plan, and the best way to do that was to arrange a submarine visit. But Base needed more than one submarine to keep them from being cut off from the outside world.

...

It was a refreshing change, sitting at the table, rotating his *sight* from Factory, to New Home, and then taking five minutes to hunt for Cerik on the mainland. He paused a moment when, after several turns looking at Holana sitting at her table reading some book, he *saw* her chatting with Sally.

He waited. He suspected Sally would sent a message to him once she heard that Cyclops had been injured, but it never came. When he went ahead to check Bernard at Factory, there was a message from Ford, replying that he'd get to Ace's report after the collapse of the walkway. The next time he looked at New Home, Holana was alone again and Sally was walking toward the kitchen.

I guess I'm not the center of everyone's thoughts. They must have been talking about something else.

. . .

Joshua was almost surprised his bed was still there. He'd been on the move for far too long. Not that his own bed was any softer, it was just familiar. As soon as he had left the nursery and put aside being a cutie himself, he had been busy. He was putting Ash through the same routine.

The quake woke him. Instinctively, he *looked* outside. The moon was high.

And then he remembered, Ford was going to time the avalanche to match the time the moon normally triggered quakes. He forgot that was in the middle of the night this time.

He stood up. Across the bay, a wave of shattered rock was tumbling down the cliff, obliterating the walkway, and entering the bay with a explosion of white nearly as tall as the cliff.

It's a wave! Joshua tensed, remembering a tsunami he'd seen when he was younger. It had caused lots of damage at both Factory and Base.

I hope this one isn't like that. Had they planned for the splash? He should have mentioned it at the last meeting.

He threw on some clothes and ran down to the dock.

The lights were on and dock workers were already moving storage boxes up the ramp. They were experienced with the effects of quakes. He grabbed up a bundle of nets and ran them up to higher ground.

"Here it comes!" one of the dock workers yelled.

The entrance to Base was an underwater tunnel that blocked most of the wave action, but when a large tsunami arrived, there could be a surge even here. He watched as the water level on the rock walls rose. It approached the level of the dock, but then it peaked and began running back out.

There was a loud, "Whew!" from Hoop. "That was close."

Joshua let them get back to work, putting everything back where it was supposed to be. He *looked* over at Factory.

He gripped the railing next to him, overwhelmed at the distruction he *saw*.

Cyclops Updates

Joshua sat beside the bed where Cyclops was strapped in place. His father breathed evenly, but hadn't said a word since the hike. The healers were worried that his spine wouldn't heal properly if he thrashed around, so they'd taken precautions.

But for now, all they could do was check on him every few hours and make sure the healing was proceeding correctly.

"It was a disaster," Joshua said. He wasn't sure Cyclops was listening, but he was so used to giving the man his reports that he couldn't imagine doing anything else.

"Everyone was so used to tsunami being tied to quakes that we didn't really consider a rockslide triggering one—at least I didn't. Ford's little *flick* went off just as he'd planned, cracking the rock and starting the slide. It took out the first section of the walkway, just as we'd hoped, but the rocks kept going, shattering another ledge below it. The whole mass of tumbling rock crashed into the bay, starting a wave.

"Over here, across the water, the surge got as high as the dock, but there was no damage. However, Factory's dock was much closer to the wave's source, and with only seconds warning. The wave ripped through sideways. Boat C slammed into Boat B and it went on to hit the tub. The tub twisted and smashed the submarine up against the dock. Everything got dents and scrapes. Boat B's raft had major tank damage and began to sink. Carson climbed into his boat and took off before it went down, but the wind blast was concentrated right there at the docks. It ripped the draperies free, and what wasn't soaked by the wave was drenched by the spray.

"Carson chose to take his boat over to New Home right then. He reported once he got there that his boat was intact, but only had enough power to make the trip there—not enough to return. It'll have to be recharged later.

"The damaged raft has been winched back up onto the dock. Patrick's boat is being charged as rapidly as possible so he can leave, too. Swimmers recovered the draperies, and workers are doing their best to get them back up before the Cerik search party arrives. All the dents and scratched paint will have to wait until the immediate danger is past.

"The orders have been given to move everything that might smell—and that includes the dock workers themselves—inside the airlocks for as long as the Cerik are in the area. Robert will be bringing the submarine here within a couple of hours, once he's finished his safety checks."

Cyclops shifted slightly. Joshua paused his report, looking carefully for any sign that his father was awake.

His lips moved. Joshua leaned over, straining to hear anything.

It was the faintest of whispers. "Joshua. Scroll twelve. Code four-nine."

He squeezed his father's hand. "Got it. Hang on there. I'll get Debbie."

His mother was only two rooms over.

"He's awake!" Debbie and Sylvia hurried.

Debbie leaned over Cyclops and took his hand. She said, "I'm here." He smiled.

...

Cyclops was in and out of consciousness. During the times he was awake and coherent, everyone wanted to talk to him. But the next day, he requested a private moment with his children.

Joshua held his hand on the right side of the bed and Veronica held his left.

"You two are going to have to work together." He gave them a squeeze, but it was weak. "Joshua knows things you don't and you, my extra special little girl, you have a talent no one shares." He sighed. "I'm not going to be able to help. My mind is fuzzy. There are noises I can't shake, and I don't trust my *ineda* any more. Until I heal, I don't even want to be briefed about our people. I don't want to know anything that I might leak. Do you understand?"

"Yes, Daddy."

Joshua hesitated. "I understand, but it will be hard, not knowing. You might worry less if you were told."

"Perhaps. But I need to heal. I will need to trust my own mind before then."

Joshua nodded. "I'll pass the word. It will be difficult not bringing problems to you."

Cyclops sighed. "Your mother will keep me busy enough. She has years worth of her gardening concerns that I was always too busy to listen to. Now, maybe I can pay her the attention she deserves."

...

Joshua took over a shift from Paul and used that time to pass on the report about Cyclops to the people at Factory and New Home. He didn't describe details, other than to let them know that Cyclops was awake, alert, and requested to be left out of the day-to-day operations.

Ford immediately sent a status report for Cyclops, describing how well the repairs had come. Joshua started a pile for reports to give his father when he asked for them.

He knew all of his father's codes, so he decided to read everything, just to make sure that nothing critical was overlooked.

All the codes except for four-nine. When he had a moment, he went into his father's workroom and rummaged for scroll twelve.

He found it, a fairly fat one, and written entirely in code. There was no hint as to its content. He unrolled it part way and found the slices where new sheets had been added. It looked like a project that had grown far beyond the original plan.

Should I start at the beginning?

He found a gap that looked like a place where one section ended and another began. The problem with some of these substitution codes was that unless you started at the right place, it wouldn't decode.

Code four-nine was a formula code. Entering the two digits into the formula provided a translating circle. This one proved to be fairly simple, once he worked the math. Did Cyclops keep this in his head? If it was a long-running project, then maybe he could translate it on the fly without a written circle to assist.

He decoded a stretch of it.

George's secret log appears to be a collection of every reference in the Tales of the Cerik that mention the position of the moon or the sky demons. I watched as he determined that Katranel moved in the sky, by references to it being eaten by Hae, which is the mythological name for the moon. George appears to know of a star chart begun by Abe the Father which lists Katranel in a position too far in the north of the sky to be eclipsed by the moon. If George's work is true, then Katranel is a star that moves and may be another planet of Ko's parent sun.

Joshua was puzzled. This appeared to be some secret investigation done by his father that he never shared with the rest of the status team. Why was it a secret? Was it just not important enough to share?

He unrolled another section of the scroll and applied the code.

After an emotional meeting between Bruce and Aarison of Kakil Home, Bruce retreated to his private room and wrote a message. He paced in his room and worked on it for several hours, but in the end, he tore it up. Here is what I was able to transcribe:

"If I should be found dead, I need to point the finger at Aarison. It has become obvious to me over the course of the past few years that Aarison is much more loyal to Elehadi than to the people of Kakil Home. As has been obvious to everyone, we have not replaced the other elders that have died over the past years, leaving only us two in charge. What may not be public knowledge is that the elders of several years ago were pressured to accept Aarison into our number even though he lacked the experience and skills necessary to take care of our people. At the time, Elehadi, through his telepath Stakka, strongly suggested that they liked Aarison and that it would be good to train him and add him to the elders.

"We thought the man would mature and step into the demands of the job. Unfortunately, as his reputation has demonstrated, he is much more interested in collecting adoring, impressionable young girls than he is in the people's welfare. In addition, he has successfully blocked every effort to expand the number of elders, even as we drop away.

"Elehadi has usurped the traditional function of the elders, leaving the U'tanse of Kakil unable to take care of our own interests. I have fought this battle alone for too long, while Aarison waits out the day when he will be the sole voice to control the lives of everyone, backed

by the good will of Elehadi. If our Name decides to wipe us out, as he did the Rikna, there will be no one to even call out for help."

There was more to his message, but Bruce tore it up before I had completed my copy of it. From the intensity of the argument, I suspect more bad changes are coming to Kakil Home. It is sad that Bruce de-cided to tear up his warning. I can't guess his motives.

Joshua saw that it was dated several months prior. Again Joshua had no memory of this revelation having been shared with the others. Scroll twelve had to be a log of his father's unique ability to read text via his clairvoy-ance. It was all important enough to write down, but sensitive enough to hide until he needed it.

What does it mean that he shared this with me? It was the first message out of his mouth. Is he that worried that he won't recover?

Joshua looked at the size of the scroll. It would take him several days to decode and read it all. The code was coming easier. He was referencing the decoding circle less and less. He'd have to pace himself, and not slack off on his other tasks, but he needed to know it all.

He carefully unrolled and re-rolled the scroll in reverse so that the earli-est entries were at the top. Carefully, he began decoding the entries.

Weeding

As the Cerik search party from Kakil approached from the north, Base and Factory both shut down all machinery. That included the air circulation pumps. The original Delense designers must have had a situation like this in mind, because even with no blowers, there was some limited circulation through the facility. The Delense had not needed to filter their air, since they were native to Ko and adapted to the contaminants the volcanos were constantly spewing into the atmosphere, but they had gone to the trouble of hiding the air intake and exhaust among natural cracks in the rocks. There were no troublesome pipes to be discovered on the surface.

Although there was no evidence that the search party had any telepaths among them, the natural response among the residents was to concentrate on their *ineda* and tighten it up. They were all telepaths, and that's the way they thought.

Joshua found himself doing it, too. *Luckily, we don't need to worry about that.* The cuties and babies in the nursery were as happily noisy as ever. Sylvia and Comfort, handling all the usual chores, were adept at hiding adult worries from the little ones.

Veronica had no new nightmares, so that was the best news he had.

Ash came into his room, panting. Joshua asked, "What's up?"

The boy sank into a chair. "They're running me all over the place. Nobody wants to put out the effort with this stale air, so they just call for me to do it for them." He took another few breaths. "I've delivered the messages you gave me."

"Good. Rest for now. Paul will be back on semaphore duty in another hour or so, but nobody is sending. Everyone is waiting quietly for the Cerik to pass by."

Ash griped, "Everyone but me." He paused, then asked, "Where are they?"

Joshua had been watching. "They're spread out, in shouting distance from each other, but they stretch from the shoreline up into the hills. Each is moving south. I'm sure they've already seen the trails and scars from where we removed the old storage sheds, but all that has seen months of weathering. It hasn't been enough to trigger a call—at least not yet."

Joshua focused on the leader of the party. The Cerik had chosen the coastline for himself, since that was the only real clue they had about the rogue U'tanse. The hunter was following a footpath. Joshua had walked that way himself, and if all the tales he'd heard about the Cerik were true, even after all this time, the hunter could probably smell traces of his passage.

Joshua reached for his thoughts. There was no *ineda*, but a hunter on a path was very much a beast searching for prey, and all he could get was a flood of sensations, most of which didn't translate well to his human mind. There were no subvocalized thoughts he could read.

Then, the Cerik paused. <Kolnsssss>

Joshua didn't know the word, but he got the feel of it. The hunter had come up to the fresh landslide, the hiss at the end of the word had the feeling of treachery and slipperiness. The ground was an enemy, waiting for one incautious step to throw him down to the more patient and overwhelming killer below, the endlessly moving ocean. He never looked down at the water—never looked along the cliff where a very perceptive eye might have noticed something odd.

He turned and put more distance between the edge of the cliff and himself. The Cerik would never run from a foe that could bleed, but his claws could do nothing about the waves.

Joshua whispered to Ash, "Looks like the search party has already passed the Base, and now, they're moving on past Factory. It'll be another few hours before we can turn the blowers back on, but the main risk is past."

"The sooner the better. The air is stuffy."

...

After Ash left, he checked Factory, but Bernard was just reading something. He checked New Home, and was surprised to see Holana looking his way with her hands over her head.

He sent the ready signal. It was a message for him.

"Sally came by and said that if there was a time when you didn't look busy, to send her best wishes for Cyclops. And for you. She said, 'I know you'll do your best, but I want you to do your own best, not your father's.' I don't know what she meant, but there it is."

He replied that he understood, and then asked if Bernard was giving her more instructions. She said he was, and said he was taking his new duties seriously. *"It's nice,"* she said, *"having someone to answer my questions all the time."*

They chatted some more, until Paul came back to take over the semaphore work.

Joshua was pleased that she was handling her own position so well. Of course, the real test would be whether she could train a helper to be as good as she was.

...

Joshua waved to Debbie, who was weeding the potatoes in her garden. "How are you doing, Mom?"

She looked up, puzzled. "Mom? Since when did you call me that?"

He shrugged. "I've heard it around. People *do* call their mothers that. I thought I'd give it a shot. How are you holding up?"

She shook her head and ripped a tiny vine from the soil, shoving it into her tote bag. "I can't..." She stopped and looked off into the distance. "Cyclops has always been strong. Even with the eye problem. Even with his fears. In spite of everything, there was always a strength there. I could always count on it."

Joshua plucked a star-thorn just edging out of the soil and added it to her bag. "He'll come back. His first words when he woke up were all business. Give him time to heal. He's been through a lot."

"I know that! I'm just complaining because it's you. I can't complain to anyone else, now that he needs me to be strong."

He chuckled. "Go ahead, then. I'm the same way. I'm desperate to report to *someone*, and everything is funneling my way instead."

She nodded. "People have gotten used to you being his messenger."

"That's what I think, too. I just hope I don't say something stupid and cause the whole place to come down on top of us."

She chuckled. "You're not that important. Everybody's doing their job. Just let them do it."

He nodded. "I'm ready for him to be well again."

"Me, too."

Something flickered. He blinked. Maybe he was just letting himself get too tired. He stood up straight and took a deep breath.

"Problem?" she asked.

"No. Just stretching. Nothing gets to your back more than weeding."

She chuckled. "You always have some excuse not to get down in the dirt."

He smiled and spread his arms in apology. "Not everybody..."

The light dimmed throughout the gardens.

"What's that!" she said.

Joshua *looked*.

All through Base, people were stopped, looking up at the lights. He checked Factory. People were running in the corridors. Someone was ripping down the 'All Is Well' flag.

"Mom, the power is going down. Something's wrong at Factory."

She looked around to her gardens, frowning up at the artificial lights that kept all her crops growing.

The lights were fading, and this time it didn't stop. They were underground and soon everywhere would be pitch black.

Debbie said, "The nursery!"

"Right!"

They ran.

Blackout

The lock to the nursery had already unlatched itself with the voltage drop. Joshua barely noticed when he hurried in. Some of the babies were already crying, afraid of the change.

Debbie's strong voice called out, "Hey, everybody. I've got a great new trick to show everyone. Come gather around while we bring the lights down."

The cuties all focused on her. Her cheerful voice was just what they'd been looking for.

Joshua was about to go signal Factory to see what the problem was when she snagged his arm. "Wait," she whispered.

"Is everyone here?" she said. She plucked some of the cotton fluff from the changing station and rolled it together in her hands. The light was fading fast, and everyone was struggling to see what she was doing.

"A very wise man I once knew, Aaron, told me a story. He was lost in the darkness, and it was cold. No one was going to come to rescue him."

The light finally went all the way out, and someone whimpered.

Debbie said, "So Aaron took some dry plants and fluffed up the edges. He carefully focused all his attention on them. Now, let's all do the same. Those of you closest, reach out and lightly touch the cotton."

Joshua could *see* them huddling closer. Arms reached out, and some of them touched it.

Debbie pulled it back. "Now, everyone, put everything out of your mind. Think only of the cotton, and imagine it hot. Think of how nice it would be, hot and bright. Think of fire. Make it hot."

Debbie leaned close to the cotton and there was a gleam of red. She breathed on it, and it flared up brighter. She breathed on it again and a flame popped into existence. There were several gasps, and a squeal.

"It worked!" came a little girl's cheer.

Joshua could see the little flame reflected in many eyes.

Debbie whispered, to him, "Go get the candles I made. In my closet with my breather and leathers. And see if you can find some wind-up lights anywhere."

He nodded and ducked out. Children's voices were calling out. "Do it again! Do it again!"

His mother had tamed the panic, keeping the nursery from collapsing into screaming chaos.

. . .

He found the candles and found two of Debbie's workers stumbling around. Not everyone had sufficient clairvoyance to navigate in total darkness. He led them to the corridor and matched them up with Ash, who was hurrying to the nursery.

"The three of you take these candles to Debbie. Help her keep the cuties calm and under control. Ash, when you're done there, find me."

He kept one of the candles and hurried up to the map room.

Debbie had told him the tale of Aaron and the flame when he was still in the nursery himself, but although he'd tried to make the fire himself, he'd never succeeded before. *Seeing* things was one thing. Making them move was another. But he'd been practicing his healing for some time now. Influencing the cells to heal and making the fiber heat up were similar.

He concentrated on the wick of the candle. Sweat was beaded on his forehead before there was a flicker of red. Carefully he breathed on it. There was light.

Once he had the candle established, he faced Factory and put his hands on his head.

Perhaps Bernard didn't need the candlelight to locate him, but it wouldn't hurt.

Bernard was distracted. People were talking to him, and he was gesturing. But then, he looked toward Base and noticed the signal.

"Joshua, the turbine is down. Word from Ford is that there are rock chips in the water flow from the dam. There's damage to the turbine blades, possibly. They had to shut it down to check. How are things at Base?"

Joshua felt a shiver run through him as he understood the problem. The turbine was the sole source of power that ran both Factory and Base. Everything flowed from that power.

His mind swirled with the implications.

Without power, Base and Factory would be unlivable. They would have to evacuate, and that would be hard. Both transports were at New Home, with limited power. The submarine would be required to evacuate Base. And with their population, there was no chance everyone could be moved to New Home before the power cells were exhausted.

Not to mention that they'd be giving up any chance of developing the technology to hold off the Cerik.

He wondered, could they power Base and Factory with power cells, just like most of the Homes? It wouldn't last long without a recharge, and the longer they kept the crops growing and the lights shining, the fewer trips the boats could fly.

Joshua moved his arms.

"Base is without power. We're making do with candles, but without some power soon, the crops will die. I'll get a estimate of minimum power requirements before we have to evacuate."

Bernard acknowledged.

"I'll pass the word. People here are moving to the dock where they can see. Biggest fear here is that the rockslide also damaged the channels that feed the water from the dam. No one knows if the trouble was a one-time thing or on-going."

Joshua sent, *"Arms tired,"* and then began a careful scan of the Base, level by level. It was as he feared. Although there were clusters of people at the dock and at the nursery, where even more people had arrived to check on their children, there were still isolated people in ones and twos who were trapped by the darkness without enough *sight* to navigate.

Ash arrived, and Joshua gave him a list of where the lost people were.

"Take them down to the dock. That's the largest open-air place we have, other than the gardens, and we don't want people tripping over the plants. Hoop has a fire burning there, and I'd rather keep the fires to a minimum, now that the air circulation has stopped."

Debbie showed up a little later. Cyclops had waved her away when she tried to tell him what had happened. He said to discuss it with Joshua. So they discussed her gardens, and the rate at which the candles were being used.

"Surely they can send us some power," she complained. "Some of these plants will go dormant, but some will die if I can't get the lights back on. They don't care about turbines or rock chips!"

"But how much can you get by with? Can we turn off every other light, or something like that to reduce the electricity necessary?"

"They won't grow well like that. People need to eat. If the corn doesn't mature, there's no need to grow it at all."

"Then give me numbers. I'll be making the argument with Ford in a few minutes. I'll swim over there to convince them we're hurting. But I can't say anything without numbers to prove I'm being reasonable."

She grumbled, but she went to the gardens with a candle to walk the rows and get a better estimate.

. . .

Ford was with Bernard. He talked and Bernard waved his arms.

"The turbine began to vibrate dangerously and we had to spin it down to check. It looked bad when I scanned it. The main turbine has eighteen blades, and two adjacent blades were warped by the impact of a rock. I saw other scratches and nicks too, so I pulled in Carl. He did a microscopic scan once we drained the chamber and he could get in there to touch the blades. One of the blades could be beaten back into position, but the other has numerous fractures and is likely to shatter under pressure. There's no way we can repair it."

Joshua could see the expression on the man's face. Ford looked as beaten down as the blades he was describing. Joshua asked:

"Is it your opinion that the turbine cannot be fixed, or that it will take a lot of time to fix it?"

Ford listened as Bernard relayed the question. Then he talked.

"Joshua, the existing turbine fan cannot be repaired. With a lot of time researching the Delense archives, and a lot of power to run the fabricator, a replacement fan might be built. Even then, the anti-corrosion coating they used to keep the metal intact isn't something we can produce in that size. We can do thinner coatings on things like the eggs, but not a thick coating on anything the size and complexity of the turbine fan."

Joshua could see that Bernard's movements were getting sloppy. Long complex messages were a strain on the arms, and even if he was struggling to keep going, Joshua could tell that Bernard's arms were very tired. Joshua decided to delay more questions.

"Ford, I will swim over to Factory so we can work out details in person. For now, give top priority to ways we can get partial power back on line. Just enough to light the corridors and keep our crops from dying. Arms tired."

Bernard spoke the translation and Ford nodded. Bernard signaled back, *"Arms tired."*

Damage Report

All through the night, the lights eased on and then faded back to black, for hours sometimes. From what Joshua could *see*, Ford's people were trying to rebalance the damaged turbine blades with strategically placed blobs of hardened putty. They turned the water flow back on at slow speeds and checked to see if the damaging vibration returned.

At Base, Debbie was taking the moments of reduced power to turn off every non-critical light or motor. Over the years, power on the Base side of the transmission line that ran under the bay had fluctuated and one of the more clever engineers had installed a heavy box full of spools of cable that allowed Base to adjust the voltage distributed through the various chambers. Hoop worked with Debbie to feed the highest voltages to the most critical of the garden lamps. It didn't take much glow in the corridors to let people walk without stumbling, but the plants were picky.

She gripped his arm as he was preparing for the swim. "Make sure they know what we're doing here. We need early warning if the power comes back up to normal so we can back out all the changes. It'll burn out my earth-lights if the voltage spikes back up."

He nodded. "I already sent a message to Ford, but I'll remind him. I don't think that's our problem. If the fractured blade shatters, it might be days or weeks before they could get anything running again."

He had spent a few minutes sitting with Cyclops during breakfast. His father took his hand, but didn't attempt to talk about the problems. He had to be aware of the power failure, although he didn't bring it up. Joshua told him that he'd be gone for a few days, and Cyclops just nodded.

Joshua packed his tow bag and checked out his breather.

Running footsteps made him look back to the hallway. It was Veronica, looking frightened and puzzled as she made her way across the unfamiliar dock in the semidarkness. Ash was chasing after her. She was heading straight for where he was packing.

"Joshua, I'm glad I found you! Ash said you were leaving, and I didn't get a chance to say goodbye."

He smiled at his little sister, "Sorry, but that's my life right now. I'm always on the move, going from place to place. I don't always get time to tell you."

She gave him a hug. "That's okay, I guess. It's just... Ash was telling me about the... turbine." She struggled with the unfamiliar word. "And I realized it was something I could have told you about."

"Really?"

She nodded. "It's just, it wasn't a nightmare, just a strange dream. And I didn't know what it was."

He gave her an encouraging smile. "Explain."

She looked flustered. "You know that picture book, in the nursery? The Life of Old Earth one? There was a flower, a daisy. Well, I dreamed about a giant daisy, and there were people coming around to look at it. It's just... I didn't realize it was anything real. Sometimes my dreams are just nonsense, you know?"

He took her hand. "It's okay. Even if you'd told me, I wouldn't have understood its meaning either. And if you did, I wouldn't have known how to stop the damage from happening in the first place. Don't worry about interpreting every dream. Just pass on your images to Ash, like we discussed."

She nodded. "I'll still worry."

"And I'll worry about you. That's just how it is." He caught Ash's eye. The boy moved closer to Veronica. "Now you two get back to your real jobs. How are the little ones handling the darkness?"

She shrugged. "It was scary at first, but they're getting used to the low light and the occasional candle. Jinger was grumbling that it was just a ploy to get us to go to bed earlier."

They laughed. Jinger was one of the older ones, and often the voice of grumpiness.

Joshua pointed, "Now, you two get back to work."

He waited until they were gone, then stashed his tunic in his tow bag, adjusted his breather, and slipped into the water.

...

Joshua spent the whole swim across the bay wondering. What could have been done, if Veronica had mentioned the giant flower in her dreams?

I wouldn't have understood. I never even knew what the turbine looked like until they started working on it.

Come to think of it, if she had warned us, and we had understood her dream, we would have shut down the water flow and the turbine wouldn't have been damaged. We'd have never had to empty the chamber and her vision of people around the giant flower wouldn't have happened in the first place.

He tried to shake off the tangled confusion of it all. Maybe it was better not knowing the future. At least it wouldn't give you headaches.

He was welcomed by quite a crowd at the Factory's dock. Everyone knew who he was, even if they'd previously spent all their time off in some workshop in the depths of of the burrows. For a group of telepaths who had effectively blocked all use of chatting mind to mind, gossip was the next best thing. All the eyes on him were a little unnerving. He'd been the topic of speculation since he first started running errands for his father, but it was more serious now.

Factory was not working. The air circulation was running at minimum—just enough to prevent toxins from collecting in the depths. Even with the furnaces shut down, there were enough chemical residues to stink up the place. Workers had to decide whether to stay in the dark interior, slowly being poisoned by the chemicals, or wander around on the dock in breathers, letting Ko's atmosphere damage their skin.

Not that the breathers were going to last forever, either. The filtration chemicals had to be heated periodically to bake out the nitrates that contaminated the air. There was a stockpile of the treated chemicals, but unless the power was restored, that would be exhausted before too long.

Ford and Robert met with him in Bernard's chamber. Bernard took notes.

Joshua listened as Ford gave him the latest information, and from the way he talked, it seemed that Ford still didn't really believe that Cyclops wasn't being kept in the loop. Maybe he couldn't believe it.

"The turbine is spinning, and we're getting a little power, but we just can't bring it up more than about twenty percent without it showing signs of stress. Most of the water from the dam is going through the bypass. We don't want to force the reservoir to rise so much that the spillway over-flows—I don't want to make the same mistake we did back when we had that chemical spill."

Joshua nodded, although he had no memory of the event. Ford was prob-ably talking about the shash plants along the river that were washed away some time back, but he didn't want to interrupt the report with side issues.

"Ford, just how stable is the cracked blade? Twenty percent would give us enough power for some things—some of the crops at Base, refreshing the breathing powder."

The old engineer shook his head. "I can't guarantee it won't shatter to bits in the next minute. And when it goes, it'll cause even more damage. The rock chips have been causing problems all along the water course. Valves are sticking, feeder tubes are getting blocked. You've even got to watch your feet at the bath.

"When the blade shatters, it'll be like slivers of knife blades. The major water channels could be scoured, and more parts of the system will fail." He sighed. "Some parts of the water flow can't even be reached. I don't know if we'd ever get the place repaired.

"Joshua, our source of power is fatally injured. It was hundreds, maybe thousands of years old when Aaron reactivated it. We all thought it would last forever."

He looked down at the floor. "I killed it. I may have killed us all."

Joshua could understand his feelings. He remembered all the times he'd made his own mistakes and how Cyclops dealt with it.

"I can understand, Ford, but how we got here isn't the issue. What do we do to get ourselves out of this fix? New Home cobbled together a paddle-wheel at first. Can we do something similar? Retire the turbine but install some home-grown replacement?"

Ford looked up, staring at the blank wall. "Possibly. Of course we're talking about just a fraction of the original power. Maybe enough to keep us breathing, but not enough to charge the boats or keep the fabricators working." He rubbed his forehead. "I've been thinking ... we should evacuate most of the people here and limit Factory's life support needs to just a small crew—just enough to keep the turbine ... or whatever, running."

Robert asked, "Where would they go? From Joshua's report, Base is on limited food and air as well. Getting everyone off to New Home would take multiple boat trips and submarine runs. We don't have the power cell capacity for that."

Joshua noticed Bernard pausing in his note-taking. He suggested, "I'm short on ideas, but maybe our friends over at New Home might have something. Let's let Bernard send the notes, and then we'll meet back here in a couple of hours."

Status Meeting

There was a status meeting at New Home as well, and Joshua was a little puzzled by the group of people he *saw* there. It wasn't just the displaced Factory people he'd expected. There were Otto and some of his people as well. All together, Holana's little chamber was quite packed.

As Holana read out Bernard's notes, the conversation there appeared quite animated. Joshua would have loved to have listened in, but everyone there had solid *ineda* and there were no Ba on New Home's island. At least, he didn't think there were.

Hugo and Ace were discussing something intently while Betty listened. Otto, Lonna and Derry were questioning Patrick, and Sally would sometimes comment. Both groups were talking at the same time, not like the orderly rotation used by Cyclops. Holana was trying to take some notes, but Joshua doubted she was keeping up.

It'll be a while.

He settled back in his chair and checked on the various parties of the Cerik. The searchers who'd passed through were still on their trek south along the coast. There was a party of hunters in the Rikna mountains near where the other heads were taken, probably hoping to find more of the same group.

After a few minutes, Joshua located the nomads. They were still hiding at the same place, but two of their hunters were missing. If he had more time, he'd hunt them down, but as long as there was no immediate danger to Base or Factory, then that would have to wait for another time.

Over at Base, Paul was with Ash, looking over some papers. It looked like more training. But then suddenly, Paul looked straight at him. He had to be using his *sight*, but he probably was looking for Bernard, his usual contact. Bernard was bent over the table, transcribing the notes.

Joshua put his hands over head.

Paul turned to Ash and probably told him to make the contact.

The boy held out his arms.

Joshua sent a message:

"Bernard is busy. If there is a message for Factory, send it to me."

Ash picked up the paper and positioned it where he could easily read it. Slowly, he sent.

"Bruce elder of Kakil Home has died. Multiple reports from various homes. Some reports say food poisoning. Arms tired."

Joshua closed his connection a little stunned.

Why now? This means I've got to monitor Aarison closely and I don't have the time!

Did Aarison kill Bruce, as Bruce had feared? The message he'd written was destroyed. Only Cyclops had ever seen it. They couldn't pass the information that Aarison was an unreliable elder on to Kakil or the other Homes without revealing Cyclops's ability to read text with *sight*.

. . .

A message came from New Home. *"Ace has idea. Needs overnight to work on it."*

Ford nodded. "I say, give him the time. I can use the time myself. Let's meet again tomorrow."

And most of the others agreed.

Joshua retired to the kitchen area. It was nearly deserted.

A familiar-looking girl took pity on him and showed him where the dwindling sacks of rice cakes were stored.

"Most of the meals are fish, down on the dock."

He nodded. "Yeah, I knew that. It was just habit, coming here. Do I know you?"

She smiled, "Jaesel. We came back from New Home on the same boat. It looks like I made a mistake, doesn't it?"

He made the connection. "The weaver. Right. I thought you'd be going over to Base."

She shrugged. "The men are here. I put it off. Maybe I should have gone when they first offered."

"Base is in the same shape. My mother is desperate to keep her crops alive, with the power gone. People eat down at the dock there, just like here."

She waved at the pale lights in the ceiling. "At least you have some power. Back when we moved into New Home, we had to burn sticks for lighting."

He smiled, "Maybe that makes you kind of an expert here. Who are you working for, right now?"

"Ciara."

"She was from New Home, too, wasn't she? Are you giving the old timers here advice on how to deal with the darkness?"

Jaesel looked puzzled. "I guess. I've just been taking orders."

"Do more than that. And do me a favor, go tell all your old friends from New Home that they should be sharing anything they know about living with reduced power. We'll all be grateful for your help."

. . .

A habit pattern of *looking* at a dozen different places on rotation, every chance he got, gave him a break. Resting on the shash mattress he used at Factory, he saw Elehadi and Stakka moving together toward their private meadow. He connected with the Ba to listen.

<Your pet U'tanse is now the name for the Kakil burrow. It took long enough, but he is second no longer.>

Elehadi *pree'd* his satisfaction. <Now we can rid ourselves of the troublesome ones.>

Stakka asked, <What shall I tell him?>

<We can't spook them. Let them honor the dead one. But by the next full moon, that pest with the questions should be sent to some place dangerous. Maybe he could run into a *haeka* at night?>

Stakka eased back on his rear talons. <I have just the task for him. I will tell your pet to assign him to repair the Sek Valley overlook, but to wait until the U'tanse have gotten used to his rule. One by one, we can have the U'tanse get rid of their own troublemakers.>

. . .

The next morning, Bernard stood and read aloud the report he'd received from New Home.

"Ace and Betty have altered one of the water pumps to produce a low level flow. During tests overnight, they have confirmed that attempting to pump upstream with a subcritical push builds levels in the embedded power-slip. They have already begun fabrication of a larger version that can be inserted into the bypass channel access port. It will be available in two days."

Joshua looked at Ford's face. The man looked thoughtful and intrigued.

"Okay, I didn't understand that," Bernard added. "I just copied the codes."

Joshua nodded. "I'm not technical either. Ford? Could you enlighten us?"

The man said, "If I'm understanding it correctly myself, they're saying that one of the new pumps can be used just like the turbine blades."

All the faces showed sudden interest.

Ford continued, "All the turbines and paddle wheels we've used *could* have pushed the water back uphill, if they'd been driven with a big enough motor, in theory. Pumps and generators are the same thing, essentially. If you add power to them—if the water flow is weaker, they pump the water. If the water flow is stronger, then it makes power that we can bleed off for our use.

"Ace has confirmed that when they take one of those new-technology pumps and run it backwards in a water flow more powerful than the pump can push, it builds power in its cell. We could transfer that excess to regular power cells, and then with a converter, make electricity."

Robert asked, "Can this replace the turbine?"

Ford shook his head. "There are so many questions. We don't know how efficient the pumps are. There's two added steps involved, moving the power from the pump to a power cell and then using a converter to make electricity. If Ace is already making one for us, then he must have some confidence we can get some power this way, but I doubt it can replace the turbine. It may just be like the paddlewheels, only something we can use in our existing plumbing.

"I'm most excited about the possibility that we can have a backup power supply that would allow us to dismount the turbine assembly and attempt a real repair."

They put together a workplan for moving the necessary converters and power-transfer equipment into the chamber next to the bypass-channel access port. Bernard and Holana at New Home exchanged more details. It would take Boat B, with its larger hatches, to move the new pump to Factory. Patrick had already moved power from his boat over to the large transport. The raft that had been damaged during the flood would be fixed by the time it was needed. They set up a provisional schedule, assuming the New Home fabricators worked as planned.

Just as it appeared that the meeting was winding down, Joshua raised his hand.

"I'm afraid there is one more issue that we need to discuss."

All eyes turned to him. The sudden good spirits that had come with a temporary solution to their power problems had put some variety of smile on everyone's faces. But at his words, concern appeared.

Joshua didn't make them wait.

"Bruce of Kakil Home has died, and it is quite possible he was poisoned by Aarison, the only other elder there. Based on notes Cyclops gave me, it appears that Aarison is taking his orders directly from Elehadi and Stakka, and has, over time, consolidated his power at Kakil Home. Those people no longer have any real elders. Elehadi is already planning to systematically kill off any Kakil U'tanse he considers troublemakers."

He gave them a moment to take it in. For the entire history of the U'tanse on Ko, their people had been protected by the covenants originally established between Father and Tenthonad which designated the elders as the protectors of U'tanse life. Cerik could kill any U'tanse they wanted, but the covenants meant that Names had to support the elders in protecting all the U'tanse of the Home.

Elehadi had been severely sanctioned for his effort to bypass the covenants when he shut down Rikna Home. Now he was trying again, but usurping the protections given by the elders. It was plain he'd been working on this for years, putting his own man in the group and then waiting for the others to die off.

Now he could kill the ones causing him trouble and never have to take the blame for it. Who knew what plans he had for his U'tanse? This was the Name who took Samson the U'tanse into his personal guard, trying to make a U'tanse into the Cerik ideal. Was Elehadi trying to make a new kind of U'tanse, a slave more subservient and less concerned with their own welfare?

Bernard asked, "What can we do about it?"

Robert said, "We rescue who we can. You guys rescued me."

Joshua said, "I'll be the first to volunteer for that, when the time comes, but today, there's something we have to deal with—something a lot closer to home. Base and Factory don't really have anyone in charge, and that has to change.

"Cyclops is healing and can't be a part of this, not right now. For all my life, the members of the status meeting have really been running things, with Cyclops being the man who had the final say."

He looked at all the faces around the room. "All of you are in charge. Each of you is in charge of your own area. Ford controls the manufacturing workforce. Robert runs the submarine and tub. Bernard is the leader of our communications. Terry keeps the electrical systems of both Factory and Base running. There are others who could be here. My mother Debbie controls our food supply. Hoop and Larson are our Dockmasters. Patrick keeps the boats flying.

"We argue and debate, and most of the time we all know what we have to do to survive. But we miss having Cyclops listen to us all, give his words of wisdom, and then end the discussion with a few simple words that send us off to our tasks. We need someone to fill that position. What's more, we need to prevent this happening again. Any of us could be injured or killed. We don't need the Free U'tanse to come to a grinding halt every time someone important is put out of service.

"We need to agree that the status meeting people will always decide who is in charge, and we need to agree when we have to make that decision. Kakil Home elders let themselves fall apart because they didn't take that job—succession—seriously. They let themselves be swayed by Elehadi, and now they are dead and all the Kakil U'tanse are in serious danger."

Out of Power

Robert declared, "You should be the leader."

Joshua shook his head, "Absolutely not. A leader needs knowledge, wisdom and experience. I'm a kid with no experience. Any words of wisdom I spout are just echoes of what my father said. And I'm just starting to gain the knowledge I'd need for a job like that.

"What's more, I work best on the move. Cyclops used me to visit New Home, to act as a messenger, and to learn new things that he was restricted from doing because of his eyes and his difficulty with travel. He was training me, but that training is far from completed. If Cyclops was here, he wouldn't recommend me as a potential leader."

Ford said, "It sounds like you've been giving this some thought."

Joshua nodded. "I've had to. Nobody wants to give up on the idea that Cyclops is sitting here in this circle, and too many of you want to think I'm just Cyclops with eyes. That's not the case, and I know it better than anyone. I'd suggest you Ford, Frank, or Patrick, or my mother. You all have the experience I lack, but we need suggestions from everyone, from everyone who sits at these meetings. I don't expect we will make the final decision soon, but it's important we do it, and do it right."

. . .

The group took his proposal seriously, which was all he had hoped for. Bernard sent messages to Base and New Home, asking for leadership suggestions from all the missing members. As they broke the meeting for lunch, Ford put his hand on Joshua's shoulder.

"Come with me. I want to show you something."

Ford unclipped the flashlight from the sash he wore and cranked on it as they walked. Taking a ramp down to the next level, where the lights were off, he pointed the beam of light to a work area.

"We were working on this when the power went out."

Joshua knew exactly what it was. Veronica's sketch had prepared him, but the reality was exciting.

The egg, nearly twelve feet long and about four feet in diameter, was resting on a work cradle. Six of the pumps from New Home were clustered around one end, built into a metal frame.

Ford pointed out features. "The egg isn't strong enough to take the forces the pumps can put out, so the pumps are fitted into a strong cage that holds them, as well as the egg. If we make a mistake on the egg, we can ... could, just form another one and replace this one."

Joshua pointed at the elliptical hole cut into the egg's skin, on the top-side as it rested on its side. "That's where the pilot enters?"

"We had planned to build a protective hatch over that, so the pilot could close it and be protected from the water. There's room for two people to sit, or a pilot and some cargo. Unfortunately, we didn't get that far before we lost power."

Joshua moved around it, fingering the pumps and the framework that held them in place. "I see a tow ring. You could drag another egg behind this one, couldn't you?"

"That was the idea." He sighed. "If we just had more time."

Joshua asked, "Is it usable?"

"What do you mean?"

"Even with no hatch, and the egg full of water, I could imagine getting in there with the air tank Ace made and punching the button. It would be a little scary, but it might work."

Ford gave an uncertain chuckle. "It'd sink like a rock. With no air inside to balance the weight of the metal, it'd go straight to the bottom."

Joshua looked inside the top opening. "There's a control pad. It's more complex than what we used at New Home."

Ford nodded. "The center button turns all the pumps on or off at once. The buttons on the ring around it each control one of the pumps. The idea was that you could steer the thing by selectively turning on some of the pumps."

"Is there any speed control?"

"Nope. Ace said the next pumps could be fabricated with selective power, but these were built in a hurry to help you move rocks."

"Right. That reminds me, are these charged?"

Ford sighed, "Yes, for now. We might have to drain them for power unless we can get the turbine fixed."

Joshua patted the metal. "Okay, other than putting some air tanks inside for buoyancy, what do we need before I can drive this thing?"

Ford shook his head. "This is why I wouldn't have wanted you to be the leader anyway. You're too eager to jump into danger."

Joshua grinned and nodded, "Exactly right!"

...

It was hard to get to sleep. The whole team at Factory had a worshipful respect for Ace's ability to invent things, but Joshua knew things never worked out smoothly. Ace had never promised that this was a solution, only a backup plan. Joshua worried that if the new pump/generator was too inefficient, Ford would bring up his evacuation plan again. Joshua had a gut feeling that if the Free U'tanse ever started that retreat, moving themselves into a single Home, that they'd never recover. Without power for the boats and the sub, they couldn't rescue anyone new, and without power for the enclosed gardens, the Earth crops would die out and their restricted diet would lead to greater health problems and fewer new children.

On the emotional upswing, the new sub was tremendously exciting. Not only could that free up the old sub for runs between Base and New Home, but Joshua had seen enough of the ocean floor to fire his imagination. What else had the Delense left behind that was hidden under the waves? Maybe this experimental sub, only partially completed, wouldn't take him any deeper beneath the waves than normal, but it would greatly expand his range.

But worry and anticipation kept him up late. He forced himself to monitor the Cerik search parties. Their numbers were dwindling, but the serious hunting parties were still at it. The idle workers who had been caught up in the excitement of the chase and possible rewards were now heading back to their original jobs. Hunting on their own on the rugged mountain terrain had lost its appeal.

Joshua was surprised to find the nomads on the move. They were keeping their females safe by moving them at night. He sampled their thoughts. One of the hunters who had been spying on the recent search party had found better caves and more food prey. Joshua followed them several times through the night, until he was confident that he could find their new location again.

. . .

People running down the corridor woke him up. It was dark. Not even the dimmed lights were shining. Joshua had refused the windup flashlight that was offered him the night before. His *sight* was good enough to navigate with. He regretted his choice as he made his way down to the turbine access room.

Ford was there, shining his flashlight into the darkness. Ankle deep in water, Ford's assistants were fishing down into the water-filled chamber. Ford didn't look his way, intent on the work, but he explained.

"We felt a vibration start and shut everything down immediately. It looks like one of the balancing weights we had installed has come free. Now we have to fish it out and rebalance the turbine all over again."

Joshua nodded. "How soon will the new pump arrive?"

"Hours yet. They're still loading it into the boat. And we have no idea how long it will take to install it here. We're back to flashlights and candles for the rest of the day, at best."

"Is there anything I can help with? I can hold a flashlight, in case you need to be working on something else."

Ford shook his head. "You were right. You're better on the move. Go talk to Larson and make sure everything is ready for the boat's arrival. Make sure Base and New Home are up to date with the latest problem."

And Joshua was off. Running errands always felt better than worrying.

. . .

Joshua was in the water with the swimmers, keeping the metal raft in position as Boat B raced in from the west. Carson, the pilot, had been told to watch the flags, which would signal when the skies would be clear of Cerik boats, but a monitor at Base reported a new boat had taken off from Dallah to the south, and no one had an idea where it was going. They were able to predict Kakil's overflights now, but other clans were still in the air.

A warning flag had been draped, but Carson continued his approach. They had to move the raft out into the water, exposed in the bay in broad daylight. Joshua hoped the Dallah boat wasn't headed their way. He hadn't located it himself, and while Carson was able to watch the flags, he wasn't trained in semaphore.

Joshua barely heard the approaching transport before it arrived, moving in fast.

The large boat blasted the water into spray, and Joshua was blind, just hanging onto the rigging, feeling it settle lower as it took on the weight of the boat.

"Pull us back!" came the call as the boat went quiet.

It was a slow, unsteady pull this time, with no power to winch in the raft. People on the dock were pulling the cable by hand. Joshua and the other swimmers were doing their best to push, rather than just be dragged along.

Once they were under the drapes, the combined relief of the crowd was audible. The raft was secured, and the hatch on the boat slid open. Carson stepped out onto the dock and sat down on the stonework, looking exhausted.

Joshua dried off and dressed quickly.

There were others in the boat. Ace came out and began directing the helpers to move a set of wheeled platforms into place. The pump was large, and although made of light-weight materials, it took a dozen people to lift it out of the boat and carefully position it on the carts.

"Carson. How did it go?"

Carson shook his head. "I barely made it. I *saw* the warning, and Paul at Base was standing beside the warning flag, pointing off to the south. I found the boat, moving along the mountains so I had to slow down, nearly to a stop." He sighed. "I was just hovering, hoping that I would be invisible in the sea haze, but I couldn't turn back! I didn't have the power. But, by the time it was out of sight, there was just enough energy left to make a straight shot in. I just prayed you'd have the raft ready for me."

He waved back at the boat. "It's drained. Boat B isn't going to go anywhere until we can charge it back up."

Joshua nodded. "Good job. You delivered. Now it's up to the geniuses to make us some more power."

Carson gave him a little smile. Joshua smiled back, trying to look more optimistic than he felt.

He looked back at the hatchway as the crowd moved the new pump toward the airlock into the interior of Factory. There was motion at the boat. A woman, Betty, came out, carrying a large bag. And following her was Sally.

Test Run

Joshua reached out and took her hand. "I wasn't expecting you."

Sally smiled. "And here I thought I could never surprise you, what with your excellent *sight*."

He shrugged. "If you don't look, you don't see. I was distracted."

She nodded, with a wistful smile. "That's your life, I think."

"Could be."

They stood there, holding hands for a moment.

Then Sally looked over at her traveling companion, and said, "One of the reasons I came along was to make sure Betty was properly taken care of. Do you have somewhere she can rest, away from all this noise?"

Joshua nodded to Betty, wincing whenever a shout came out from one of the workers. "Sure. I know just the place."

...

When the Delense built Factory and Base, doors were not on their priority list. Doors were to keep noise and fumes from escaping, never for privacy. When the U'tanse moved in, they had to make do with what they found, so privacy was often a matter of custom, turning your head when passing someone's sleeping chamber, for example.

Ace had a more active way of looking at things. He was a *tenner*, with no telepathy and no *sight*. People walking by were a constant distraction. When he decided he'd be able to work on his projects better if he could close a door and avoid annoying footsteps, he built one. Joshua had been there before and knew how to work the latch.

They had scavenged a pair of candles from the kitchen on the way, and by the flickering light, Ace's bedroom clutter was plain to see.

"I'm sure he wouldn't mind you resting here."

Betty nodded, taking the candle without a word, and sat down at a table strewn with papers. She picked up a diagram and peered at it intently.

Sally said, "She's fine here."

They left both candles with her and closed the door behind them.

Sally said, as they walked down the dark corridor, "Ace spent most of the flight talking to her and making sure she knew what to expect at Factory."

Joshua steered Sally slightly to the left as the corridor bent. "She's so timid, I was surprised that she came."

"Nobody can separate those two. With the uncertainty over power, there was no chance they'd risk being stuck with an ocean between them. Joshua, is it really this bad? Patrick was saying that we have only a few flights left, and then we'll have no way of recharging any of the boats."

He squeezed her hand. "That really is one of our possible futures. Everyone here is cheered up enormously by Ace's arrival. He's the only *tenner* genius we have, and everybody feels like he can find a solution."

She leaned against him. "People are saying great things about you, as well. 'The next Cyclops', and things like that."

"I've put a stop to that. I've let everyone know I'm just a messenger. We'll be deciding on Cyclops's replacement soon, and it won't be me."

"That's good, I was worried about you."

He stopped. They were alone in the darkness. "There were things I couldn't let myself worry about. The idea that we'd always be apart was too horrible to be real. But now … I don't want to be stuck on the other side of the ocean from you."

She eased into his arms. "That's why I came."

. . .

Ace looked up from his work when they entered.

Sally said, "Betty is in your room."

He looked relieved. "Thanks. She couldn't handle this." He waved his hand at the eight men struggling to move the huge cylinder into the tight quarters of the bypass channel.

Joshua nodded. From what he'd seen, Betty's skills did not include working with a large group of shouting men.

"What's her official reason for coming with you?"

Ace smiled. "It's not just a whim. You've had the theory explained?"

"A pump running backwards generates power."

"Right, but there's a lot we don't know. The pump will have to be tuned to this situation. Just how much 'stiffness' to the resistance will produce the most power? How much will this reduce the flow of the water? How much physical pressure will this place on the pump hardware itself? Betty can play with all the parameters of the pump, testing and adjusting until it's working the best it can. And nobody knows how much power that will be."

Joshua nodded. "So you've got to anchor it firmly."

"Right. And the bypass channel wasn't really designed to hold it. There's a lot of work to be done before we can start testing."

"So ... we can't get power from it quickly?"

"No. But we brought an improved converter that's designed to work with the pump. For now, we can use it to drain any power cells we have here at Factory. Ford is out scrounging up whatever he can find. We're going to need at least enough power to weld the supports into place."

Joshua sighed, thinking of his new sub, likely to be drained. "I hope this all works before—"

Ace looked at him, waiting for him to complete his sentence. Then he said, "You have a thought?"

"Boat A has a charge, off in its sea cave. We should bring it here. I need to go check with Ford."

. . .

Sally ran beside him through the corridor. He grinned at her.

"Want to help me try out the new sub?"

"Is it dangerous?"

"Probably."

They found Ford, and Joshua made his argument.

"Now is the time to bring Den and his boat back to Factory. That's our most accessible source of power right now. It'll also give me the opportunity to try out the new sub."

Ford gave him a sour look. "It's untried. Now is not the time."

"All I need is hands to carry it to the water. We've put in those ballast tanks like you wanted. If I can't get it to work right in the first hundred yards, then I'll just swim the distance. But the sub would be faster."

Ford waved his hand in frustration. "Fine! Get Robert to approve, and you can go."

...

Sally stuffed her tow bag with what she'd need, then put on the goggles. They climbed in through the top opening and settled in place, him sitting in front and her behind. The sub was awash with water, but the ballast tanks, mostly filled with air, gave the sub enough buoyancy to keep it just above the water.

Joshua handed her the air hose. "Breathe through that when you need to, and keep your head low. The water turbulence might be too great to deal with, and we might have to give up on it. Be sure to let me know if you're having problems."

She took a breath through the hose and then said, "I will. I don't want any stunts from you, either."

Sally leaned up against him and put her arms around his waist. It was a lot more intimate than they'd been in months. Joshua was conscious of the smiles on the men helping them. He'd be smiling too, if they were alone.

"Ready?" he asked.

"I guess."

Robert called down, "Remember, you don't have any reverse, and no way to slow down. If you get stuck, get out and push."

Joshua laughed. "Did you ever do that?"

Robert said, "There were a few times I wanted to."

Joshua couldn't imagine that one. The old sub was far too massive for a single swimmer to push.

"Okay, here we go."

The sub was pointed out toward the gap between the draperies. Sally gripped tighter, the warmth of her body a contrast to the chill of the seawater. Joshua tapped two of the six individual pump buttons. On opposite sides, the middle pumps shoved them forward.

Water splashed up over the top, threatening to take off his breather. He ducked his head low, out of the flow, relying on his *sight* to guide him. The pumps were designed to stop after a few seconds, and they did. Joshua started one of the pumps a fraction of a second before its mate, causing the sub to swerve, giving them limited steering.

"It's working," he said when he raised his head above the water after they were out past the draperies. The sub slowed quickly once the pumps timed out.

"Are you going to ride on the surface the whole way?" Sally asked.

"Are *you* ready? If I can't control the ballast, we'll have to abandon it and swim back."

"Do it."

Beside him was a lever. He pushed it forward a couple of strokes, pumping more water into the ballast tanks, compressing the air. The sub began to sink. When they were three feet under, he worked the lever back, letting some pressure out. They stabilized, both of them breathing from the stored air in the separate breathing tank. He tapped buttons, never more than three at a time, pushing them on ten-second runs.

He paused after a few minutes and raised them back up to the surface.

"How are you doing back there?"

Sally said, "This is fun. How far out are we?"

"Farther than I expected. I doubt a Cerik could see us now. I think, just for safety's sake, I want to run on the surface."

"Okay. You're driving."

He pulled more water out of the ballast tanks and made the sub ride a little higher in the waves. It also meant he could see where he was going without having to rely on *sight*.

Ten minutes later, the line of rocks that led out to the sea cave came into view.

Den walked out to the cave entrance when he heard them approach. Joshua waved. Hesitantly, Den waved back, his eyes on Sally.

Visiting Home

Joshua brought the sub close enough to scrape on the rocks, and then Den helped guide them inside the cave. Sally pulled out a tunic from her bag to cover herself.

"Den," Joshua said, "we need your boat, Angel, back at Factory. We have a critical power problem." They retired into the filtered air inside the boat.

Den had observed the flags and the activity at Factory, but since the avalanche he hadn't received any updates. His mouth was open as he absorbed the extent of the disaster.

"So the turbine is down?"

Joshua nodded. "And it'll be a while until we can generate any new electricity. Not only is Factory shut down, but the electric feed to Base is gone. With no lights the crops over there are dying as we speak. Unless you want to eat fish the rest of your life, we need Boat A at Factory so we can convert your power-cell capacity into electricity."

Den was ready, but he'd let his tools and supplies get scattered all over the cave. Joshua and Sally helped gather them all up.

Den asked, "Are we bringing back your baby submarine?"

Joshua shook his head, "We'll be riding it back."

Den looked at Sally and smiled. "Off joyriding with your girl, I see."

She blushed. Then she said, "All business; I'm just keeping an eye on him."

Den nodded slowly. "Okay, then. Now we have to get the boat out into the water. Normally I'd wait until high tide, but if you don't mind a little dust, we can do it now."

Joshua signaled Bernard what was happening and got a clearance that there were no known Cerik boats in the area.

With the sub moved out of the way and Joshua and Sally in their breathers, Den climbed into Angel and started up the high-pitched buzz that shook the air and gently started to lift the boat. Clearance was very tight inside the cave, and the torrent of air was fierce. Joshua felt a sting on his leg as a pebble zipped his way. Then he and Sally began pushing the boat from its resting place, guiding it out onto the water. Like before, the spray made everything impossible to see through their goggles, but *sight* was enough.

As the boat reached clear sky, the blast of air increased and Den took off, heading immediately in the direction of Factory.

Sally took Joshua's hand. She said, "I'm a little bruised and maybe deaf, but that was amazing. I've never been that close to a boat on the outside when it was taking off. I could feel the engines shaking me, just like they did the air."

Joshua nodded. "Yeah, that probably wasn't the safest thing to do, but it worked."

He sat down on a wave-smoothed boulder and patted the space beside him. She joined him.

He smiled, "You know people are watching us."

She tilted her head. "Aren't they always?"

"Yeah, but I'm on a mission, so Bernard, Paul, and maybe Holana are checking up on me like clockwork, just in case I have to send a message. I thought you should know that—just in case you had any ideas."

She nodded seriously, then pulled off her breather. Hurriedly, he did the same.

She said, "That's good to know. Did you have any particular ideas in mind?" Then she leaned closer and they kissed. And then kissed some more. Joshua seriously wished they weren't on a mission. He needed a long time with her, preferably when he didn't have to worry about anyone but her.

But everything had changed. Somehow, Sally had made her decision, if the ocean became a life-long barrier, she chose him over her family at New Home.

After a bit, they reluctantly put their breathers back on.

Joshua took her hand. "You know I'll do everything I can to help New Home, don't you?"

She nodded. "I think I knew that all along. It's just that when Base and Factory went black, and I knew you might be stuck there forever, I couldn't bear the thought of being apart."

He squeezed her hand. "It's great to have you here, now. Are you okay with a visit to Base?" he asked.

"I'd love it."

"We're still testing the range of the sub. We didn't exhaust the pumps on the first lap, but the run to Base from here is longer. We could still run out and have to swim back."

She shrugged. "I'd like to experiment, too."

"Oh?"

"I'm going to wear my tunic. It's already wet, and I'm not really swimming, so I don't have to worry about the fabric dragging me down. Plus, the water is a little colder when I'm not constantly exercising. That is … unless you mind."

He grinned. "Maybe a little. But I wasn't really happy at how Den was looking at you when we arrived, either."

She chuckled. "Just an experiment. Working in the water naked is a little harder when there's so many men around."

"Hey, I was at New Home. People were looking at me while I was working in the water, too, you know."

She poked him in the ribs, "And not just looking, from what I heard."

"Hey, I got up and told them off when they got … touchy."

"Like getting up is any better."

He sighed. "I threatened them with you!"

She giggled. "I heard that one, too."

They had to take another break from their masks so he could make a proper apology.

Eventually, Joshua signaled their intent to visit Base to Bernard, who had been watching everything, and told him to pass the word to Paul.

...

With the warning flags in mind, always conscious that a Cerik boat could head their way, Joshua experimented with various ways to drive the sub. Riding on the surface seemed faster, but rougher, and with the added disadvantage that only the lower pumps gave efficient propulsion. Riding under the surface had more water drag, but all pumps could be used at once, if there was a need for speed.

Sally shook her head after a run using all six pumps. When they surfaced, she said, "The turbulence is awful when you punch the center button. You said there was a plan for a top hatch? I think that's a good idea."

"It all depends on getting the power back. They can't fabricate the hatch covering without it."

But in a shallow spot, Joshua took them deeper, until the pressure on their ears was uncomfortable. By pushing along on one pump at a time, they wove through beds of vegetation that looked like ribbons, and saw long-legged animals walking along the bottom of the sea. Fish scattered as they approached. One beast was nearly as long as the sub, trailing arm-like fins that hinted that it might even be able to drag itself ashore. It gave them a look, and then swam away.

Joshua pointed out corroded machinery, long abandoned by the Delense.

Back again on the surface, she said, "I've always wondered what the seaweed looked like and where it came from. It's like an underwater forest."

He grinned. "I've always wanted this—breathing underwater like a fish and moving along in places that nobody can see. I always just got a glimpse of it when riding in Robert's sub."

"I wonder what it's like even deeper?"

He shook his head. "I'm not going to risk it. The ballast was sluggish returning to normal this last time. Our engineer types will have to make a better one, or something. I get the feeling that once we go a certain depth, there's no return."

She held him tighter. "Good to know, but no unnecessary risks."

Shortly, they approached the imposing rock dome that concealed Base. Joshua took them down and they slowly entered the tunnel through the rock. Navigation was horrible. There was no reverse, so he only used one unbalanced pump in order to avoid racing in and crashing against the dock.

As it was, he pulled up inside, but short of the dock. As he surfaced, Hoop was there waiting for him, as well as his mother.

Hoop yelled, "Heads up!" and tossed him a line.

"Got it!" Joshua yelled, and then Hoop pulled them in next to the ladder. Joshua got out and tied the line to the rear tow loop, and then helped stabilize Sally as she reached for the rungs.

"This tunic weighs me down, drenched as it is."

Debbie was there at the top. She took Sally's hand. "I'll get you a dry one. Sally, it's so good to see you again."

. . .

Cyclops looked worse than Joshua remembered, but the grip on his hands felt a little stronger. The flickering candlelight etched deep shadows across his face. The bandage across his 'eyes' was a different cloth than Joshua remembered.

"Sorry I can't get up," Cyclops mumbled. "The healers are having a hard time with my spine." He looked at his new guest. "Sally, you look healthy. New Home must agree with you."

She'd been coached about keeping quiet about any details that the man might accidentally leak. "Oh, they've been keeping me running." Debbie gestured to the chairs lined up around the bed. They sat.

Joshua was dismayed that he could feel his father's thoughts. There was a sense of weariness coming from the man, in spite of his genuine pleasure at seeing Sally again. There was a struggle, and then the leaking thoughts closed off as Cyclops regained his *ineda*.

When Joshua had first graduated from the nursery, one of his chores was taking meals to the older men who still lived at Base. He'd seen this same deterioration among them. But his father wasn't that old! Had the injury weakened him that much?

Debbie was on her feet, bringing him a sip of water, carefully helping him drink it from the pouch. Joshua suspected she could read a lot more of her husband's thoughts than he could. She looked tired, and there was a worried look to her eyes that never seemed to go away.

They couldn't talk about all the things that mattered the most—his health and their missions. Debbie filled the silence talking about her plants and about the little ones in the nursery.

Joshua looked at Sally, and she nodded.

"Um. I guess it's time we told you. Sally and I wish to be considered a long term couple."

His parents paused, and then smiled. Cyclops said, "Good."

Debbie came close to give Sally a hug. "I've always hoped you two would get back together."

Joshua shrugged. "Nether of us could back off from our opinions."

Sally nodded, "But the things that kept us apart seem to have evaporated. We've got more important things to do, and we work best together."

He held her hand. "Yeah, this way I won't have to worry about her as much."

She giggled, "And maybe I can keep you out of trouble."

. . .

After a few minutes of simple family time, Joshua said, "I guess I'd better get back to work."

Sally was on her feet with him. "Me too. It's been good seeing you again."

His father clutched Joshua's hand. "Could you stay, just a minute longer?" His focus was on Joshua alone, so Debbie and Sally went out.

Cyclops gestured him closer. Joshua leaned down.

Cyclops whispered, "There's something I've never written down, and it's been worrying me."

"What is it?"

"George at Kakil. His mother came from Tenthonad Home." His grip tightened. "She arrived from All-Ko Festival the year before Elehadi threatened to get into the power cell business. I don't know if there is any connection there. George might know something from his mother. We have to get him out!"

Thoughts leaked in a flash from Cyclops—the pain in his back, general worry for everyone, fear that he was draining Debbie. His grip loosened, and he tightened his *ineda* again. He closed his eyes. "Maybe I can stop thinking about that now. Go on, Joshua. You're doing well. I'll leave everything to you."

Sally's Run

Joshua stopped in the hallway, faced Factory and waved his hands in semaphore. Sally asked, "What's up?"

"They're ready to feed power to Base, converted from the power cells in Den's boat. I need to warn my mother."

They hurried to catch up with Debbie. She ran off to protect her lights.

Ten minutes later, the corridors brightened.

"About half power, it looks like," Joshua said. He couldn't be sure. He'd gotten used to the candlelight.

Sally said, "I wonder how long they can keep it going."

Joshua wondered too. Once the cells in Boat A were drained, there was no handy replacement. The only other power was at New Home, and they couldn't drain Patrick's boat and leave the U'tanse with no active boats at all. They needed the power for critical repair work at Factory. Power for Base was just a side effect.

"We need to get back to Factory. Let's see if we can make more of this visit than just a whim."

They held a meeting in the map room, discussing the leadership issue, the usual telepathic monitoring of nearby Homes, and the status of power at Factory. When questioned, Sally gave them an overview of what New Home had to offer if it came down to evacuating Base and Factory.

Debbie asked, "Aren't we already past that point? If we don't have power for the sub and the boats, how could we possibly evacuate everyone?"

Sally nodded. "It looks impossible to me as well, but if it comes to that, just moving some of the people to New Home would reduce the resource demands here and enable you to survive longer."

Joshua kept quiet during most of the discussion. It was clear to him that the Free U'tanse needed a new source of power. Even before the turbine problems, they couldn't keep up with the demands of Base and Factory. Now with New Home's fabricators, and more extensive travel between the island and the mainland added to the mix, there would have been a power crisis anyway.

What if Cyclops was right? What if George was sitting on the solution? How could they rescue him from Kakil? Would he even want to be rescued? If George was even aware of the Free U'tanse and their capabilities, then they had a bigger problem than just a broken turbine. If Elehadi knew, he'd do everything in his power to blast them out of existence. It was just the kind of grand play he liked, and something like that would make him more popular than ever with the other Names.

Stop thinking like that. If we're dead, it doesn't matter if Elehadi gains more power or not.

The discussion turned to the new sub. "It's only half-built. But it works. It's a lot faster than swimming to Factory, and we have the possibility to tow another egg behind us. And that's what I think we should try to do next."

. . .

Corn and rice filled most of the egg, but they had to add quite a few rocks to weigh it down. Once they had it sealed off and balanced for neutral buoyancy, they tied a ten-foot line to secure it to the sub.

Sally asked, "You're frowning. Are you afraid it won't work?"

He sighed. "It all depends on the power left in the pumps. If we run out of power half-way back, we'll have to swim for it, but we could easily lose the sub and the cargo as well."

He remembered swimming the run between Base and Factory dragging a tow bag. That had been bad enough. He'd never be able to tow all this mass on muscle power alone.

Steering was rough with the egg tied to the rear. Even a single, unbalanced pump didn't cause much of a twist to their direction. Joshua had to push off the stone wall by hand as they drifted too close on the way out. The egg bumped and scraped behind them.

When they reached open water, he surfaced and swam back to check for damage.

Sally asked, "Any problem?"

"Just scratches. But either I'm going to have to learn to steer better, or Ace will have to redesign this thing."

"Are you going to be the only one driving it? Don't you have other jobs?"

He nodded. "You're right. It's not mine." He got back in and steered in slow, wide curves until they were dead on course for Factory.

After a bit, he came to a stop. The wind was mild and the waves were lower than normal. He turned back to Sally. "Your turn."

"What?"

"You drive for a while." He smiled.

"I don't know how."

"Neither did I. You've seen what I did. That's better than I started out with. And you said you wanted us to work together. So it's your turn."

They got out and switched places. As he settled in behind her and put his hands around her waist, she mumbled, "Now I know why you want me driving."

He chuckled. Denying it would be a waste of breath.

Since her clairvoyance wasn't as good, he gave her landmarks to steer by. "Aim for the bay, which will be lined up with that notch just to the left of the larger peak. We can ride on the surface for half the way, but when we get closer, we'll need to go all the way underwater."

Sally was hesitant to start, but she got into the spirit of it quickly enough, rotating among the pumps, keeping their speed low but making solid progress.

After checking with him, she worked the ballast lever and took them five feet down. He tapped her shoulder from time to time. Left shoulder to steer left and right to go right.

Then she tapped a button, there was a surge, and then it quit after only a second. She twisted her face to try to look at him. He gave her a reassuring squeeze. One pump had run out. But he'd expected it.

She kept going. Near where the waters started to get darker with the mud coming out of the river, two more of the pumps quit in quick succession. She worked the ballast and they rose enough to talk, just their heads out of water.

"Will we make it?" she asked.

"Maybe. The pumps we used the most gave out first, as they would. The top pumps were used the least, so those should last the longest. Just keep rotating among the positions like you've been doing."

"Are you sure you want me to continue?"

He nodded. "Hey, driving is fun, and I want to go more places in the sub, but what you said before is right. The sub is a tool for all of us, and Robert will be in charge of it. When we arrive at Factory's dock with you doing the driving, we'll have shown that it's not just a tool for one person. Any of them could learn to drive it, as well."

She sighed. "Okay then. But if I break it, it's your fault."

They ducked down under the surface again, like any good sub should. Joshua enjoyed the passenger position, and not only because his arms were wrapped around Sally. The bay area near Factory had the heaviest concentration of abandoned Delense relics. There were pipelines, trenches, corroded tanks, and what Joshua was sure was the power cable that ran from Factory to Base. He saw it snake off into a trench where it disappeared. He'd seen something exactly like it at the Base entrance. The Delense had taken the effort to hide it, even though he couldn't imagine a Cerik sticking his head under water to look for it.

The fish scattered as they approached. Just over their heads, the tips of the draperies swirled in the waves. They were very close. Joshua raised one hand and pointed to where the hull of the big submarine was visible. She tapped one button, and they surged.

They were swinging a little too wide, and there was no time or room for any more pump action. Joshua held out his arm, outside the hull, hoping the drag of the water on his hand would help steer them. Sally did the same. Their little sub twisted slightly, and they slid up beside Robert's sub with a bump. They stopped, and a few seconds later, their cargo egg slid up beside them and nudged the dock with a a thud.

Sally worked the ballast, and they rose to the surface.

Faces were looking out over the side of the dock, watching them.

Joshua said, a little loudly, "Good job, Sally. Nice driving."

She gave him an elbow in his ribs.

The dock workers had been notified that they were coming. Joshua told them of the food in the cargo egg and asked that both it and the sub be lifted out of the water.

When word spread that there was likely to be more than just fish for dinner, more workers appeared.

Joshua helped Sally, again sagging under the soaked tunic.

"Joshua!" Bernard came up to meet them, looking harried. He saw them dripping water on the dock. "You two get dressed. There's a meeting at Ford's workroom. You're needed."

Aarison's Speech

Betty was waiting in a nearby room, Joshua noticed. He brushed his fingers through his hair. There hadn't been time to rinse the saltwater off, and he knew he'd be feeling it. Sally was hurrying a dozen yards behind him. Her hair looked like it had seen a brush. He was jealous.

Ford's workroom wasn't designed for meetings, and Ace was already sitting on one of the tables. Joshua stood by the door. Sally came in a few seconds later and stood with him.

Ford nodded. "Good. You're here. We needed everyone to make this decision."

Ford pointed to Ace. "Describe it again."

Ace slid off the table to stand. "The bypass pump is working, and we're still tuning it for efficiency. The weaker the pump force, the faster the water flows, but the power is lower. Raising the force of the pump increases the power—up to a point. You can imagine if we stopped the water flow completely, there wouldn't be any power either. So finding the peak power level is important. But there are also structural issues. The bypass tunnel was never designed to hold the pump, so we've had to chip bracing struts into the rock and to install metal beams to support the pump. Under the full turbulence of the water, we can't count on the supports holding."

Ace made shapes his hands to help them visualize how the bracing was cut into the rock as he talked.

"We need to switch between draining the boat for power and using the pump's power, on and off for several days while we work out the best engineering compromise. I doubt we'll be able to achieve half of the turbine's power, at best.

"So I have a suggestion, but it's hazardous. I think we should dismount the turbine—take it all the way out of its mounting. Once it's free, we should then shear off the damaged blades completely, and two other blades in the balancing positions."

There were frowns around the room. But Joshua could also see some thoughtful nods.

Ace continued. "With opposite blades missing, we can precisely balance the turbine again. Put back in service, even with the gaps, we should be able to achieve eighty percent power. With our furnaces back on line, and with our careful measurements of the original turbine, we could probably manufacture a replacement fan within a year."

"That long?"

Ace nodded. "Yes, think about the precision we'll need—the alloy we'll have to create and test, and the anti-corrosion coating we'll need to lay down—all to make a perfectly balanced turbine. Honestly, I only give us a fifty-fifty chance of creating an exact duplicate. We may have to settle for a less-efficient version."

Joshua asked, "Ace, so you're saying that we're going to be underpowered for a year at best, but we may achieve a workable power level to charge our boats and resume rescue operations?"

Ace sighed. "Yes, but honestly, we were always underpowered. We just didn't know it, not down in the gut like we do now. I also have alternate suggestions.

"We could design a pump-generator or combination of pumps to be installed *in place* of the turbine. Another possibility would be to run the turbine and bypass pump at the same time, putting a lower stress on both branches."

Ford said, "We'll need a power systems crew, full time, to keep everything running. We have people who are probably up to the challenge."

Ace added, "Keep New Home in mind. They need power, too. The new generator we put in place there is more efficient than the paddlewheel, but it'll never be powerful enough to run those new technology fabricators."

Joshua noticed that Bernard ducked out of the room in the middle of Ace's presentation. He kept an eye on the door. Someone had signaled him.

Sally was in a whispered conversation near the door. Ciara had a smile on her face, and snuck a peek at Joshua as well. The news that they were now officially a couple couldn't be stopped, but people had expected it anyway. Other people's romances was the most popular entertainment around. He felt a lot of eyes on them.

Ace was describing the New Home power system that had replaced their paddlewheel. It was only five percent as productive as Factory's, but that couldn't be helped. There was no water flow on the island as powerful as that the Delense had built for Factory.

Bernard appeared in the doorway and beckoned with his fingers. Joshua eased out of the room.

"You had Rachael monitoring Aarison at Kakil?"

Joshua nodded. Monitoring Kakil Home was one of her regular duties. With Cyclops no longer actively holding their status meetings at Base, she reported to him before they left.

Bernard said, "She reports that he's going to be making an announcement at mealtime. There's some worry at Kakil about what he's going to say."

"Thanks. I'll be ready to monitor."

Sally had followed him out of the meeting. "What's going on?"

Joshua looked back at the meeting. "I've got to be ready to monitor Kakil in a couple of hours. They don't really need me to discuss power systems. Let's eat early and find a quiet place where we can listen in."

...

Factory's bath was deserted, with everyone else off to eat. With all the furnaces shut down, it was much cooler than before.

After some serious kissing and more energetic activities, the water felt just right. Sally cuddled in his arms.

"What are we going to monitor?" she asked.

"Aarison is the only elder left at Kakil, and he's taking all his orders from Elehadi. He *should* be announcing the new elders to replace the ones that have died, but that's not going to happen. I fear he's going to start killing off workers who are causing Elehadi trouble."

"Really?"

Joshua nodded. "Kakil Home is just another annoyance to him, and putting the blame for more U'tanse deaths on the U'tanse themselves is just a way to divert complaints away from himself."

Sally pulled herself tighter to her husband. "It's like Rikna all over again."

"Right. And we've got to be ready for more rescues."

"How?"

Joshua sighed. That was the big question. It was no longer a matter of swooping in with a boat to rescue an abandoned worker. All the boats were tied up keeping everyone alive.

"It really depends on what we learn next."

...

It was embarrassing, listening to the thoughts streaming out of the girl at Aarison's side. Sally, in the water with him, shifted her position.

Sally whispered, "We're slurking on official business, right?"

Joshua's arm was around her. He gave her a squeeze. "We can't help what she's thinking. They're sitting at a table, eating. Just because she's...."

Sally finished for him, "Planning to get pregnant within the hour."

"Yes. And we're not the only ones embarrassed."

All of Kakil Home was squeezed into their dining area. Every table was packed and some were standing against the wall. All eyes were on Aarison, and inevitably on the girl about Sally's age who had chosen to sit beside him. She was thrilled to be sitting next to the most powerful man in her world. Even more so because he was paying attention to *her*. Even the streaks of gray in his hair just made him more impressive to her.

Aarison was basking in all of the attention, and he made little effort to hide it. This was the place he'd always wanted to be—the center of every-one's thoughts. They were waiting for him to speak, because what he was going to say, whatever it was, mattered to their lives.

Joshua thought there were a surprising number of people who thought Aarison could do no wrong, even with all his focus on women. Less than a tenth of the people were using *ineda*, so all of the adoration, and suspicions, were out there for any telepath to absorb.

And the girl on his arm wasn't the only one who desired him. Scattered through the crowd were others who had been there, and still more who were waiting their chance.

But there were many who despised the man.

A fearful woman thought, *He thinks he's a Name. If something's not done, all of the children in the nursery will be his.*

A father frowned at his daughter, *No, Ellen, don't look at him like that!*

A sad carpenter with still-aching hands from a rough day thought, *If only Bruce were still alive. Who will protect us now?*

Joshua looked over the crowd—both with his *sight* and listening to their thoughts. He was overwhelmed by the turmoil. It was difficult, often impossible, to fit the thoughts to the faces. He knew Sally was getting the thoughts alone, perhaps seeing through their eyes. It would be easy to pull away, focus elsewhere. But they needed to know what was going on.

Aarison gave the girl a smile and then rose from his chair. Like the ripple in a pond from a single stone, quiet spread through the room. Joshua had to admit, he made an impressive figure. The man was tall, fit, and wore an embroidered tunic that looked more like a ceremonial robe than everyday work clothes.

He smiled at a few people, then spoke quietly, although everyone could hear him.

"This has been a time of change for us. We've lost loved ones, of course, but it is more, much more than that. I want to talk about that, but first, let's think back to those missing faces."

He started with a short eulogy of Bruce, then continued on, mentioning everyone who had died recently, all the way back to Samson, their giant son who had made such waves among the Cerik.

Joshua was listening to his thoughts—the overtones that put emotion behind his words. There wasn't a whisper of deception there. His mind was open and clear, concentrating on his audience. As he went down the list of people who had died, he talked directly to their families, or in the case of one woman who had been a nursery worker for forty years, all of the people who had been touched by her efforts. When he talked about Samson, his eyes were on Omelia who had Samson's son Sterling in her arms.

Her thoughts were hard as crystal, *You will never get my baby!*

Aarison's face never showed if he heard that. His gentle smile moved on, across the crowd.

"As we change, so do our efforts. Kakil Home has become, over the past few years, the most important U'tanse community of all."

He let that statement settle in.

"In part, this is because our Name has become the foremost leader among the Faces. As his influence and his lands expand, so do ours."

225

Joshua wasn't the only one to have strong reservations about Aarison's claim, but the speaker wasn't going to let it drop.

He talked about the recent accomplishments, both Elehadi's military expansions and the Home's efforts to keep up with the demands the Name had placed on them. He phrased it consistently.

"The Name asked for more fence lines in the southern foothills, and we succeeded!

"The Name asked for new huts as he gained new warriors, and we succeeded!

"The Name asked for repair work on two dozen boats, and we succeeded!"

The level of pride was growing, notching up every time he shouted the tagline. Every kind of worker—carpenters, herders, weavers, healers, cooks, and all the rest—had their moment of recognition.

"And finally, as the Name calls on us again to work together, to take on new duties, and to take our skills to even higher peaks, we will succeed!"

There were cheers, and he raised his arms, letting them relish the moment.

When the noise died down, he said, "In the next few hours, I'll be talking with some of you about new projects. I'll be asking some of you to expand your skills, to take on duties you've never handled before, but we all know you can do it. We are the best. It's time to show our Name, and the rest of the U'tanse on the planet, just what we can do!"

He finished to the sound of more cheers, and then began walking among the crowd.

Sally asked, "Is it done? Did you learn what you needed to know?"

He pulled her a little closer and gave her a kiss. "No, and I've got to keep monitoring for a while. Some of those new assignments are death traps, and we have to know how many there are and who is involved."

"Oh. He didn't sound so bad. Otto would never get away with all that cheering and stuff, but I thought it sounded okay."

Joshua nodded. He kept part of his mind following Aarison through the room, listening to the thoughts of people he talked with. It was mostly innocuous thus far. But he could talk with Sally, too. Not much more than talk, however.

He asked, "Did you notice, the most important person at Kakil Home, an *elder* no less, just died, and Aarison talked about him less than anyone else? He had to honor the man, but he didn't want to praise him too much. Instead, he made him just one of many, and praised all those others."

Sally exclaimed, "You're right! And you're sure about this poison thing? Aarison killed him?"

"I have no evidence. Nobody watched him do it. It's just a suspicion, but Bruce expected it. He was going to warn people that it might happen, but then changed his mind."

"So Bruce didn't tell anyone? Then how do you know?"

He gave her a smile in the faint light of the bath chamber. "Trust me to tell you later."

She sighed. "More secrets. I'll hold you to that."

He squeezed. "I'll gladly hold you more."

"Down, boy. I'm waterlogged as it is. If you have to do more monitoring, I think I'll get out for now and dry off."

He sighed. "Okay. Sorry."

After she left, he focused all his attention on the Kakil Home activity. Aarison was making more new assignments. Some were innocuous, swapping out some workers, putting a higher priority on some of the building repair near Elehadi's High Perch, and some personal requests as well. A weaver was requested to take measurements for a new decorative robe. From the lady's thoughts, she knew it was a more intimate request than the words indicated.

Three of the tasks stood out in Joshua's mind. An elderly fisherman, who had already given up outdoor work because of his health, was requested to bring in a monthly quota of *jarka*, a long, skinny fish that he had been famous for catching in his earlier years.

Another was a cook who was told that since the herders were going to be staying out longer shifts in the fields, it would be up to her to prepare and deliver their meals. The lady was quick with her tongue, challenging Aarison that it was just a way to keep her quiet, and that with the extra work, she might be out at night, well after it was safe. Aarison told her that they all had more work to do, and everyone had to work longer hours. Friends kept the lady from throwing a screaming fit right there, and Aarison moved on through the crowd.

Joshua tensed up when Aarison zeroed in on a familiar face.

"George, I have a few words for you, as well."

The *tenner* frowned, uncomfortable with all the faces looking at the two of them.

Aarison smiled, "All of us here have been grateful for the research you have done. In particular, Kakil Home has been able to trade copies of your *Tales of the Cerik* to other homes quite successfully." He sighed. "Unfortunately, our masters can't seem to understand your type of work. Written documents are ..." he waved his fingers, " ...invisible to them.

"So, we need to show the Name that you are a valued worker and capable of doing something *tangible* and visible that he would value. I'm going to assign you the task of rebuilding one of the mountain overlooks."

George's face was wrinkled in thought. "By myself? I haven't any experience in carpentry or stonework, or whatever it will take."

Aarison smiled, "But you are very smart! Everyone knows that. Take three days and check with the other workers. Find out what tools and materials you'll need. It's a remote location, so a boat will drop you off with your supplies and food. Remember that it's outdoor work, so you'll need leathers and a breather as well."

George was stunned. He'd worked indoors all his life. He didn't even have a breather, certainly not leathers. "Three days?"

Aarison nodded. "I've already made arrangements for your transportation. It will be a good learning experience for you." And then he walked away.

Joshua's heart was beating, too. He had no idea why Elehadi had singled out George as a person to kill, other than keeping his *talespeaker* for a while after Samson had died. What was clear was that, starting in three days, the person his father had urged him to rescue was going to be in great danger.

Upstream

Joshua shrugged. "I can't tell you. All I know is that it is *likely* that these three people are being set up to be killed in a way that would appear to be accidents."

Ford frowned and glanced back at the papers describing the progress on the power systems. "You can't tell us how you know this. I accepted that from Cyclops, because we all knew he had his ways of finding out things. But you insist that your father is still keeping himself isolated."

Joshua looked at the others in the room. He couldn't read everyone, but there were some frowns that matched Ford's.

"I can't share certain information. Part of this is because of a promise I've made, one that protects the source of my information. Part of what I know comes from notes my father made that he has shared with me."

Ford sighed. "From what you say, nobody is in immediate danger, right? I agree, what we've always done is rescue those who've been abandoned. We have no boats available to rush to the rescue this time. Everything is tied up. Three separate rescue attempts in the heart of Kakil while they're still searching for us... That seems reckless."

Joshua nodded, "I agree. No Cerik is rushing toward them with claws extended. This is the patient side of the hunter's game. Elehadi is pushing these people into hazardous situations, and he may be willing to wait it out—wait for the accident to happen. His claws would be clean of U'tanse blood, but it would have been a killing to his satisfaction. How many years did he wait to put his pet into the leadership position of Kakil Home?"

Robert said, "Are you suggesting that this *isn't* urgent? That's not what you said at first."

Joshua rubbed his forehead. "This is why I'm not in charge. If this was my call, I'd start the rescue efforts immediately, but you're probably right. I was monitoring Aarison as he ordered them into danger. It *felt* immediate to me. Clark, the fisherman is old and experienced. His danger is failing health, or slipping on the rocks. I'd like to rescue him, but it could probably wait.

"June, the cook who has been ordered to trek out into the fields after dark is tough and opinionated—probably the reason she's being targeted. She will take precautions and it would be difficult to make that rescue, as you say, right in the heart of Kakil. I would appreciate anyone's thoughts on that problem.

"But George, the *tenner* who translated the *Tales of the Cerik*, was specifically ordered into *haeka* territory by Elehadi. He wants him dead, and if George manages to stay clear of the wild animals, a Cerik hunter will arrive to fake a *haeka* attack. George will be moved to the Sek Valley overlook in two to three days, and after that, his hours are numbered."

Ford nodded. "So, we could take more time with the other two—monitor them for now and make plans for a rescue if it's clear the danger is high." He looked around. "What do the rest of you think?"

The meeting ended up agreeing with Ford. The man was growing into the leadership position, and Joshua had a feeling he'd be taking Cyclops's place once the final decision was made.

Joshua was given the task to come up with a rescue mission for George—one that didn't require a boat to fly in and get him.

...

Sally shook her head. "It makes no sense. George's biggest danger is the *haeka*. What good will it do for you to hike into wild animal territory alone to try to rescue him?"

Joshua looked out the window of the sub. The water was getting a little more murky as they approached the mouth of the Sek River. He checked the map once again. Robert had added a few fresh updates, marking a couple of underwater rocks, and those lines were darker than the rest. The Sek River was farther north than the submarine usually traveled. They had been cruising for hours.

Robert said, "I have mixed feelings, myself, Sally, but if Aaron hadn't pulled a crazy rescue, I'd have died alone a long time ago. The Free U'tanse have always done whatever they could to get abandoned workers to safety."

Joshua took her hand. "I think I'll be okay. With my *sight*, I'll have an advantage over the *haeka*. They can't attack if they never see me. George has to rely on his eyes and ears."

He pointed out the window. "Robert, just surface over there. Just enough to let me out the hatch."

"Okay."

Sally clenched Joshua's hand tighter. "Take me with you. We're supposed to work together."

He kissed her forehead. "Can't. The mini-sub can only handle one passenger, and I have to bring him out somehow."

She fumed. "If you get injured ..."

He smiled. "You'll just have to fix me up. You said I didn't know how to heal myself."

She hugged him tight. "Don't joke."

Robert pointed as the window brightened and waves started splashing on the surface.

One last kiss, and Joshua was out the hatch, carrying his tow bag. The hatch clanged shut, and in the water he could hear the latch seal tight.

Trailing fifty feet behind the sub, on a thin cable attached to the hull, was the mini-sub, dragged backward through the water by its own tow ring. Joshua stuffed his bag in the mini-sub and attached his air hose. He had to disconnect both ends of the cable and roll it up. He hated to have to carry it along, but he'd need it.

Once he was free and clear, he moved his sub around to the front of its big brother. He waved to Robert and Sally, watching through the glass. Sally waved back. Robert nodded.

No time to dawdle. He hit two buttons and blasted away toward the mouth of the river. The turbulence of the water wasn't horrible, but when he looked back, Robert had already pushed away and was gone.

...

The Sek River was large enough to be an effective barrier between Kakil and Graddik. Occasionally, one or other of the clans would fly warriors across into the other's territory, but the incursions never lasted. On Old Earth, humans would have built bridges or run water craft to ferry the warriors, but the Cerik had never invested any resources in such things.

He'd scanned the route, and if his *sight* hadn't betrayed him, he'd be able to navigate underwater all the way upstream to the position of Kakil's overlook. Getting up the mountain to where George worked would be a more difficult task.

Sally's anger worried him. It had been so nice resolving their previous problems. They were meant to be together. But he had to go on this rescue, and long hours arguing with her had felt just like the previous round.

He had tried to explain. *"It's not just a matter of rescuing an abandoned worker, although I'd volunteer to do that as well. George knows things that might save us all. I know you don't want to hear it, but Cyclops believes that George knows critical information about the Tenthonad clan, and maybe how they get power from space."*

Sally had said, *"I agree we should rescue him, but why you? And why go alone into dangerous lands?"*

Sally had given in, but she came out on the sub with him to the mouth of the river and had made sure he'd brought all the tools he'd need to climb the mountain. His tow bag was twice as heavy as he'd intended. Bringing it along was going to slow him down.

Oops. He stuck his right arm out, dragging the water and turning more sharply to the right than he could manage with the pumps alone. Even so, the sub scraped a sand bar that had suddenly appeared.

Navigating the river was more challenging than the ocean. *I can't let my mind wander.* He stretched his sight ahead and located the deepest channel.

The freshwater plants and animals were a change from what he'd seen before. He recognized some of the fish, but the plants were all new to him. Streaming with the current, they were smaller than the seaweed he was used to.

Then, he saw something quite different.

A patch of the river bottom shook free of the mud and began flapping many feet, pushing it sideways through the water.

Is that a Ba? It was small, three feet wide at most. The Ba he'd *seen* before were much larger, fifteen to twenty feet wide. But this one was the first he'd seen with his eyes.

The surface was a patchwork of dark brown scales, each rough hexagons. The feet were smaller, but rippled through the water in a synchronized fashion. Joshua let the sub slow to a halt. It began drifting with the current. He couldn't keep that up, but he watched the Ba in fascination. Seeing it helped him understand in ways that *sight* had missed.

The Ba was keeping pace with him, not making any move, but not trying to run away like a wild animal. On a whim, Joshua reached into his tow bag and brought out a hammer, one of the tools Sally had added. He struck the side of the sub three even strokes. What the Ba made of that, he couldn't tell, but it was an overture at communication.

But the sub was drifting out of control in the current, and he had to move on. He hit one of the pumps, steering wide of the Ba, and continued on upstream. Behind him, the Ba went on about its business.

Up the Mountain

Joshua found the perfect place to hide the mini-sub. A tributary coming down from the mountains spilled off a lava dike, forming a large, noisy waterfall. A deep pool had formed below, giving him nice, clear water in which to position the sub for a quick escape, if necessary. In any case, there was no chance of getting the sub any higher up the creek. He barely finished mooring it and climbed out of the water before all daylight faded away.

No chance of climbing in the dark. Better camp for the night.

He pulled out his tow bag and found a rock overhang where he would be protected if the rainclouds off to the north drifted his way. The rocks were still warm from the afternoon sun, so he took the opportunity to dry off before bundling up in his outdoor suit. His body shivered from the cold. The water was comfortable at first, but hours in the flowing water had leached the heat out of him. It had been much better riding with Sally's body next to his, sharing their warmth.

He wished he could risk a fire, but the best choice now was to get dressed and notch his metabolism up a little. It would make him even hungrier, but it was better than shivering all night.

He frowned at the muddy-colored cloth, with patches still showing recent repair work.

I would have preferred my leathers.

He sniffed, smelling the oils that saturated the cloth. This was Sally's idea. This had been her outdoor suit, suitably altered to fit his larger body.

"This is what I've been using back at New Home, and it works just fine to keep your skin protected from the raw air. There are two big disadvantages," she lectured.

"One is that it's less sturdy than the leathers—more likely to tear if you scrape against sharp rocks. The other is the important thing. The oils smell bad. Your nose will get used to it fairly quickly, but I'm thinking that if you're trying to sneak into that overlook, neither Cerik nor wild animals will know what it is they're smelling. You certainly won't smell like a U'tanse. If they come to investigate and George is missing, you don't want to leave the smell of another U'tanse there, do you?"

He had to agree with her logic, and he was glad to have her working to help with the rescue, rather than fighting him all the way—not that she ever gave up trying to talk him out of it.

He fitted into the smelly garment. There was one other disadvantage she hadn't mentioned. The cloth was rougher against his skin than the leathers. If this did prove to be a superior costume for rescue work, it might be better to make one out of a softer fabric.

Partly to get his mind off the smell, he ate his crunchy trail biscuits and out of habit, checked the warning flags. Not that the warning of a Cerik flying over Base and Factory would mean anything to him, up in Sek Valley. Bernard at Factory wasn't paying him any attention, but over at Base, Ash was looking his way with his hands over his head.

Joshua stood up and acknowledged, pleased that the boy had been able to track him down.

"Veronica just woke up with a nightmare. She came to me rather than draw it. A Cerik was sneaking up behind you. No other details."

Joshua signaled back, *"Thanks for the warning. I'll take extra precautions. Arms tired."*

He sat back down, thinking about the warning. That was one vision he didn't want to see happen in real life.

No other details. I don't know if I like that or not.

It was better than seeing him sliced open. But where? And when? Was it daylight when this would happen?

He just had to trust that they would have given him more details if they had them.

He cleared his mind of extra worries and started scanning the valley. He wanted to know where every Cerik was that might be close enough to worry about.

...

Two hours later, his brain getting numb from the effort, he had to admit there were limits to searching by *sight*. He had found warrior overlooks on both sides of the river. A Graddik hunter was even aware that there was work activity going on at the Kakil overlook. Apparently, hammer and chisel on a rock cliff rang quite a distance, enough to be noticed on the other side. It was something to be reported, but he had no intention of doing anything about it personally.

Up the river, where the Sek was small enough to be crossed by a hunter, there were a party of Kakil warriors patrolling the area. They had their job and weren't thinking anything about others downstream.

He'd also located a nomad party, not the same ones he'd *seen* before. This group was three males and four females, two of which were younger. From the looks of the pen where the females were kept, this group might have been nomads long before the destruction of Rikna. There was a bone pile nearby, where old carcasses had been discarded. It looked too large for a recent party.

Joshua had stumbled onto them by accident, following one of their hunters back home. Their home was quite secluded among the rocks. His first pass searching that area had seen nothing.

It's a shame you can't just will yourself to see Cerik and then all of them instantly appear to your sight. You had to search the ground and find them, just like you would with your eyes. Considering the Kakil and Graddik warriors watching this valley as well, Joshua was surprised the nomads had remained undiscovered for so long.

But, in any case, he hadn't found Cerik anywhere close to him. He'd just have to trust that none would find him while he was asleep.

One last check for any messages from Base or Factory or New Home and he saw Holana *looking* his way. She must have followed him on his trip to know his exact location. Was he so visible to every clairvoyant? She wasn't requesting contact, but on a whim he put his hands over his head.

She signaled.

I've been monitoring you, are you okay?

He signaled back.

Everything is going as planned. Thanks for watching.

She smiled. *Bernard and I are trading off so we can each get some sleep. Not that there's anything we could do if you get in trouble.*

He nodded. *It's comforting, in any case. Thanks.*

She paused, then moved her arms. *If you've got a moment, I have a personal question. I've been reading the Book. Is the Bible section real?*

Joshua thought a moment on how to answer that. It was a question that he'd had when he read the Book written by the Father of them all. A big portion of what Father had written was his memories of an important religious book that he had read in his early years.

Joshua began signaling.

It is clear that Father was a believer. Just read the introduction and you can see how concerned he was about the text. He said clearly that what he wrote in the Book was just his paraphrase, and wasn't to be treated as an infallible record. Yet he spent a great deal of effort to include as much of the original as he was able.

There are believers spread out through all of the U'tanse, more in some Homes than others. Personally, it is comforting to believe that there is a greater power out there looking after us—looking after me—even if we can't detect it.

There have been moments when I have prayed for help. If the hivers can cut through our ineda *and know our thoughts, surely the God that Father wrote about could do the same.*

But you'll have to read the text and make your own decision. Smarter people than us have read it and made many different interpretations.

Holana replied. *Thanks. That actually helps.* Then she signed off.

Joshua put into practice what he'd said, praying for a little luck in the coming days. Then he made sure all his gear was out of sight and stretched out behind some boulders.

...

The nightmare didn't totally wake him up—just enough so that he realized it was a dream. The Cerik had jumped at him, slicing his leg, and he fell into the ocean.

No, that happened to Cyclops, not me.

He shifted his position on the rock slab, trying to ease the ache on his arm.

I knew I was going to sleep outdoors. Why didn't I bring something a little more comfortable to lay on?

The answers ticked away; weight, bulk, more things to pack in a watertight bag.

That didn't help when his arm hurt. It nagged at him. He even *looked* at it, out of an irrational fear that he'd been injured and forgotten about it. Nothing was wrong.

He *looked* over at the pool, checking on the mini-sub. Nothing was wrong.

Nothing's wrong, nothing but me. Veronica's vision had spooked him. He was afraid.

Why am I walking right into a Cerik trap? One of them is going to catch me unaware. I should turn back, right now!

But he couldn't do that. Could he? How could he abandon a rescue, right in the middle of it?

Sally wouldn't mind if I came back early.

Or would she? They met during a rescue. *She gripes about me getting into danger. I rescued her. That's the Joshua she knows. What would she think about me if I ran away?*

And what would happen to George?

He had instantly volunteered for the job when he realized George needed to brought out of danger. Maybe that was stupid. He wasn't the only person who had gone into hazardous territory to rescue someone, other people had been doing that all his life. He had experience with the mini-sub, but that could have been taught quickly enough.

Well, it's too late now. My encounter with a Cerik is sometime in the future, but it might not be during this trip. I just have to be on my guard.

He sighed. There was a pale brightening of the sky. Dawn was coming. No chance for more sleep. He got to his feet and stretched out the kinks. From his vantage point at the waterfall, the mountain looked imposing.

...

George grunted with every stroke of his axe. By Joshua's count, he'd been at it an hour. The climb had gone slowly, following the mountain stream so he'd know every bend and waterfall. To disguise George's scent, that's the way they would have to make their escape.

The last fifty feet was a steep cliff face, difficult for a U'tanse, impossible for a Cerik. Joshua pulled on the cable, hoisting his tow bag up to his resting spot and making it secure before climbing the last few feet. He could hear George's every move and he was surprised the man hadn't noticed him yet.

Joshua's head and shoulders were above the platform ledge when George came along, dragging a five-foot-long timber with fresh-cut notches.

"Hello," said Joshua.

"Aaiii!" squealed the man, dropping his timber and falling backwards on his rump.

Joshua raised his hand, palm out. "It's okay. I'm here to rescue you." He tapped his forehead with his finger, the gesture requesting *ineda*—but with George, he probably didn't need to make the request. He'd never been able to read the man's mind.

George's eyes were wide and he panted, openmouthed. "You're human! How did you get here?"

Joshua finished pulling himself up onto the ledge. He sat, catching his breath. "You're George bar Ted, of Kakil."

"Right. Did Aarison change his mind? Am I going back home? I mean, all this outdoor stuff is character building and all, but I'm not really any good at it."

Joshua slowly shook his head. "I'm not here to *retrieve* you, I'm here to *rescue* you."

George frowned. "From what?"

Joshua explained, "On the day that Bruce died, Elehadi rejoiced. He then ordered Aarison, through Stakka, to assign you to an outdoor job where you would be killed by *haeka*."

He gestured at the stack of lumber and the ruins of the previous overlook. "This is just an excuse. Elehadi has a list of people he wants killed, but with the restrictions on him from the Rikna affair, he has to make the killings look like accidents. You were first on the list."

George frowned. Then he got to his feet. "You just stay put. If what you say isn't just the ramblings of a crazy person, then *somebody*, probably one of the Smileys, will be checking up on me from time to time to see if I'm dead. So, I need to be working away, so they won't notice you over in the bushes."

"Smileys?"

Lifting one end of the timber, George dragged it a few feet and propped it up against the one already in place. He wiggled it until the notch locked with the crosspiece.

"Oh, there's a half-dozen young guys who see all the privileges that Aarison has and want to be in line to get some of that themselves. Every time Aarison looks at them, they're all smiles. They'll do anything he says, no questions asked."

His tone of voice said everything. Joshua sighed. Kakil Home was in worse shape than he'd thought.

George asked, "So, who are you? One of the Rikna escapees? You heard about the hunt? Right? Elehadi wants to kill off everyone he can. I can almost believe what you said about him wanting to kill me."

"I'll tell you more, a lot more, about who I am once we're gone from here and safe."

He grunted, and then lifted the other end of the timber into place. "I'm not sure I believe any place is safe. Besides, I'm getting the hang of this timber cutting. Maybe I'll just stay put."

"You think you can stay safe from the *haeka*? You're pretty smart. You just might take the right precautions, but Stakka has a warrior waiting, ready to make sure your corpse ends up with the right kind of teeth marks. The Sek Valley overlook was chosen for just this purpose. It has a reputation for *haeka*."

George had a sober expression on his face as he hammered at the timber, forcing it tightly into position. "I've heard them, at night. Thus far they haven't been brave enough to approach the fire I keep burning at the cave opening."

"You know the jawbone Samson wore as part of his warrior costume. That was from a *haeka*."

The man looked at Joshua sharply. "How did you know about that?"

"I'll tell you later."

George sighed, "It doesn't matter. I can't leave anyway."

"Why not? They're going to kill you."

He looked down at the hammer in his hand and tossed it aside. "I can't leave because I promised Samson I'd take care of Omelia."

Sally's Choice

Joshua stood up, faced Factory and raised his hands over his head. George paused in his work, looking puzzled. Then Joshua made contact with Bernard.

Once the handwaving stopped, George asked, "What was all that?"

Joshua sat back down in his semi-secluded spot. "Telepaths who live all their lives under *ineda* must have other ways of communicating."

"Some kind of code that clairvoyants can see?"

Joshua nodded.

"Then what did you say?"

"I said you couldn't leave until Omelia and her son were rescued from Kakil Home."

"You didn't even try to argue. Why?"

Joshua managed a shrug. "I know you meant it. I just hope they can pull together a rescue mission quickly enough."

George shook his head. "It's impossible. Aarison or the Smileys are always around her. You see—"

"Elehadi wants the son of Samson. As soon as the child is able to survive out of the nursery, he'll take him away and train him to be a warrior like his father."

"Exactly." George's eyes tightened. "How do you know all this?"

"I'll tell you later."

"I'm getting tired of that sentence."

"It's necessary."

George looked at his stack of lumber. "How long do we wait? I've got to get back to work."

"I'll keep you updated. It will take days to get something going. I've been working on your rescue for five days."

George looked thoughtful. "Since Aarison's speech?"

"Yes, I tried for three missions, Clark the fisherman and June the cook as well, but your rescue was highest priority." Joshua paused. "If a rescue is started, will you agree to escape with me then, or do we have to wait until she's safely out?"

"Keep me informed as to what's happening. If it's real, I don't want to stay here with the *haeka* any more than you do." He gestured toward the bushes. "But stay out of sight. I guess I'd better get back to work."

Joshua retreated into the shade of the vegetation. It was frustrating to be waiting like this, but just having been through this argument with Sally, he could sense trying to talk George out of his duty would be a lost cause.

He'd been there, in Samson's mind, when the U'tanse warrior faced his final battle. His biggest regret was losing Omelia, and her final thoughts to him, revealing her pregnancy, had given him strength.

George had been Samson's friend, and the giant was nearly alone in the world, his size and strength forcing him out into the world of the Cerik warriors. When Omelia chose him, she put herself out at the fringes of society, as well. It was only natural that George would have stepped in to help when Samson died.

Echoes from the nearby rock cliffs matched every stroke of the axe. Joshua spent the time searching the area, checking in on all the Cerik he'd located the night before. As far as he could tell, none had moved any closer to the overlook.

He checked Factory and Base. There were meetings underway, but no one had any information for him. New Home was quiet. Holana was reading something.

He checked the sub, where Robert and Sally were waiting for him.

Both were facing his way with their hands on their heads.

He signaled that he was ready to copy.

Robert spoke to Sally. Slowly, she began to form the words.

"I can do it. A woman could sneak into Kakil Home and get her and the baby out. The Cerik wouldn't even pay me any attention. Robert can get me

close to shore and I'll swim in. We've talked it over and it's possible. Getting George to leave with you is important. You convinced me. Now I'll do my part. Don't argue. I can't see your hands. Arms tired."

"No!"

He signaled to Robert.

"Don't let her do it. It's too dangerous."

Robert replied.

"Fear for my life if I don't do as she says. Besides, she's right. Give her your blessing."

Joshua glared her way, even though he knew she couldn't *see* him. He waved his hands.

"Kakil Home is different. Dangerous place. Be very safe. I love you."

Robert spoke to Sally, and she waved back, *"I love you, too. Be safe."*

George asked, "What was all that about?"

Joshua sighed. "My wife has volunteered to get Omelia. She has rescue experience, and she figures a female can sneak into Kakil Home with no Cerik attention."

George frowned. "Your wife. Is she pretty?"

Joshua smiled. "Yes, she is."

The man didn't look happy. "I wouldn't send any pretty girl into Kakil. Not now."

"It's too late. I couldn't stop her. She's already on her way."

George put down his axe. He took a deep breath. "Okay then, I've got to trust you. How do we get out of here?"

...

The sun was low on the horizon. Joshua hated the thought of climbing all the way down in the dark, but there was no help for it. George was ready to go, and Joshua didn't want to give him any chance for second thoughts.

It helped that the *tenner* was getting into the spirit of the thing.

George winced, then said, "I've got to leave a blood trail. The Cerik will expect that when they come to check on me." He pulled out his healing kit—salves and bandages, mainly. He'd been prepared for a long stay with no healers around to take care of him. "But where should I put it?"

"Over the cliff, maybe."

They decided on a story: George was eating his evening meal near the ledge when the *haeka* arrived. The *haeka* slashed at him, and then George, bleeding, fell off the edge. The *haeka* then made its way down and dragged the body away.

They left a half-finished meal, partly to attract the *haeka* so there would be the proper scent on the ledge, and George cut his forearm enough to bleed a smeared trail to the edge before they bandaged him up.

"That hurt more than I thought it would," he grumbled, as Joshua hooked him to the cable and lowered him down the first leg of the drop. With the cable doubled over one of the timbers, Joshua followed and then let one half of the cable loose so it would slip free. After that, they followed Joshua's route, getting to the stream as quickly as possible to hide their scent.

George stumbled more than Joshua did, but urgency kept their spirits high. They needed the cable more than he'd expected. There were places where holding that cable made crossing loose rubble possible.

They didn't talk much, other than about where to put their feet and where to secure the cable. George did have regrets. "Simp told me never to leave my tools out where they'd get rained on. I wonder when they'll come check on me. He'll fret over the rust."

A little later he said, "I wish I'd have known this was going to happen. I've got so many notes back at my place. I'm sure they'll just throw them into the mulcher. I worked so hard on that stuff, too."

Joshua said, as he handed George the cable end, "You've got a good memory. Duplicate them. I'll be interested in your work. I really enjoyed *Tales of the Cerik*. That was a good job you did on the translation."

George looked at him, taking another look at the stranger who had come to rescue him. "I don't think you're Rikna anymore. Just who are you? And how do you know I did a good job?"

Joshua shrugged, moving on down the trail, splashing through the water. "I heard some of the originals through the ears of people who came by your place as you worked. And I read your translation. There are places where the Cerik just doesn't make sense in English, but you always did a good job catching the gist of it."

"So you're a telepath who was monitoring me?"

"No. Monitoring Samson. But you were his best friend—really, his only friend there until he met Omelia. But I had to watch the people around him. You were difficult, because your *ineda* never cracked. I was really puzzled by the secret notes you took as you made the translations."

George walked on silently for a while after that.

. . .

They were approaching the main waterfall when Joshua gripped George's arm. He whispered, "Take a look down in the pool. Can you see it? That long egg-shaped thing in the water. Go down there quickly. Get into the water and look at it closer."

Joshua watched as the man scurried down and splashed into the water, not even worrying about his leathers.

Joshua waited just a moment longer, and then said, <You are an excellent hunter! This is the second time you've approached me when I didn't see you coming.>

Behind him, a voice snarled, <U'tanse-who-swims? What are you doing here?>

Encounter

Joshua raised his voice to talk to the Cerik who had snuck up behind him. He'd never seen him—just sensed a whisper of his thoughts, and that was enough to identify him.

<I am hoping to be able to talk with you. Of course, I could leap into the water from here and swim away, but then you would not learn all the interesting things I could tell you.>

That was a bluff he didn't want called. He was at the top of the waterfall and maybe he could make that leap without injury, but it would be a big risk.

Joshua slowly turned to face the Cerik. He was very close. Joshua said, <I saw that you have moved your people, but is it really wise to come this far north? Kakil has many warriors walking the trails, looking for U'tanse like me and nomads like you.>

The Cerik shifted slightly forward. <Where I hunt is my business. What are these interesting things you speak of? My people are not hungry.>

Joshua had picked up some Cerik body language from when he was monitoring Samson. He shifted his weight to his heels. It was a minor thing, but the Cerik recognized it as being at ease, dismissing any threat.

<The U'tanse-who-swim recognize greatness when they see it. It is a shame that there are so many barriers between now and the day you walk among the other Names at the Faces.>

That got a reaction. This hunter had ambitions. The highest aspiration was to be a Name, to have a clan of his own, and to be recognized as an equal at the Faces meeting. His *ineda* was very limited, more like the calm of *kadan* before a kill than a true telepathic block. Joshua could read his hunger for status. He could also see frustration.

<Are you so hungry to impress your right-eye that you need a U'tanse skull as a trophy?>

The hunter growled. <A prey shouldn't taunt the hunter.>

Joshua had hit a sore point. The other lead hunter of the nomads had taken a *haeka* and kept its claw as an ornament. The one facing him now might just have to compete for the leadership within his own nomad group. Without something to show off his strength, he might end up being the right-eye to the other.

<I want to see you achieve more. If you continue to listen, you will have more runners, more lands, and more females. Would you like to hear those words?>

<You still breathe.>

Joshua acknowledged the truth of that. He described in detail what he knew of the other nomads in Sek Valley. He felt a twinge of guilt revealing the others. They had never posed a threat to him, or to any U'tanse, as far as he knew. Was gaining the limited trust of this hunter worth putting them in danger?

Still, he did it. To the Cerik, gaining those females was the primary appeal, but the others could always call *uuka* and pledge their loyalty to a new leader. Conquering others was the Cerik way.

The hunter turned, <Breathe some more. I will listen to you again another day.> He bounded away. His thoughts were already aimed at planning an ambush that would bring him more females, more warriors, and greater status.

Joshua sagged. He had been far too close to the edge of the waterfall and even a slippery stone could have sent him over the edge. It had also been his last line of defense. No Cerik would attack if the leap would risk ending up in a deep pool of water.

Carefully, he made his way to the stable path down to the pool below. He wondered, if he had to make good on his boasts, how did a U'tanse teach a Cerik warrior how to strengthen his *ineda*?

I despise Elehadi for trying to make U'tanse over in the Cerik image. Am I doing the same thing here? What use would there be for a tame Cerik?

...

George hadn't noticed a thing. He was still drenched in his leathers, although he'd probably clogged his breather, because his head was bare.

"What is this thing? It looks new. Did you make it? What does it do?"

Joshua smiled. The scholar was five-to-ten-years older than he was, but he sounded like the kids in the nursery.

"You've read the Book. Do you remember something called a submarine?"

"Old Earth technology, right? This looks Delense."

"Both of us invented submarines. This is a new version, the core technology is Delense, you're right, but we invented this one. It's not done. Riding it in will be a little rough, but staying underwater will keep us safe from the Cerik."

George put his hand on the nearest pump and felt how sturdy it was. "I can't imagine how you made this."

"The safer you are, the more I can tell you."

George nodded, still in his own thoughts, absorbing this newest revelation. "How soon do we leave?"

Joshua looked up at the sky. "We have a little daylight left. I want to get as far down the river as we can, but we'll camp on shore for the night."

He unhooked the mooring, stowed the tow bag and cables, and taught George how to breathe through the hose from the tank. They were moving downstream quickly, and the farther he got from the waterfall and the area of the overlook, the safer Joshua felt.

But he was right. As the light fell, he had more trouble keeping the minisub moving in the deepest channel. It was complicated by his limited use of the pumps. He had counted on using the flow of the river on the way back.

He found a place in the valley with a large boulder pile, and they pulled ashore.

George, once he had his mouth free of the breathing tube, was excited by all the fish he'd seen underwater. Joshua smiled. He'd been the same way, his first time. He answered questions when he could.

After a bit, sitting by a fire sheltered on all sides by the boulders, George's leathers and Joshua's cloth suit were draped on rocks to dry out. Unfortunately, the cut on George's arm had opened back up, and the bandages were red and soaked. They made an effort to wash them out and dry them. The rest of the bandages had been left at the top of the cliff, and they didn't have any other cloth to use.

George asked, "You look distracted. Am I too chatty? I've been told that."

"No. It's just that I've been monitoring other places. You know my wife? She left the big sub about the same time we came ashore. She's about to come out of the water near Kakil Home."

"The *big* sub? Okay, I'll ask about that later. I'll let you monitor her." Joshua was grateful. He narrated while he watched.

. . .

Sally came ashore on the rocks just north of the bay where a fishing dock had been built. She pulled her tow bag out of the water and found a ledge where she could dry herself off with a towel. Hurriedly, she slipped on a tunic and shoes. She wasn't wearing a breather, although Joshua knew they had extras on the sub. He tried peering into her bag and thought there was one, no, two breathers in there. She hid the bag among the rocks.

She turned abruptly, peering into the twilight.

Joshua looked in that direction. There was a man, sitting on a flat boulder just high enough to keep him dry. He was a fisherman slowly pulling in his net. There was no ineda.

"Sorry to startle you," he said.

Sally was poised to run, but then she calmed down. "Uh, it's my fault. I shouldn't be out here."

The old man shrugged. "No problem here. I'll take any excuse to watch a pretty girl come out of the water." His thoughts were a little more explicit.

"Sorry," Sally said. "You won't tell on me?"

He shrugged. "Why should I? I'm no Smiley. But don't you have a breather?"

She shifted. "Not one I'd admit to."

He nodded. "Don't admit anything. Don't even let them notice you exist. I celebrated just a little too much when I retired, and look at me now, fishing after hours so I can get a crazy quota filled."

Sally asked, "You're Clark?"

He chuckled. "I thought everyone knew me. You must have come from a recent Festival."

She said, "Not to be nosy, but can you swim?"

He laughed harder, "Not by choice, but I wouldn't be this old if I couldn't. These rocks get slippery at times."

"Good to know. Well, I've got to sneak back in. Maybe I'll see you later."

He raised a hand. "Just wait. Let me drape my net and I'll help you get through the door. Sometimes a Smiley will question people, just for the pleasure of it."

"Thanks. My name is Sally."

Joshua frowned. He whispered to George, "She shouldn't have told him her real name."

George whispered back, "Why?"

"She supposedly died in the Rikna Home explosion. Many Free U'tanse take new names to protect themselves or their family. There's always a chance, even if it's slight, than their name will be discovered and put their 'death' in question. My father chose the name Cyclops."

George nodded thoughtfully, taking in the new information.

"And you? Is Joshua a chosen name?"

He smiled, "No. I was born a Free U'tanse."

Sally and Clark walked the half-mile back along the stream bank toward the Kakil Home. Clark was considerate, but greatly enjoyed the presence of a pretty girl, even if she had gotten dressed.

He entered first, then waved her in after he'd checked the entrance. She thanked him and then took a step down the left corridor.

"Do you know where you're going?"

"The nursery?"

He pointed the other direction. She thanked him again and turned around.

George asked a few minutes later, "What's she doing now?"

Joshua shrugged. "Still walking down the corridor. She's passed several people, but nobody is saying anything."

"Yeah, it's a shame. People don't talk to strangers anymore. You only talk to people you trust."

"There's a man calling out to her."

His mind wasn't blocked. He was puzzled. He thought he knew everyone.

"Hello, what's your name?"

"Uh. Sally."

"Where are you going?"

"I'm headed to the nursery. I'm running late."

"Hang on, now." To him, the girl looked worried. It was a mystery, and he wanted to know what was going on.

"I'll be late. I'm needed in the nursery."

"You can wait if I say so!"

George said, "It sounds like one of the Smileys. What's his name?"

Joshua tilted his head in thought. "It's not on the surface of his mind. But I get the feeling, big, jum … jumbo?"

George sighed, "Roland. He's got the nickname, Jumbo. He likes to throw his weight around. She should just nod and agree with whatever he says."

"Unfortunately, I can't communicate with her. We're under *ineda*, and that's how we'll stay."

Joshua frowned. "Another man is walking up. Oh, no. It's Aarison."

George's face showed his disgust.

Sally's Escape

Aarison strode up to the two. His mind was open and he smiled. "What's going on here. Roland?"

"This girl. I don't recognize her, and she's acting suspicious."

Aarison took a good look at the girl, but Joshua was surprised at how he saw her. From the patina of her skin that had frequently seen raw air to the muscle tone of her legs to her posture to the drape of her tunic, poorly made by his standards, he knew that she wasn't a Kakil Home native.

"You're new here, I can see. Did you come in from the last Festival? I apologize for not greeting you earlier. Our late elder Bruce was in charge of that."

She made a smile. "Oh, I know you. I was there when you gave that speech—about how we all have to work harder—and I'm late getting to the nursery. He won't let me go."

Aarison gave Roland a gentle frown, but he talked to her. "Oh, he was just trying to make sure things flow smoothly. But he won't mind leaving you with me."

Roland gave a nod and hurried away.

Aarison held out his hand. "Why don't I walk with you, and make your excuses?"

Hesitantly, she took his hand.

Joshua ground his teeth. Sally was just doing her job, but he didn't like that man moving so close to her.

George said, "I wouldn't worry. Not yet. The guy knows every girl is trapped there in the burrow, and he's the most powerful man any of them will ever know. He's got plenty of girls ready to come when he crooks his finger."

"I know all that! But ...." *This was Sally!*

As they walked toward the nursery, Aarison explained how things worked at Kakil, nearly always working his role into the flow.

Joshua was surprised to sense surface thoughts from Sally. He knew she could put up a front like that, because she'd done it to him from time to time. But now, floating at the top of her mind was a disturbing sense of the man beside her—his strength, his scent, and the rumble of his voice.

And Aarison was soaking it in.

As they approached the nursery, with cries and a certain familiar scent in the air, she stopped and put her hand on his chest.

"No, please. I've got to go in there by myself. I don't want anyone making excuses for me."

"It's no trouble."

She shook her head. "People need to trust me or not based on my own actions, not on who I know."

Aarison raised his palm. "However you want. Just know that you can come visit me at any time, for any reason. I am willing to help."

When the door closed between them, Sally's ineda locked tight. Joshua took a deep breath and tried to relax.

. . .

Joshua tossed a stick on the fire. "You'd better get some rest. Tomorrow will be a busy day, and you can't really take a nap with an air hose in your mouth."

George frowned, "But your girl. What's happening?"

"She's handling nursery duties. The other women in charge didn't ask too many questions and they were glad for the help. Really, young girls come in all the time, wanting to help with the babies. Sally is older than most, but she can play the role. She's just waiting until Omelia shows up, I guess. I wasn't in on the planning for this rescue. I'll wake you if something happens."

. . .

256

George shook awake, startled and confused. "What...? Oh. What's going on? What time is it?"

Joshua shrugged. "It's about an hour before dawn, I'd guess. They're on the move."

"What? Omelia?"

"Yes. She showed up just a few minutes ago. She found Sally holding her baby."

"Sterling's his name. Big baby."

"Yes. Sally flagged her to go to *ineda*, and they've been silent ever since. She must have been more persuasive than I was with you, because it didn't take them long to get sleepy juice from the cabinet and bundle him up. Omelia made some excuse to the others and they went out into the corridors. Omelia's leading the way."

George got up and stretched. "Omelia would have taken any excuse to get out of there. Elehadi has plans for Sterling, but Aarison had his own plans, as well. Omelia is a big, strong girl. She was the perfect mate for Samson when he was alive."

Joshua chuckled. "Yeah. Sally looks like a young cutie beside her."

"But Aarison is a big man himself, and he's got it in his head that siring a boy by her would be a great thing. She's holding him off, but it's hard, now that he's undisputed leader of Kakil Home."

Joshua growled. "Isn't anyone going to stand up to that man?"

"How? All the other elders are dead. The Name speaks through him, so he can reassign work duties as he sees fit. And he has his Smileys if someone needs to be shut up or forced out of the way. People on his side get the best work hours, the best food, and ... the women."

Joshua nodded. "And the others get sent out on hazardous duty to be *accidentally* killed. Still, if people got together and acted together ..."

George shook his head. "People learn *ineda* only when they need to, and you'd never keep a secret meeting quiet at Kakil. We've learned. If you speak out about Aarison, he'll find out and act—quickly. We should have acted back when Bruce was alive, but it's too late now."

Joshua held up his hand. "They're at an airlock. Not the same one she came in."

"Near the feed bins?"

"Um. Yes."

George said, "That's the way I snuck out when I wanted to look at the stars at night. There are spare breathers handy."

"But she needs to get back to the bay."

"There's a trail that goes over the hill. Most people take the shortcut through the burrows, so it's usually vacant."

Joshua nodded. "They're fitting a breather over the baby. The straps are loose, but maybe it'll help."

"Those breathers don't work in the water. I found that out the hard way. Yours does, though."

"Special design—I do a lot of long-distance swimming. But they'll have to make the swim to the sub without them."

They prepared to leave their campsite. Joshua intended to get started the instant the women were safe aboard the sub. He wanted to leave the place as clean as he could manage. An abandoned campfire could only mean "U'tanse were here."

Joshua was scraping the old coals into the water when he yelled out, "George! How is Omelia's *sight*?"

"Close stuff, of course. I don't think I've ever heard her talking about it."

"There's a warrior on the hill. I don't think Sally has noticed."

"What!"

Sally jerked and gripped Omelia's hand. She whispered.

Joshua had broken ingrained habit to send a brief telepathic warning, *"Sally, look out!"*

The warrior had already sensed something—whether it had been a sound or a smell, he had shifted out of erdan and was actively looking for prey. He leapt to a higher rock, using his superior night vision to hunt for anything out of place.

Sally took the lead, pulling mother and sleeping baby into a gap in the rocks.

Joshua's heart was beating fast, and he could only imagine what Sally's was doing. His memories of the Matt bar Keith family being easily tracked down and gutted were still fresh. Nighttime curfews were the rule. The only U'tanse allowed outside after night were those working on special tasks. Anyone else was fair game.

He didn't know what Kakil's rules were, but this Cerik wasn't acting like a patient guard.

The Cerik's thoughts were open enough. His hunter's instincts had caught a scent. U'tanse female. He was a little disappointed. It would have been more satisfying to take out a male.

He leapt to another boulder, closer to the scent.

Sally's gripped Omelia's hand tighter.

Joshua gasped, "Oh, no!"

George asked, "What?"

"The Cerik moved closer, and ... Omelia shoved the baby into Sally's arms and started running."

George frowned, closing his eyes. He had no *sight*, and no telepathy, but his imagination was vivid.

Joshua related what was happening. "The hunter is following Omelia. The *'eeh* is on him—he's all instinct now. Omelia is fast, for a human, but he's having no trouble following her. Her panic is leaking past her *ineda*. She's trying to make it back to the airlock, but ..."

Joshua winced. George cleared his throat. "Tell me."

Joshua shook his head. Then he raised his head to look at George. "It was a fast death. Omelia ducked down and grabbed a rock, swinging at him. But his claws were faster. He speared her through the chest and ruptured her heart. I'm sure her telepathic cry will bring out people to investigate quickly enough."

Joshua sat down on a rock. "The hunter's fear of the U'tanse poison has kept him from eating any of her, but just barely. As the *'eeh* is fading, he's starting to worry. He might be penalized by his boss for being out of position. He's just hoping this one was the female he was supposed to kill."

"What?"

"I'm guessing it's the cook, June. It's not clear."

"Your girl? And Sterling?"

Joshua nodded. "Sally started running for shore the instant the chase started in the other direction. She's not used to running carrying a child, but she's doing okay."

George said, "Omelia sacrificed herself for Sterling." He stumbled and sat down on a rock.

Joshua nodded. "Probably, although she would have been happy to kill the Cerik. That's how I see it. George, I'm really sorry."

He wasn't ever going to describe the subsequent details of her death. The Cerik had been angry that he'd been attacked by a female and shredded her.

Joshua had never really understood whether the *tenner* had personal feelings for Omelia or it had just been a deep loyalty to his friend Samson. In any case, he'd been willing to give up his own rescue to protect her.

George hit his knee with a clenched fist. "We have to get Sterling to safety."

"Sally is half way to the bay, and there's no sign the hunter noticed her."

"She'll swim the drugged baby out to this other submarine?"

Joshua nodded. He had his worries, too.

To the Sea

Sally stumbled along the shoreline. With the baby in her arms, walking the boulders taxed her balance.

Joshua assumed she was looking for her tow bag. She should have already been in the water.

Robert must have been watching her with his clairvoyance, because the sub moved position, following her. The sub had to stay in deeper waters, not only because of the rocks, but because the Free U'tanse weren't ready to reveal something as major as their freedom of the ocean.

A man appeared in the dawn light. It was Clark.

"I am glad to see you. I thought for sure, when the cry went out, that the Cerik had killed you."

Sally tapped her forehead, and Clark's thoughts closed off.

Joshua would have loved to know what they were talking about, but she was right. If he could listen in on Clark, then so could any of the Kakil Home people.

From her gestures, Sally was arguing with Clark to swim out into the bay with her. He shook his head and gestured toward the fishing dock.

Sally followed, looking around as the landscape became lighter minute by minute. Joshua wished she'd just get out into the water. Someone would see her soon.

Clark pulled a cover sheet free and revealed a log raft. Hurriedly, they all got on and started paddling out into the bay. Clark had a woven fan on a stick that he used to stroke the water. Sally helped what she could with one hand, the other clutched protectively around the baby.

The waves were a little choppy, and Sally had to retreat to the center of the raft for balance, but the old fisherman worked slowly and steadily.

Still, when the submarine surfaced close by, he stumbled and fell to his hands and knees at the sight.

Joshua chuckled.

"What?"

"Clark, the fisherman, was a little startled as the submarine appeared. But Robert is there, helping them inside. Clark is a little uneasy, but he's going with them."

George asked, "But now they're safe?"

Joshua nodded. "A lot safer than we are. Enough talking. Let's get moving."

...

He used the pumps intermittently, only when he needed steering. If there was a demand for speed somewhere up ahead, he wanted the power available. The river's flow kept them moving. The gentle pace gave him time to monitor.

Kakil Home was in turmoil. People died—but this was a Cerik kill, and once it was clear that Omelia was the victim and that her baby was missing, nothing could stop the angry speculation. Everyone knew of the conflict between Aarison and Omelia. Everyone knew that Elehadi had plans for the baby. How it all fit together wasn't clear.

June had the biggest voice, and a lot of people heard her.

"That might have been me out there! Aarison can't expect me to trek out to the fields and stay after dark if Cerik are on the prowl!"

There was a question that few were speaking, but many were thinking. "What was Aarison's part in all this?"

There was another question as well, "Why haven't we replaced our dying elders?"

Aarison was doing what he could, talking to people one on one, where his charm had the most sway. And then Stakka called for him, a personal talk, not by telepathy. He had to go.

Joshua wondered, what was the chance that Aarison would be blamed for the loss of Sterling? Was there any chance the people of Kakil Home could name new elders and kick him out of power?

George slapped his back, hard. Joshua craned his neck to see him flailing his arms. Something had happened. He released the ballast pressure and didn't even wait for the sub to rise. He dragged George to the surface. When they reached air, George was coughing, spitting up water. Joshua kept him stable.

When he calmed down, George said, "The sub! Don't let it get away!"

"We're drifting in the same current. What happened?"

"The air hose got away from me. I was tired of keeping it clamped between my teeth and tried something different."

Joshua looked over at the sub and saw the air bubbling out of the hose. He stroked his arm, pulling the both of them closer. When George gripped the sub with one hand, Joshua reached in and shut down the air flow.

"Let's take a rest. There—in the shade of those trees." Joshua pushed them all with strong strokes until the hull of the sub ground on the gravel bed. He dug into the tow bag and pulled out a breather. He shook it well to make sure there was no water clogging the filter and then helped George fit in on. Joshua worried about George's color. He'd lost more blood than they'd planned, and he moved his arm only with difficulty. The water dripping from his leathers was tinted pink. Joshua wished he had the skill to heal others, but he could barely work on his own body as it was.

"Are we going ashore?"

Joshua shook his head. "I haven't searched the area. We might still have to make a dash into deep water. If that's the case, remember to pull off your breather."

The *tenner* grumbled, "I've had more raw air in the past couple of days than I have all my life."

"It won't kill you. We have good healers that'll take care of everything once we get to Base."

"Base? Where's that?"

"I'll tell you later, if you need to know."

George grumbled, but Joshua ignored him, half climbing into the mini-sub to check the air system. The pressure gauge on the supply tank was much lower than he'd expected. The slow trip back had preserved the pumps' power levels, but they'd used more air that way.

"Problem?"

"There's enough clean air for you, but I'll have to be using my breather's filter from now on."

George nodded. "But we're on breathers now. Tell me what's going on in the outside world. I'm almost getting tired of fish swimming by."

Joshua gave him a summary. George didn't look happy. "There's no way Elehadi will let us go back to traditional elders. Aarison is a sleaze, but if Elehadi took him out, the Smileys are worse. When will you know what has happened between Aarison and Elehadi?"

"When it happens? Easily thirty minutes more, and I don't think we can wait that long."

George sighed, "I've lived my whole life being the last person to find out things. I can take it."

They got back into the main channel, George gripping his air hose between his teeth and Joshua trailing his breather's floater hose behind them. He risked speeding them up a little. The mouth of the river was still a ways ahead.

. . .

<Where is the get of Samson?>

Aarison winced at the shout. He was a different man, curled forward and subservient. To Joshua it looked like he expected to be killed. The secret meadow was intimidating to him.

<For your Name.> He mumbled the honoring greeting. <The child has vanished. The mother took him. We know that she carried him from the nursery. There were others around. They saw this. No one has seen him since. The mother was . . . taken while running back to the burrow, alone.>

Elehadi took a pace closer, <I gave you a task. You failed.>

<I admit . . . that I have failed. It is possible that others assisted the mother to take him away. Another female was with her.>

Stakka spoke. <Your thoughts say that you saw this female. You led her to the nursery yourself.>

Aarison sagged even more. <She did not seem to be a threat.>

Elehadi paced in a circle. <So. You do not even keep control of your females. Why should I let you live?>

Aarison said nothing.

Elehadi strode back to him, just inches from his face. He raised a claw and casually sliced the man's face from his left temple down to his jawline. Aarison shivered, but held his ground, even as the blood ran down, staining his embroidered tunic.

<I will tell you what will happen, little name of the U'tanse. You will go back to your people and discover what happened to the cub. Your people will do everything you say, because if not, then they will have breached the Pledge of Tenthonad, and I will take great joy in staining the river with all of their blood. You will be the first to feel your obscene blood flow away. Now go!>

Aarison bent his head, <For your name!> He backed away.

Stakka gestured in the direction of the Home. <You should run.>

Aarison did, racing down the trail.

Joshua wondered if there would be any other hunters tempted by a prey already bleeding as he ran. The Cerik were hunters, and blood scent was a powerful goad.

But a revolt among the Kakil U'tanse would be just the excuse Elehadi would need to purge his last U'tanse. Whether he would take that step or not, he'd certainly thought about it.

Technically, by the wording on the pledges that bound the Names and the Homes, Kakil Home might already be in violation, because the agreements always spoke of the elders as a plural body. Did the Cerik get that picky about language? Joshua didn't want to find out.

Elehadi, back in the meadow, spoke. <What are the thoughts of the U'tanse?>

Stakka the telepath said, <There is great confusion. Many suspect the cub was eaten.>

<What about this other female?>

<No one knows. Some saw her and spoke with her, but they all look alike—I can get no sense of her. Some think she arrived at the last Festival, but every time they talk together, they doubt their own memories.>

Joshua was glad to hear that. Sally wouldn't like to know that she was identified.

The conversation went on to discuss how to deal with the hunter who had killed Omelia. As far as they were concerned, he did nothing wrong, but he had killed a slave that the Name had wanted safe, at least until her cub was ready to be trained.

Suddenly, through the water came the sound of three taps, as if someone had struck metal.

Joshua looked through the water, but he couldn't see any sign of the Ba. Still, it had to be out there somewhere. Joshua returned the taps. George tapped him on the shoulder, but they couldn't risk surfacing to talk.

Joshua would have liked to monitor some more, but the river was widening out and there was a taste of salt in his breather tube. They had reached the mouth.

Open Mouth

George asked, "What now?" He gripped the opening in the mini-sub's hull. Riding on the surface out in the ocean was a lot rougher than in the river. They were so far out that the shoreline was just visible in the distant haze. Not even a boat flying along the shore would see them. He hoped.

Joshua shrugged. "We wait. Out here, no Cerik is going to get us. Of course, if a boat shows up, we'll submerge out of sight, but we don't have much air for you left in the tank and we don't have enough energy in the pumps to make it all the way to Base. The big sub will come to get us before too long."

"What was that banging noise? Was that your friends? It sounded close."

"No. I won't explain it, and I'd prefer if you never mentioned it to anyone, either."

George hesitated. "You're keeping secrets from your people, too?"

Joshua chuckled. "It's unfortunately the reality of my life. I'm always keeping secrets from people. They expect it. But seriously, never mention it, okay?"

George nodded. "Okay, but you're going to have to open up more than you have been."

"I promise. The instant we're picked up, I'll tell you a lot more. I'm looking forward to it. But right now, I'm going to take a nap."

He closed his eyes and let the gentle swells rock away the tension. The sea was safe. The Delense should never have abandoned their underwater bases to seek safety in space—not after having given their masters access to space as well.

Less than a minute later, he was asleep.

...

A wave shook the sub, and George winced when he was shoved against the side. Joshua woke, automatically gripping the hull metal at the opening.

There was another wave that shook them. George griped, "Are the waves out here in the ocean always this rough?"

"Sometimes. Depends on the weather." Joshua *looked* around them. The waves were larger than in the bay, but for some reason, they were shaking more than they ought. Was there a tsunami?

And then he felt it. The thoughts were even, cool, and predatory. It was a beast, and he could only interpret a little of it. There was a taste in the water, and that meant food!

Joshua blinked. Then he located it.

"George! Crawl down as deep into the hull as you can! Use the hose!"

"What?" But Joshua was fumbling with his own hose connector. George grabbed for the hose and stripped off his breather. He pushed himself back, up next to the rear ballast tank, and tried to make himself small.

Joshua did the same, only into the nose of the sub.

And then the mouth closed on them. Teeth like spears, as long as his forearm, poked into the hull's opening. The beast shook the whole sub in its jaws. Joshua had to shove his feet against the teeth to wedge himself in place.

The shaking was violent, turning the water into foam, and it was bouncing him back and forth in the metal cavity. He worried about George, on the other side of those teeth.

It was endless. The beast was trying to shake the mini-sub to death, changing its bite for a better grip. The metal was bending. He could hear it.

I can't wait for it to give up. Or wait until they were swallowed whole.

He reached behind his back and stabbed the center button.

All the pumps blasted on full power. The sub lurched in the beast's mouth. Joshua worried that they might be shoving themselves down its throat, but a flash of light from the surface gave him an instant of bearing. They were thrusting sideways. Twisting sideways in the enormous mouth.

The pumps timed out. Joshua stretched his fingers and hit the button again. The instant of quiet had hinted to the monster that its prey was dead, but the resurgence of power angered it.

There's blood in the water. The foam was pink. Was George still alive? Joshua struggled to focus, in spite of the thrashing of the beast and the force of the pumps. George was still there, but he couldn't tell any details.

A third time, he hit the pumps and with a wrench, they broke free. The sub, still with ballast tanks full of air, broke free of the surface, and for one long instant, sailed through the air before slamming back down into the surface.

Joshua looked back. George was still there. His eyes were wide with fright, but he was in one piece. He was looking at two huge teeth wedged in place, ripped from the mouth of the beast.

Joshua grabbed at his hand. George looked his way.

"Where is it?"

Joshua located the beast, swimming large circles some distance away. It was tinting the water with its own blood. The injury to its mouth was attracting the attention of other predators.

"It's that way. We're going to go the other way."

"Good idea!"

Joshua steered them south. Not quite in the opposite direction from the beast, but he didn't want to get any closer to shore, either. He pushed them on the surface with half the pumps for a couple of minutes.

"It's not following. Are you okay, George? Did you get injured?"

"My heart will never be the same again. It's still pounding. I'm beat up, but those teeth..."

"Yeah. I know. I'm keeping one of them. You want one?"

George laughed. "Like Samson's jawbone?"

"Why not?"

Joshua alternated between checking on the beast and George. The *tenner* was excited, but pale. Joshua worried that he might save the man from the Cerik and then lose him to physical collapse from his blood loss and other injuries. Sally's rescue had gone horribly wrong. He didn't want the same thing to happen here.

The beast, at a distance, was fascinating. The mouth was a formidable forest of teeth, the head was just a bulb on a long snaky body, with lateral fins every so often all the way down.

"Just at a first impression, I'd say it's closer to a *lulur* than a Cerik or a *haeka*. But it probably could have swallowed the sub. Certainly either of us would just be a bite."

George sighed. "I have mixed feelings. This was my only chance to see a *jandaka*, and all I saw was the inside of its mouth. But don't get me wrong! Let's keep our distance!"

"I've never heard of a *jandaka*."

"One of the lesser tales. The Talespeaker device didn't include it, but after I finished translating all those stories, I heard that the tale tellers who raised cubs had some other ones. Oral history stuff. One of them was a horror story about a Cerik who tried to use a log raft to cross over a river and was swept out into the ocean, where it was swallowed whole by a *jandaka*. Just another nightmare tale to keep the cubs away from the water, I thought."

Joshua smiled. "It smelled your blood in the water. That's what brought it here. It thought you just might be tasty."

George shivered.

Joshua gripped one of the teeth and looked at it closer. It had ridges running from tip to the base, where torn flesh still clung to the root.

"I've seen other large beasts in the sea, but nothing like this. However, most of my swims have been in shallower waters. I'm going to have to keep a better lookout in the future. Even a *jandaka's* baby brother would make a mess of an unprotected swimmer."

George blanched. "I'm staying inside this hull."

There was a sway, unlike the easy swells they'd been feeling. George stuck out his hands to brace himself. "Is it back?"

Joshua grinned. "No." He nodded to the left. "Take a look."

The water was churning, rocking the mini-sub. And then the big sub rose out of the sea.

George nodded. "Impressive. Not even a *jandaka* could swallow that."

Back to Base

George was weak—too weak to stand, in fact. Robert helped him into the hatch. Joshua took the cable and attached the mini-sub to its big brother. The last thing was to hoist the tow bag and the teeth up to the hatch.

Sally pulled him in and secured it shut.

Joshua took a moment to kiss her, then whispered. "George has blood loss, an unhealed cut on his arm and numerous bruises. Get him stabilized."

She nodded. "First come look at Sterling." Her eyes shimmered. "I'm so sorry. It happened so fast."

He held her tight. "We do what we can."

Clark was minding the baby, still asleep from his potion. "He's a hefty one."

Joshua held Samson's son with a strange feeling he'd been there before, even though he knew he'd never seen the boy. He counted the boy's fingers. A normal five on each hand, not like his father's six. But that had been Omelia's doing, when she filtered the boy's genetics.

"Hello, Sterling." He felt comfortable holding him.

Sally was slicing the leathers off of George. "Sorry to do this, but leathers soaked this bad can't usually be salvaged anyway." She frowned at the cut on his arm.

"What caused this?"

George shrugged. "I did it. We left a blood trail to sell my death."

She nodded. "I understand, but the wound has been infected. It'll take some work. Drink this. It'll help with the dehydration. Just lay back and let me work."

George sipped, then downed the whole pouch.

Sally had her eyes closed, concentrating on the man's cells.

Joshua met Clark's eyes. "You're the fisherman. Thanks for helping Sally."

The old man nodded. "Sounds like I helped myself."

The submarine began moving, the engines barely turning. There was a little shake when the cable to the mini-sub went taut. Robert said, "I'll be taking it slow. It'll be hours at best, but I've got to conserve power. We're going to Base, right?"

"Right. I want to get Sterling into the nursery before he wakes up and the sleepy juice will only last the night."

Clark nodded toward the teeth. "Looks like you caught a whopper."

"Other way around. George and I are the ones that got away."

He told the story of the beast, and Clark was all ears. "I knew something was up. Young Robert there ..." Robert chuckled at being called young. " ... he knew what was going on. He revved this thing up to full speed. But he was tight-lipped at the time."

Robert added. "I've seen one of those before. I've always tried to give them a wide berth."

George was asleep. Sally probably had done something to him. Joshua told them about the *jandaka* attack. Sally sniffed, as if it had been his fault they'd gotten into danger.

After a bit, Clark asked, "They tell me you people rescue the abandoned and those in danger. Now I can understand the baby, and the *tenner* over there. But I'm old. Why rescue me?"

Joshua held the baby and thought about it. "Well, we've never put an age limit on rescues before. But I ask you. Wouldn't Kakil Home be in better shape if they'd made *you* an elder?"

Clark winced. "I'd try to be modest, but that's not even a question. Anything would be better there than what's happened to us."

. . .

They made good time on the way back to Base, in spite of towing the mini-sub. Sterling woke when the morning sun came in through the window, but Joshua was experienced in keeping babies calm, growing up in the nursery himself.

Sally finished what she could do to help George and then came over to sit with Joshua.

"There's something I've got to tell you." She took Sterling in her arms. "When Omelia handed him over, she knew she was giving him up for good. I think he's mine now. I never thought I'd have a baby so soon, but…"

Joshua nodded, "We'll raise him as our own. He's bigger than most U'tanse. He'll have problems being different."

"He'll need a mother and a father."

"And more than that, he needs to know that his gene-parents were both heroes. I was there, if just by *sight*, at both of their deaths and I can tell him what I saw."

George coughed, shaking off his sleep. He'd been listening. "I promised Omelia that I would train him. She wanted Sterling to be exceptional, not just a man desired for his strength and ability to fight. She came to me when she was trying to find a name for him. There's a metal, silver. We don't use it much here on Ko, but it's pure white, like aluminum, and a lot more dense, with many exceptional qualities. In the Book, it mentions Sterling silver as model for purity."

George sighed, "It's a lot for a boy to live up to, but she knew how Samson was influenced by his name. She tried to do the same for his son."

…

Clark and George had the same expression on their faces when they docked at Base—open-mouthed amazement at the huge underground facility, only accessible via an underwater tunnel. Joshua had given them the rules, and neither of them had any problem with the constant *ineda*. It was obvious to them. Clark went off to talk to Base's fishermen. George was handed over to the healers, although Sally's efforts were already starting to show their benefits.

Debbie was amused that she was suddenly a grandmother, but due to her position at Base, all of the babies in the nursery were her charges, so it didn't throw her off stride. The biggest problem was his size. They decided to pretend he was older than his true age, just to keep the other cuties from spilling thoughts about the huge baby. Once they got used to him, hopefully, it wouldn't be an issue.

Veronica visited Sterling with them.

"I may have moved my bed out of the nursery, but I still like to spend a lot of time here. I'll try not to spoil him too much." Sterling's fist clutched her fingers, and she smiled.

Sally said, "I'll be grateful for the help. Being a mother scares me a little."

Joshua said, "Thanks, Very, for that last warning. I was prepared because of it."

She nodded, her eyes still on her new nephew. "I'm sort of getting the hang of it—my dreams." She talked low, because there were plenty of cuties wandering in and out of the babies' play room. "The future doesn't have to be like falling off a cliff. It can be just looking at the obstacles in your way. Maybe you can't move them, but sometimes you can go around."

. . .

George was recovering rapidly, once the healers and the cooks got him under their care. He looked up from the table with a smile when Joshua walked by.

"There you are! You promised me some answers."

"Okay. You up for a walk?"

He took the last bite of his snack and stood. "Where to?"

"Spending one night at home in my own bed was great, but there's always so much to do. I'll be heading out a little later today. I need to say goodbye to my father, and I thought you might like to meet him."

George nodded, "Okay. What was his name again?"

"Cyclops, from the myths in the Book."

"Right. One-eyed giant from Odysseus?"

"That's where he took the name, yes. Although he's hardly a giant."

Joshua coached George on the rules—no talking about current events. No questions. "My father used to be in charge of the Free U'tanse, but he's recuperating now."

Cyclops was sitting upright. "Hello, Joshua. You caught me on a good day."

"How's your back?"

"Well, it's pretty clear I'll never walk again, but the pain is gone. My arms are getting a workout. It's the only exercise I get."

He turned to face the guest. "George. I'm glad to see you. I've enjoyed your work over the last couple of years. I hope we'll have a chance to talk once I've recovered a bit."

George seemed a little thrown off by the bandage across the man's face. Although even with that, Cyclops seemed well aware of their every movement.

"I'm glad to meet you, too. Your son has been taking good care of me. Even if…"

Cyclops smiled, "Go ahead. Like I said, it's a good day for me."

George nodded, "Um. The guy is very secretive."

Cyclops laughed, "Then I've been raising him right."

There were a few more jokes, and some simple questions about Sterling. But Joshua didn't want to tire his father, and they left.

George asked, when they were well down the corridor. "Your father's eyes are bandaged?"

"He lost them, years ago. He only wears the bandage to keep from unnerving people. Makes it easier for us to imagine him with eyes."

George nodded, "Ah! I understand the name now. Should I take a new name?"

"It's up to you."

...

Sally joined them at the dock, where they were looking over the damage to the mini-sub. She shivered, looking at the scrape marks on the outside of the hull.

"Those are teeth marks?"

Joshua nodded. "Yeah. It almost makes me understand why the Cerik are so afraid of the water."

"Almost?"

He shrugged. "The *jandaka* are deep-water creatures, so a Cerik would hardly ever see one. And it's in their nature to charge after any threat. I'd almost think it would be a challenge to them."

George groaned, "I never want to get close to one again, that's for sure."

Joshua grinned, "So, you don't want the answers to your questions? I'm about ready to take the mini-sub over to Factory. I thought you'd want to come along."

George's eyes lit up. "Factory? You didn't say anything about a factory."

"That's its name. This is Base, across the bay is Factory. It's close enough that we get all our power through a cable laid by the Delense on the bottom of the sea."

George frowned. "Shallow water?"

Joshua nodded.

Sally asked, "Are you feeling up to it, George? You're probably still weak."

George looked down at the teeth marks. "We can't take the big sub?"

Joshua shook his head. "It's almost out of power. One run back to Factory is all it can do, so the plan is to load it up with food supplies over the next few days and make the most of that last run. I can't wait that long."

Sally frowned, "How much power does the mini-sub have left?"

He shrugged. "It's hard to judge, but I *think* it has enough. At worst, I'll tow it the rest of the way myself."

George said, "It sounds like you have power problems. I thought the lights were dim. Is that why?"

Joshua nodded. "Our biggest problem. We can't buy power from Tenthonad like the clans do."

"Then how do you get your power?"

Joshua grinned. "I'll tell you at Factory."

George grumbled low. The only word Joshua could understand was "secrets".

"Okay, then. But I expect answers!"

Fire in his Eyes

They surfaced just a few hundred yards from the tunnel. The skies were clear, and the air tanks for breathing were nearly empty.

George looked back at the rock face towering above them. "I'd never imagine there was a burrow hidden in there."

"That's the idea. The Delense didn't want the Cerik ever to discover it."

They cruised on the surface for a while. George looked sinister in his dark, leather breather and the gray-tinged tunic Sally had prepared for him. Joshua praised her for coming up with the ideal clothing for mini-sub operations—the cloth soaked in oils repelled much of the water and kept it from weighing him down. At the same time, the cloth kept him warmer in the constant swirling water than just working in skin. George shook his head.

"What are you thinking about?" Joshua asked.

"I was just surprised at Clark. He'd retired, and then he'd been forced to go back to fishing by Aarison. Now that he was safe at Base, I saw him this morning, working hard, tossing his nets."

"Sounds like he's still a fisherman at heart."

"Oh, he was happy. I asked, and he said, 'Loving what I do—with filtered air, no surf tugging at my legs, and no rain soaking me to the bone.'"

Joshua nodded. "Oh, I bet he'll get lonely for the sunrises and sunsets before too long. It's one thing to live all your life in a burrow. It's another to give up the pleasures of the outside once you've experienced them."

George chuckled. "So that's why."

"What?"

"I asked people about you. They all said you'd be gone within a couple of days. They said you couldn't stay in one place very long."

Joshua nodded. It was probably true. Once he left the nursery and discovered the world outside the tunnel, he'd never stopped wanting to see more. Sally wasn't even surprised when he told her he needed to go check on how things were proceeding at Factory.

All she said was, "If you're not back soon, I'll come track you down. I can swim the bay too, you know."

It gave him a warm feeling to know that she would do it, too.

...

They were close enough to Factory that Joshua could point out the scar on the cliff where the walkway had been destroyed.

"So when the turbine had to be shut down, our main source of power was lost. Unless we can repair it, the Free U'tanse will be in real distress. No power to filter our air. No power to grow our earth crops. And no power to let us go rescue people like you."

George frowned. "And you can't buy or steal power cells?"

"The Cerik clans think there are a small handful of rogue U'tanse, mainly survivors from Rikna Home. They would notice the missing power cells. If it was a regular thing, they'd treat it as a serious threat."

Joshua looked at George. "My deepest desire is to learn how the Tenthonad get their power from space. The Free U'tanse need to be able to do that, too."

George blinked. "Oh, I know how that works, at least in principle."

"You do?"

He nodded. "It's simple, really. You know the boats fly by grabbing the air and pulling it around them?"

Joshua nodded. "The pumps on this sub do the same thing."

George took a second look at the cluster of pumps. Then he turned back to Joshua.

"Well, the boats can pull things and push things very far away, as well. If you located another world in the sky—"

"Like *Katranel*?"

George was speechless for a second. "Yes, exactly like *Katranel*... I'm going to have to find out how you know that. But anyway, this other world is moving. Perhaps it's moving away from you. So if you pull at this other world with the tractor beam that is at the heart of all our boats, but you don't have enough power to stop it . . ."

Joshua nodded, "When an underpowered pump can't slow down the water, then you can pull energy from the pump."

George nodded. "Well, yes. Like that."

Joshua asked, "So then could we point a pump at *Katranel* and get power?"

George sighed, "It's more complicated than that. For one thing, all the air gets in the way and ruins the effort. It only works in space, above the air. So that's why, without a boat, it's just a fascinating idea."

Joshua nodded. "Take off your breather and let's hope there's enough air in our tanks. We have to go underwater for the rest of the way in."

They went down and George watched as they entered the shallow part of the bay and then went under the draperies.

When they surfaced, a cry went out on the dock, "The kid is back!"

George was looking back and forth, trying to take in all the activity and machinery visible there on the docks. He frowned, trying to make sense of the tub. And then as they moved closer, he suddenly reached out to grip Joshua's wrist.

"Is that a boat?" He pointed at Boat A resting on a cradle.

"Yes, one of three we have. But we are currently draining its power cells, just to keep Factory and Base running."

George leaned close as the workmen up on the dock tossed them a line and moved a sling out over the water, preparing to hoist the mini-sub out of the water. People were starting to notice the teeth marks on the hull.

"You would rather I take a new name, wouldn't you?"

Joshua nodded. "You're well-known to Elehadi and his telepath. We really don't want your survival to be discovered."

George's eyes were shiny. "Okay then. Call me 'Prometheus'."

"Okay, Prometheus. Sounds mythological. I think I remember it from somewhere."

"Ancient god who brought fire to mankind. I'm suddenly very excited about the future."

Joshua felt his heart beat faster. So was he.

The End

Cerik Terms

Cerik Term	Definition
'eeh	The bloodlust, a heightened sensual awareness.
Cerik	Literally, 'Hunter', the name of a race of predators
chitchit	A small predator from the Cerik home world that were used to root out burrowing prey. They were also used as pets.
conek	Tall slender trees, often used for construction of lightweight structures such as huts and decorative walls. Conek trees only grow at high altitudes.
dak	A substitute kill. Used when an honored soldier is killed. An enemy is killed, the blood drunk, and the kill attributed to the honored soldier.
dakka	A swamp-living prey, wide and flat in front with a long snake-like tail behind. Cerik like the taste, but since they live in the water, the Cerik hate to chase them.

Cerik Term	Definition
dan	Cerik biology alternates between periods of intense activity and deep rest. In dan there is limited awareness, but no real thought. Many of these rest states have their own names in the language, such as erdan, or fenke dan.
Delense	Literally, "Builder," the name of a semi-aquatic race of tool users. The Delense were enslaved by the Cerik in prehistory, and existed in a symbiotic relationship for thousands of years before they were exterminated by the Cerik.
dlathe	A broad shade tree, with many low-hanging branches. It was a favorite hunting Perch for Cerik.
dul	A traditional net used to hold a captured prey
erdan	The long wait. A semiconscious trance state when no prey were expected, but instant alertness might be required.
fenke dan	The meal, and the following period of torpor. In good times, a Cerik would eat once a day. Digestion has its own heavy demands and causes a deep lethargy that is not easily overridden.
Ferreer	A telepathic, hive-mind alien species that had inhabited several planets. Some Cerik refer to attached U'tanse as Ferreer as well.
flick	To bomb an enemy with an overloaded TP core. Invented by the Delense to attack the Ferreer, the only race the Cerik could not attack directly face to face, it was also used in the fatal rebellion against the Cerik. It has the blast effects, but not the radiation, of a small tactical nuclear bomb.

Cerik Term	Definition
Ha	The Ko Moon. Large with an elliptical orbit that brings tides and triggers quakes and volcano eruptions.
Hae	Cerik mythology—the male spirit of the moon.
haeka	Larger predator, sometimes known to capture Cerik cubs or nomadic females. Generally preys on runners in the foothills
hatsen	Mid-sized predator that feeds on small prey like *chitchits*.
hurru	A Perch. The rear talons of a Cerik efficiently grip any branch large enough to hold them. The Perch of a Name was a ceremonial throne from which the Name ruled as he rested above all the others. It also came to refer to the buildings around it.
ineda	A telepathic block. This skill can be learned by any Cerik who needs to be a leader over telepaths. Before the arrival of the telepathic U'tanse, an ordinary Cerik who practicesd ineda was, by definition, a suspected thief.
jandaka	A deep-sea predator with snake-like body and large teeth that preys on a variety of other marine animals.
janji	A freshwater fish that is edible by humans. The meat is chewy. More common in the north.
jenna	Common saltwater fish that can be digested by humans.
kadan	The anticipated kill wait. Like erdan, but with heightened anticipation that prey would appear any second.

Cerik Term	Definition
katche	The "peace." During the Face, all clans are bound to refrain from clan-on-clan attacks, with the threat that all other clans would turn on the aggressor.
Katranel	A sky demon in Cerik mythology, blamed in some of the Tales for a clan's bad luck.
kede	A Broken Hunter. Any Cerik who is valuable even though severely injured. Surgery is unknown among the Cerik and it is up to the clan leader whether to support anyone crippled by injuries.
kel	A common tree that is found near streams.
klakr	The Cerik world's version of a triceratops. Twice the size of a Cerik. Large massive head with spikes and tusks. A spiked tail. Vegetarian, with easily offended sense of territory. Nearly extinct.
Ko	Literally, "all lands." This became the name of the Cerik home planet when they discovered that other planets existed.
Koee	Cerik mythology—the female spirit of the land.
koodak	A ceremonial way to resolve descisions where all parties bring competing gifts to the leader.

Cerik Term	Definition
La	Literally, "First," also referred to as "Named." The title of the leader of a clan, family or guild. A First was the only individual Cerik with a name. The First names himself when elevated to rank. All other adult males are addressed by their rank, and known unambiguously by their scent. Females and cubs are known by their scent and genealogy.
Larek	Literally, "Second," the second in command, and prime assistant to the First. Second is also heir to the First and can usurp his position with a physical challenge. In addition to the possibility of death in such a challenge, there are numerous social- and clan-level sanctions against a Second who endangers the clan by a challenge at the wrong time.
lulur	Large centipede-like creature with tubular body and a pair of legs per segment. Carrion eaters, for the most part. Cerik disdain them and eradicate them only for sport.
ooro	Coastal lizards that are a food delicacy, traded to interior clans
po	Flying reptile that nest in dlathe trees.
pree	To register personal satisfaction. Physically there can be a purring component, a salivating component, and/or a relaxing of the subdermal plates.
Rakladel	Cerik mythology—telepathic demon who could make a Cerik mindlessly crazy and who could not be killed.

Cerik Term	Definition
ralak	Speaker. A clan-to-clan personal ambassador, with various levels of importance.
rettik	Literally "right eye," a close assistant, with status over other assistants. Often personal soldiers or bodyguards.
Rotaak	Literally "Face to face" or commonly Face. A traditional meeting of clan Names on neutral ground. Historically, there were a number of regional Faces, but since the Delense gave them flying boats, there has been one central Face. The orignal grounds were destroyed when the Delense made their failed attempt to escape the Cerik.
ruff	A territorial noise and posture, a threatening purr.
sendt	Literally, "Runner," a grazing herbivore that make up a dominant prey for the Cerik. There are dozens of native varieties and several off-world species, prized for taste or for being skillful prey.
shash	A reed-like plant that grows along stream beds.
shillee	Long mid-sized lizards know for their erratic running path.
soso	A trade that both parties were happy with. "Fairness"
ska	Flying predators that prey on coastal fish.

Cerik Term	Definition
ssitt	Literally, "Take the eyes." In battle among Cerik, the ritual death stroke was to take out the eyes of an enemy and eat them. Due to the tough skin of the Cerik, the most common death stroke in duels was a blow at the weakest part of the head, at the eyes.
tetca	Literally, "dance." A guild, an organized collection of Cerik workers with their own First, Second, and lower workers. A clan First will have many tetca First's under his direct command. Some common tetca: Rear Talon - Boat and spaceship pilots Telepaths; Scientists—nearly obsolete. This tetca came into being after the extermination of the Delense. U'tanse were better scientists than the Cerik by far and took over that task; Herders; Tale tellers; Ralak—messengers.
uuka	The ritual of submission where a Cerik lays face down, defenseless and awaits either a killing blow or the opportunity to swear allegiance to the new master.

U'tanse Terms

Over time, the original language of the U'tanse, English, has acquired a number of loan words from the Cerik, but has also added new terms of their own, or redefined old ones.

U'tanse Term	Definition
attachment	A disorder of telepaths when their thoughts become so tightly linked that individuality is lost and they become a hive mind.
creeper	A bug, but the Ko varieties range from tiny crab-like species, to legless worms. Multi-legged varieties do grow larger, but many of those have their own Cerik names.
cutie	A U'tanse child old enough to walk, but too young to have come of age.
Festival	A trade and exchange of females between U'tanse Homes designed to reduce inbreeding. Over time, selected goods were exchanged also.

U'tanse Term	Definition
Home	A colony of U'tanse inhabiting a Delense burrow.
random	A person whose genetics was dictated by the random combination of the parents sperm and ovum, rather than having been controlled by the mother. A term of abhorrence, due to the history of birth defects whenever it was tried.
slurk	Monitoring thoughts or activities with salacious intent.
tenner	By policy, one in ten males is bred with no psychic abilities, in order to keep the U'tanse from drifting too far from the old human stock. In practice, tenners have proved superior in science, engineering and math.

Slave Races

A variety of species were conquered by the Cerik as they scavenged Star damaged planets. Most stayed on their home worlds. Only a few could survive the Cerik atmosphere and were valuable enough for the Cerik to make the effort to bring them to Ko.

Species	Type	Value
U'tanse (Human)	Erect bipeds	Technically talented, and could design and repair tools.
Dadada (BaBaBa)	Radial symmetric turtles, triangles at birth, add legs as they age.	Young ones used as pets, older ones as slow transport. Can carry heavy weights and understand spoken directions.
Uuaa (Wob)	Quadruped with long, multi-jointed arms and thicker hind legs for jumping.	Favorite pet of the Cerik because they jump the same way as their masters. Used to quickly climb trees and harvest fruits and nuts that the Cerik can't reach. Not vocal, but they can be trained.

The Ko Calendar

The Cerik have always lived by the moon. There are two types of cycles. One cycles through the phases, just like on the moon of Earth, but there is a more important cycle as well. Their moon, Ha, is in a highly elliptical orbit that brings it close enough to regularly trigger quakes across the globe. The Large Moon dominates the sky much more than Earth's full moon, regardless of which phase it is in. While the Cerik have noted that certain stars are in the sky following a "yearly" pattern, it makes no difference in their lives. With no noticeable yearly weather pattern, months, marked by the Large Moon, are the dominant measure of calendar time. On a day to day basis, the Large, Small, Full, and New moons make convenient markers even though these "weeks" can vary from 1 to 12 days in length.

The phases of the moon are slightly less than half of this month, with a Full Moon taking place every 24.4 Cerik days. Important days such as the Face are often marked by the conjunction of these 2 cycles, i.e., a Large Full Moon.

When the U'tanse arrived, Father began documenting what he could. There was a wristwatch, by which he determined that a Cerik day was slightly more than 20 Earth hours. A Cerik month was a little over 58 Cerik days.

The U'tanse set up their own calendar system, one that more closely matched the human norms. A Normal week was seven Cerik Days, with the same names Father and Mother were used to. Each Normal month was 5 weeks. There were 10 Normal months, which didn't quite match the Cerik year, but it was close enough. The month names were: January, March, April, May, July, August, September, October, November, and December.

Secrets of the U'tanse

U'tanse count birthdays and ages by the Normal year, which is only 80% as long as the Earth year. A 20 (Earth) year old would be deemed aged 25 on Cerik.

	Hours	Earth Days	Cerik Days
Earth Day	24	1.000	1.198
Cerik Month	1162.4	48.433	58.033
Normal Month	701.05	29.210	35.000
Normal Week	140.21	5.842	7.000
Cerik Year	6867.3	286.138	342.851
Normal Year	7010.5	292.104	350.000

Coming Soon: The Power of the U'tanse

Check out all books of the **Project Saga**:

The **Earth Branch** consists of:
Star Time
Kingdom of the Hill Country
In the Time of Green Blimps
Captain's Memories
Humanicide

The **U'tanse Branch** follows **Star Time** as well, consisting of:
Tales of the U'tanse
Free U'tanse
Secrets of the U'tanse
Power of the U'tanse

Other Novels by Henry Melton

Emperor Dad
Roswell or Bust
Extreme Makeover
Lighter Than Air
Falling Bakward
Golden Girl
Follow That Mouse
Pixie Dust
Bearing Northeast
The Copper Room
Breaking Anchor

Short Story Anthologies by Henry Melton

Henry's Stories: Volume 1
Henry's Stories: Volume 2

Childrens' Book by Henry Melton

Chipper Flies High

If you want more stories by Henry Melton, the best way you can help is to spread the word, and leave a review at the high traffic sites like Amazon and Goodreads.

To follow Henry Melton:

On Facebook, like the page HenryMeltonFan

His twitter handle is @HenryMelton

Check out www.HenryMelton.com

www.ingramcontent.com/pod-product-compliance
Lightning Source LLC
Chambersburg PA
CBHW021952010726
47494CB00003B/709